BROGNOLA KNEW THE PRESIDENT HAD HARD NEWS

"NATO plans to start a high-saturation bombing campaign over Kosovo—military targets, bases, fuel dumps. Tracking and communication sites. Power supplies. Anything and everything that feeds the Serbian military. The bombing runs will continue around the clock."

"I take it this is on a need-to-know basis?" Brognola asked.

The President nodded. "This is where it gets hard. Assuming your people locate the missing members of Phoenix Force and go in for them, we can't warn them of what's coming."

"So my people have to go in under the threat of an air strike."

"Understand my position, Hal. I don't like holding back information, especially when lives are on the line. But this time I have no other choice."

Neither did Brognola. Come hell or high water, he'd get a message to Phoenix Force about the approaching storm.

Other titles in this series:

STONY MAN II
STONY MAN III
STONY MAN IV
STONY MAN V
STONY MAN VI
STONY MAN VII
STONY MAN VIII
#9 STRIKEPOINT
#10 SECRET ARSENAL
#11 TARGET AMERICA
#12 BLIND EAGLE
#13 WARHEAD
#14 DEADLY AGENT
#15 BLOOD DEBT
#16 DEEP ALERT
#17 VORTEX
#18 STINGER
#19 NUCLEAR NIGHTMARE
#20 TERMS OF SURVIVAL
#21 SATAN'S THRUST
#22 SUNFLASH
#23 THE PERISHING GAME
#24 BIRD OF PREY
#25 SKYLANCE
#26 FLASHBACK
#27 ASIAN STORM
#28 BLOOD STAR
#29 EYE OF THE RUBY
#30 VIRTUAL PERIL
#31 NIGHT OF THE JAGUAR
#32 LAW OF LAST RESORT
#33 PUNITIVE MEASURES
#34 REPRISAL

#35 MESSAGE TO AMERICA
#36 STRANGLEHOLD
#37 TRIPLE STRIKE
#38 ENEMY WITHIN
#39 BREACH OF TRUST
#40 BETRAYAL
#41 SILENT INVADER
#42 EDGE OF NIGHT
#43 ZERO HOUR
#44 THIRST FOR POWER
#45 STAR VENTURE
#46 HOSTILE INSTINCT

DON PENDLETON'S
MACK BOLAN.
STONY MAN

COMMAND FORCE

A GOLD EAGLE BOOK FROM
WORLDWIDE.

TORONTO • NEW YORK • LONDON
AMSTERDAM • PARIS • SYDNEY • HAMBURG
STOCKHOLM • ATHENS • TOKYO • MILAN
MADRID • WARSAW • BUDAPEST • AUCKLAND

First edition June 2000

ISBN 0-373-61931-6

Special thanks and acknowledgment to
Michael Linaker for his contribution to this work.

COMMAND FORCE

COMMAND FORCE

PROLOGUE

Foothills, Mount Pastric, Kosovo

The area was remote, and bleak at this time of the year. Cold winds scoured the rocky slopes and ravines, rattling the brittle vegetation as it passed. Higher up the hills, snow clung to the bare rock, and even the lowering sky was cast in a somber gray. Isolated flakes drifted across the landscape, touching the motionless figures huddled at the rim of a shallow depression skirted by skeletal trees.

The eight men were clad in thick, padded clothing against the severe chill of the day. Their faces were pale from the cold, eyes rimmed red, mouths held in taut lines, words of rage straining to burst free. The fingers of hands thrust deep into pockets were clenched into helpless fists, and shoulders were raised in the instinctive gesture of shrugging off the bitter cold. Some wore hoods, others were bareheaded. There was a noticeable array of weaponry. Autorifles, mostly of Russian origin, hung by straps from shoulders. There were even a couple of ancient rifles of indistinct manufacture.

The tableau had remained in place for some time.

Each man was absorbing the scene, fixing it in his mind for future reference. They were noting every little detail, making certain that none of the horrors were missed. The time and the place were important to them all.

One man moved closer to the rim of the depression and squatted on his heels, cradling his Kalashnikov AK-74 to his chest. He was a tall, lean man with thick black hair framing a hollow-cheeked face. With his head down, none of the others could see the tears in his eyes as he surveyed the scene below.

At the bottom of the depression, now that the earth had been dug away, were the visible remains of at least twenty bodies. Adults and children. Male and female. Closer examination would confirm that they had all been physically assaulted before being methodically shot. A single shot to the back of the skull. An added indignity was the binding of the hands behind their backs.

The squatting man knew every person in the mass grave. They had all come from his home village some twelve miles to the north. Their only crime had been their loyalty to the cause they believed in. For that, and because they had refused to inform on the local freedom fighters, they had been herded together, marched out to this lonely place and slaughtered.

He stared in silent agony, picking out every scrap of detail. The broken bones. Lacerated and ragged flesh. The dark crusts of dark blood that had marked flesh and clothing. The twisted, unnatural formation of the corpses, frozen where they had fallen. There were still shocked expressions on those ravaged faces, some eyes still open wide, staring out at a world that had abandoned them.

Among the dead were his mother, two brothers in their teens, and his precious three-year-old sister. His only consolation was that his father had died a year ago, so had been spared this moment.

The man started as he felt a hand rest gently on his shoulder. He twisted his head and looked up into the face of his closest friend.

"We should move on, Lec. Remember there are still patrols around. Getting caught out here won't do us any good."

The man stood. The hands gripping the rifle were tinged with blue from the cold, but he ignored that. He was beyond physical pain at the moment.

"You're right. There's a lot to do."

"Lec, what about...?" The speaker gestured in the direction of the grave.

"Get our people to cover them up. But cut off those damn cords. We can offer them at least that."

"Cover them? I don't understand. Neither will the others."

"What do you expect me to do, Drago? Go running to the United Nations? The peace monitors? Send begging letters to NATO? Ask the Americans to help? And then what? I'll tell you. Just like every other time. The government will deny everything as always and wriggle their way out. Nothing will happen, Drago. It never does."

Drago stared at his friend as if he were looking at him for the first time. As if suddenly, within the space of a few seconds he no longer knew Lec Pavlic.

"So this is it? We bury them again and leave? We walk away as if nothing has happened?" Drago's anger burst free in a shout that drew the attention of the others. "Tell me, Lec, is that how it's going to be? They slaughter our people and we do nothing? We cover it up? Run away as if there is nothing down in that hole? Does it all end here?"

Pavlic rose to his feet, turning his friend away from the grave.

"No, my friend. Do not misunderstand me. This is not where it all ends, Drago. This is where it all begins."

Zittau, Saxon-Czech Border, Six months later

GREGOR RIDIVIC LEFT the boardinghouse just after nine o'clock that morning. The day was bright, the air crisp. The foothills of the Lausitz Mountains were still streaked with snow, forming a sparkling background to the activity centered around Zittau itself. Sharp sunlight bounced off the roof tiles on the houses and glittered against the windows of houses and shops.

It was here the human tide of refugees came, desperate to escape the horrors of the still embattled Yugoslavia, hoping that this was a way to a semi-peaceful life, some kind of stable existence away from the deprivation and the uncertainty of life in their former homeland. For the most part they were ordinary people. They only wanted the basics—homes, jobs, security. It was a dream for many of them, a dream that would never be fulfilled, because the German authorities had decreed that enough was enough. Germany could no longer contain floods of refugees within its borders. There were too many, putting financial and economic strain on the German state. Debates in the German parliament had resulted in strict demarcation. Refugees from the Kosovo war zone weren't to be tolerated. If they were caught trying to cross into Germany, the border patrols would round them up and they would be eventually shipped back. It had become a desperate game of cat-and-mouse—the isolated Albanians against the superbly equipped German border patrol, with its trained officers and high-speed pursuit cars.

The figures for those picked up ran into thousands. Ironically, so did the numbers of those getting through.

Ridivic wasn't strictly a refugee in the political sense. He had chosen the guise as a means of getting out of Kosovo because it had been easier to lose himself in a large crowd than isolate himself by trying to slip away by any other route. He had false identity papers, produced by the American NSA and cash money—again U.S.—that had helped to procure his passage out of Kosovo. It had been arranged by one of the so-called people smugglers he had been introduced to by some friends who were also anxious to leave. Ridivic had counted himself lucky that the party he had joined was leaving within a couple of days. Any longer might have proved fatal as far as Ridivic was concerned. His time in Kosovo was over. Added to that was the information he needed to get to his outside contact as soon as possible. Time, as always, allowed no favors. It ticked away its precious hours with unbending regularity, deaf to the pleas of anyone struggling against the odds.

So it was that Ridivic found himself walking through the town, avoiding contact with anyone who resembled an Albanian refugee, and hoping he could make his rendezvous without being spotted by the German border patrol. He couldn't be sure that he had remained anonymous. For all he knew he was being watched every moment of the day. The fact he hadn't been intercepted meant nothing. His enemies were smart enough to realize he had been waiting to make contact. It would be as much in their interest to wait out the time and pick off both Ridivic and his contact. By now they would have figured he had nowhere else to go, that his meeting with whoever came for him was the next step in his journey. Until that time Ridivic was going nowhere, so all they needed to do was keep him in view and wait.

Ridivic reached the corner of the street, paused to check the traffic, then crossed to take his place at the café where he took his midmorning coffee. This was part of the ritual he had performed for the past three days, knowing that one morning there would be someone there to meet him. He chose his usual table and waited until the waiter came to take his order. It was always the same. The familiarity with the routine had become almost comfortable to Ridivic. He tasted the coffee when it arrived and found it delicious. The rich, hot liquid eased down his throat, settling his nerves.

It would have been so easy to forget why he was here. The thought slid so quietly into his mind that

Ridivic felt a little unnerved. He watched the ebb and flow of daily life around him, wishing that he could have been part of it for real, rather than being like some actor in a movie, simply playing a part that had been written for him. Then he pushed the idle thoughts away, reminding himself where he had come from, the horrors he had seen and the reason he was here. In fact, what he hoped might result from his escape from Kosovo was a chance to experience the way of life these people enjoyed. They lived reasonably content and satisfying lives. They worked and played, built their homes and their futures, and within the strictures of modern society they were free.

Where Ridivic had come from all those things were fragile wisps, part of the dreams the people wished for daily. Their lives were shattered by fear and deprivation. By hate and intolerance and overshadowed by the rule of the gun. The destabilization of society had left their world in ruins. From day to day no one knew what was waiting around the next corner. It had become a cruel, bitter place, where trust and friendship had been replaced by injustice and deceit. The people were dictated to by politics, by advisers from other countries, by the policing organizations that had descended upon them en masse, but who seemed to have little effect when it came to organizing the simplest of directives.

Ridivic had seen the establishment of groups willing to fight for the freedom they wanted. He was as eager for change as the rest, but his initial excitement had turned to dismay when he realized that certain groups were willing, eager in fact, to take their fight to even greater degrees of extremism than all the other groups put together. In the situation the ethnic Albanians found themselves, there was always the risk of some taking their zeal too far. There were always those who saw the cloak of the patriot as a blanket for their own ambitions, who allowed national pride to become the excuse for going beyond the limits. The groups that formed were independent. They devised their own rules and lived, and died, by them. Some saw the need for talk. A forum for their desires, so that the actions they took were recognized as a cry for help from an oppressed and suffering people. Then the fringe groups stepped back, declaring that their brothers were selling out, giving in to the pressures put on them. They were suddenly the outsiders, the violence and anger they had allowed to run free isolating them from everyone around them as they blindly went ahead with their designs, and ignored the pleas from the moderates.

Here was where Ridivic had become involved. Aware that the situation within his country had spilled over into near anarchy, and that talk, the only sensible way out, had been pushed into the background so that the rule of the gun could take center stage, Ridivic had agreed to take on the guise of infiltrator. He accepted the possible mark of traitor, betrayer, because as far as he was concerned the future of his beloved country hung in the balance. If matters were allowed to progress, plunging them all deeper and deeper into violence, terrorism and the like, then it wouldn't matter in the least what he was called. By then there would be nothing left. Albania wasn't a rich country, and its economy couldn't sustain a prolonged war situation. Already deprived and sliding quickly down the slope to oblivion, the struggling nation needed conflict like a drowning man needed cool water being poured over his head.

Ridivic's role as a seeker of information had been, at first, slow and almost tedious. His infiltration of the group to which he had been assigned by his U.S. advisers had been tentative. The group he had been asked to infiltrate had proclaimed itself as the Free Albania Party, on the surface an admirable concept, but one that had been overshadowed by the far-ranging and destructive nature of the organization. The FAP had become extremist from inception. There was no middle ground for them, it seemed. The party distrusted almost everyone around them, whether Albanian or foreign adviser. Their rallies advocated resistance to everything. The vitriolic speeches were aimed at inciting armed resistance, sabotage and complete and utter denial of everything that was not for complete, unfettered autonomy. No compromise. No quarter. The party held the view that the people needed such action. There had been too much talk. Too many climb downs. Too many agreements and accords that only gave away their freedom and allowed their enemies to grow in strength. The FAP refused this kind of weakness. Albania could only become strong through out-and-out resistance to the weakness of the administration giving away their rights.

Ridivic had been nervous when he had first approached the FAP, which wasn't surprising. He was a computer engineer, not a soldier. But even the FAP needed people with his experience. Part of their strategy was the infiltration of computer systems belonging to local government, military and police. They had people within the party who were expert at devising programs that were able to alter data and so confuse information being passed between agencies. In this way the FAP was able to disrupt the movements of the military and the monitors working for the UN and the NATO forces. Part of Ridivic's work was the maintenance of the computer equipment and the installation of additional hardware as it was introduced. The FAP used the information they gained from their cyber-trawling to plan their raids on convoys and patrols. Being in the right place at the right time meant they were able to intercept and attack with ease, taking the enemy by surprise. In the bloody confrontations the death toll rose, and as time slid by Ridivic became increasingly uneasy. He was party to the crimes as he saw them, even though he was never included in any of the attack squads. It made no difference to him that he wasn't actually there. He had a hand in every death. The day came when the FAP attacked a convoy that turned out later to have included U.S. monitors and a truck carrying wounded civilians. Ridivic was physically sick when he heard what had happened. He almost gave himself away in front of his comrades. He decided then and there that his time with the FAP was over. There was no way he was going to be able to hide his feelings any longer. He had to get out, leave the FAP before his false identity was discovered. He had written notes, detailing as much information as he was able, and made a hurried disk copy from the master computer data bank.

Now, sitting in the warm sunlight, sipping coffee, Ridivic found he was unable to wipe away the images of his former comrades. Just thinking about them made him nervous. He could recall the ruthless dedication they had put into every one of their acts of resistance, and the anger, even rage, they exuded. He saw them all as men who had lost their way, had forgotten about the original motivation that had caused them to create the FAP. That seemed a distant shadow, lost in the heat of battle and the seemingly endless war of attrition they were waging. The world had taken on the unwitting role of the enemy now. The maxim for the FAP was if a person wasn't with them, then by definition they were against them.

Ridivic was in that category now. He would be seen to have betrayed the party and his comrades. So the simple edict would go out that he would have to be eliminated. There would be no debate within the FAP. They viewed everything very simplistically. For or against. Life or death. The choice was simple.

Ridivic's concern was less for himself and more for his contact. How would the FAP see the contact? As simply another nuisance to be eliminated? Put that way, it sounded cold and stark, but Ridivic had learned enough about the party to understand their abhorrence of someone who had turned against them. In their eyes, he was already a dead man. That rule would be extended to anyone in contact with Ridivic.

The prospect looked grim. Ridivic began to wonder what his chances of survival might be. It was possible he was under observation at that very moment. When Ridivic showed himself to his contact, then what? Gunfire? A moment of frantic madness that might leave Ridivic and his contact dead? He thought of the gun secure in the pocket inside his coat. He had undergone training with the weapon while he was part of the group in Kosovo, and though the sight and sound of the weapon terrified him, he had accepted the training as part of his cover. To refuse to touch a gun would have been considered more than odd. That being so, Ridivic hadn't used the weapon since he had shot at targets, and he had no idea what would happen if the occasion arose when he might be forced to draw the gun in anger.

Life had become extremely complicated.

Perhaps when he had passed along his information and his contact arranged for him to go to America things might ease a little. Not that he knew what he would do when he got there. He did have some distant family in the U.S. They lived somewhere in Seattle, so perhaps he might be able to make contact with them and—

"May I join you?"

The voice was gentle, female and with barely a trace of an accent. As Ridivic slowly raised his head, peering through the wreath of smoke from his cigarette, he caught a glimpse of a slender, blond-haired woman settling in the seat across from him. She looked to be in her early thirties, her features striking rather than delicately pretty. Her eyes were very blue and they stared at Ridivic in a way that almost made him blush. As if aware of his thoughts she gave a quick smile, leaning forward so that he picked up a trace of her perfume.

"So, Mr. Ridivic, it's time to make that trip, yes?"

"Yes."

"We'll have another coffee then take a walk back to your hotel."

"I have information to—"

"Time for that once we're on our way."

"Are you sure we're safe?"

"There is nothing certain in this life, Mr. Ridivic. Except the fact you're born and eventually you die. Between those two it's down to which side the coin falls each time you spin it. Now that is all you get on the mystery of life from me, so order that damn coffee because I'm thirsty."

Her confidence amazed Ridivic. She seemed entirely at ease with the situation. So young, he thought, and so sure of herself. If only life was so certain. He thought back to Kosovo and the bleak atmosphere that enveloped the place. The violence and the sudden, shocking death that had become endemic, so ingrained that no one made a fuss about it any longer, which was the sad part.

They sat for a quarter of an hour, drinking coffee and chatting like old friends. The woman was dressed like any tourist, and the maps she produced and laid on the table would have added to the image for any passerby. Their conversation had little to do with tourism as she explained what they were going to do, how Ridivic would go with her to the station where they would board a train that would take them away from Zittau. Dresden was their initial destination, and from there Ridivic would eventually continue on to the U.S.A. His contact had new identity papers for him, including a passport and visas. There was nothing he had to concern himself with. Everything was in hand.

Ridivic still felt uneasy, but he couldn't explain why. His nervous state prompted the woman to cut short their sojourn at the café. They would return to Ridivic's boardinghouse, collect his luggage and head for the station. Ridivic paid for the coffee, then helped the young woman to put away her maps. Folding one of them, he slipped a brown envelope between the layers and handed it to her. If she had been surprised at the bulky feel she made no show, simply slipping the maps into her shoulder bag and continuing to smile and speak to him.

They started on the walk to the boardinghouse.

Across the square, a light-colored Mercedes eased away from the curb and angled across to fall in behind them. When Ridivic and the woman reached the far side of the square, the Mercedes was only yards behind them. Some sixth sense made him turn. He saw the idling car and knew immediately what was about to happen. Without warning to the woman he broke away, running back across the square, fumbling under his coat for the gun.

Tires squealed as the Mercedes made a vicious sweep, broadsiding anyone in its path before the driver regained control of the vehicle. He touched the throttle and the big car lurched forward, rapidly picking up speed as it bore down on Gregor Ridivic.

All thoughts of his future were blanked out of Ridivic's mind as he ran. After seconds of fumbling, he slid the automatic pistol from under his coat. His training took over, and he flicked off the safety. He stumbled and slid on one knee, burning the skin against the ground. In a moment of iron self-control he turned and raised the gun, sighting along the barrel. The windshield of the approaching car reflected the sun into his eyes and he was unable to see any of the occupants. What he did see was the barrel of a weapon poking out of the passenger-side window.

He silently prayed that the woman would get away with the envelope.

It was his last conscious thought.

The barrel of the weapon aimed at him emitted a brief burst of fire.

Ridivic felt something strike his chest. There was a moment of blankness, then he was on his back, the pistol flying unfired from his fingers. His world was filled by the roar of the Mercedes as it hurtled toward, then over him. Ridivic was dragged beneath the heavy body for yards, twisting and rolling over and over. His agony was short-lived, as rear wheels crushed his head against the ground, shattering his skull and ending forever his dream of seeing a free Albania.

CHAPTER ONE

Stony Man Farm, Virginia

Yakov Katzenelenbogen was first in the War Room, ahead even of Barbara Price, the Farm's mission controller. He placed his stack of files on the table in front of his seat and crossed to check the coffee supply. The aroma teased his nostrils. Katz poured himself a mug and returned to his seat. He placed the mug to one side after a quick drink, then turned his attention to the files, a half dozen manila folders. Each contained information, in various forms, relating to matters at hand. On their own they were isolated incidents, but once drawn together and analyzed, a thread of continuity had started to show. Added to concerns that had previously been pushed at the Sensitive Operations Group, the data had produced a scenario requiring the full attention of the Stony Man personnel.

Katz had spent most of the day going over the information, theorizing, discarding, letting his instincts guide him, until he had an acceptable grasp of the implications of the data. Now he was ready to give his input and help the rest of the team put together a plan of action. Retrieving his mug, Katz sat back, enjoying the period of calm before the coming storm. It was strange, he thought, how he had slotted into his role of tactical adviser to Hal Brognola. After his long years in the field, undertaking mission after mission as leader of Phoenix Force, Katz had relinquished command to David McCarter, the British hell-raiser. There had been some doubts on both scores. One was whether Katz himself would accept a less aggressive role within the Stony Man chain of command. In truth, it was what Katz had been secretly hoping for. His own doubts as to his continuing as combat leader had been assuaged when Brognola had held out the offer of tactical adviser. Phoenix Force had deserved a new leader, someone who could take over and give it the kind of guidance Katz had over the years. No one had been more surprised than McCarter himself when he had been offered the position, yet in the event he had proved himself to have the maturity that his promotion called for.

Both men had been surprised and pleased at their individual success. For Katz it was a relief to distance himself from the rigors of the battlefield. His mind was still as active as ever, but his physical body had been unable to keep up. Katz wasn't a young man, something he admitted to openly, and the tasks he carried out at Stony Man suited him perfectly. David McCarter's intimacy with Phoenix Force, the way it operated and the men who comprised the team proved more than useful when he stepped into the shoes of the man he had, and still, admired and respected. McCarter thrived on action.

Danger instilled him with courage and the capability to tackle the problems that often appeared without warning out in the field. His brash behavior, often in the past leading him into conflict with those around him, also presented his companions with an individual who would put his life on the line for his partners without a moment of thought. That was still there. But now McCarter had to hold himself in check, making decisions that not only affected himself but also every man in his group. He was, under the skin, still the Cockney rebel, and always would be, but that rebellious streak was now tempered with caution.

"You feeling all right, Katz?" Price asked as she skirted the table, placing files for the people who would be joining them.

Katz smiled. "Feeling sorry for myself," he admitted. "I'm getting old."

Price paused beside his seat, leaning one hip against the edge of the table while she studied him soberly.

"Can't see it myself."

Katz smiled. "Now I can see why nobody around here minds putting themselves on the line when you ask," he said.

"Dammit, you've seen right through me."

The doors opened to admit Able Team. The three team members acknowledged Katz and Price before heading for the coffeemaker. As soon as they had their drinks, they sat down.

"What's on the cards this time?" Rosario Blancanales asked, flicking through his file without really looking at it.

Price took her place at the table. "You'll see soon enough when the others get here."

Carl Lyons tapped the table impatiently, his restless gaze flitting back and forth around the War Room. He hated inactivity. Like all intelligent men, he had a low boredom threshold. He needed to be on the move, meeting challenges head-on.

"Been a little quiet lately," he said. "Have we taken down all the bad guys?"

"Hardly," Hal Brognola grumbled as he entered the War Room. He took his place at the head of the conference table. "Be a cold day in Hell when we can put in for retirement."

Aaron Kurtzman was next in, rolling his wheelchair up to the table. He was followed by Carmen Delahunt, ex-FBI, a member of his cybernetics team. The rest of Kurtzman's group were in the Annex at their computers, maintaining the round-the-clock surveillance that Stony Man required.

"Aaron, you want to get set up while we wait for Phoenix Force?"

"Yeah, where are the hotshots? Waiting for a fanfare?" Lyons asked good-naturedly.

"Actually, we're here, mate," David McCarter drawled in an exaggerated British accent. "Had trouble parking the Bentley. Couldn't find a space because of all those vulgar American gas-guzzlers."

Clad in tan slacks and a cream shirt, McCarter looked neater than he had for a long time. He picked up a chilled can of soft drink from the minifridge and took his place at the table. Cool and relaxed, the Briton popped the tab on the can and sat waiting while the rest of his team completed the lineup at the conference table.

Gary Manning, Canadian demolitions expert, eased his stocky form in beside McCarter. On the Briton's left was Calvin James. The lean, black Phoenix Force member was quietly conversing with T. J. Hawkins, the newest team member. The ex-Ranger and Delta Force soldier had already proved his worth. Cuban-born Rafael Encizo sat close to Katz, his attention focused on the file before him.

Kurtzman activated a switch and a large, wide-screen TV monitor was exposed as a panel on the wall slid back. Tapping another button on the control pad set in the table, Kurtzman brought up the first image, then sat back for Brognola to open the briefing.

"The map shows Kosovo province. I don't think I need to tell any of you the problems there. We have a volatile situation with warring factions at one another's throats every minute of every day, despite the efforts of the peacekeepers and the U.N. NATO is playing watchdog, and we're all holding our breath in case one sneeze sets the whole thing off again."

"Past history suggests any kind of peace is going to be fragile to say the least," Price said. "The ethnic Albanians are set against the Serbs, and you have religious and political agendas thrown in for good measure. The Albanians want a totally autonomous state, completely separate from the rest of the country. Elections have thrown up leaders who satisfy one faction but not another. Old feuds. Resentment.

Payback time. Not an easy mess to clean up and replace with a peaceful accord.''

"We also have a regime in Belgrade that is resisting any edict that comes via the UN or NATO. Positive action has been suggested, but nothing has budged the authorities yet.'' Brognola tapped the files on the table in front of him. "You'll find all kinds of facts and figures in there. As much as you want on the pros and cons of the whole shooting match.''

Katz leaned forward, pushing aside his files. "The situation is serious. We have a fragmented society with all the baggage that goes with it—destruction, loss of property and possessions, the homeless wandering the countryside, starving and sick. They don't know where the next meal is coming from, or where they'll get medicine when they're ill.

"There's a great deal of suspicion floating around between the various groups. Sitting down at a table talking peace doesn't appeal to some. They can't believe it will get them what they want. So they go their own way and use the only thing they have left—their will to fight. They set up resistance groups. Given the way they've been treated, who can blame them. The problem is that what they're doing is only making the situation that much harder to monitor. Anyone trying to bring these people to the conference table has a hard time because they're spread out in small groups all around the province. They move around, use sympathizers to hide them and keep a low profile until they strike, then vanish. Belgrade treats these rebels as criminals. They come down hard, sometimes going to extremes.''

"The mass graves? Dead women and children?" Hawkins asked. "If that's coming down hard, I must have lost my grip somewhere."

"None of us like it, T.J., but it's a fact of life. When people are set on dominating each other, it all goes out the window."

Hawkins gazed at Blancanales. He knew the man spoke the truth, but it was still hard to accept. He'd seen the photographs, the stark evidence of what a country divided could stoop to. There was no justice in those mass killings. None at all.

"Where do we fit into all this?" Manning asked.

"This has come to us via the Oval Office. There have been some problems involving the situation in and around Kosovo," Brognola said. "Security leaks. Details about military operations are being passed to a hostile faction so that control of potential hot spots have been weakened. All of this is making the job of the negotiators that much harder. The latest incident has added some urgency to the problem."

Brognola changed the image on-screen.

"The bus was carrying UN aid workers on a mercy mission to a zone that had been hit hard during a shelling session. The bus was riddled by small arms fire on a deserted stretch of road. Six of the aid workers were left dead and a number of others were badly wounded. Americans were among the dead and the wounded. The Land Rover carrying the UN escort was hit at the same time by a rocket, which destroyed the vehicle and killed the four men inside."

More images followed, showing the carnage inside the bus and Land Rover. The scenes were stark and brutal. They showed the results of violent death, and they were far from easy viewing. The occupants of the War Room absorbed the horrors of the scene with silent acceptance. Death and destruction were no strangers to them. The combat teams had seen it in the field on countless occasions, and would again because of the nature of their business. Yet despite the familiarity of their contact with such things, they were far from blasé about what they were seeing on the screen.

"Denials have come from all sides," Brognola continued. "The general opinion is that the perpetrators were members of a breakaway group known as the Free Albania Party. Apparently this is the kind of move they're notorious for."

"It's not a name I'm familiar with," Manning said.

"Something of a shadow group," Brognola explained. "Pretty extremist in their attitude. Totally opposed to any form of peace talks because they refuse to accept any compromises. Their manifesto demands one hundred percent autonomy for the ethnic Albanians. Intel we've inherited points to this FAP being the orchestraters of some hard actions, including the disruption of UN and NATO operations. They don't want anyone in their country telling them what to do, and they've promised direct action to emphasize their demands."

"A number of what looked like random acts can be attributed to this group," Katz said. "It suggests an involved conspiracy aimed at disruption and creating destabilization in the province."

"So we're talking hard-liners here?" Hawkins asked. "Direct action, take no prisoners, push and keep on pushing type people?"

"What are you getting at, T.J.?" Brognola asked, sensing there was more behind Hawkins's words.

"We have a hard-ass group that likes to make indiscriminate strikes. Hit fast, get out, show the world they're not going to lie down and take any kind of decision made in their name. Okay? At the same time, you're suggesting they're also responsible for some pretty sophisticated operations. How does an isolated group like the FAP become strong enough to influence classified operations run by the UN and NATO? Aren't we talking computers? Expensive hardware? That's a little out of the league for a hit-and-run guerrilla group."

"He has a point," Blancanales conceded. "Call these guys what you want—freedom fighters, terrorists. In my book these people are usually short on equipment, they move around so no one can pin them down to one base and they travel light. How do we link this bunch with a computer hacking setup?"

"That was our first thought," Brognola said, "until we started pulling in more information. The first break came from this man."

The image on screen showed Gregor Ridivic.

"He's an ethnic Albanian who was working undercover for us. He'd been approached because he was against the kind of operation the FAP was running. He wanted Albania free but not by using the tactics employed by the FAP. He managed to get himself into the group and worked the system to his advantage. Ridivic was a computer engineer, and his main job was looking after the group's equipment. From the intel he fed back, it looked like the FAP did have a pretty sophisticated setup. The bad news is that Ridivic felt his position had been compromised and made a break. He was smuggled to a place called Zittau. It's a jumping-off place for Yugoslavian refugees trying to escape into Europe. Ridivic met up with his contact, but he was killed before they could move on.''

''End of story?'' McCarter asked, sensing there was more to come.

''Before Ridivic left, he managed to make a copy of some of the data stored on the FAP computer. He passed a disk to his contact along with his written notes. She got out and forwarded the disk to her department head at the NSA.''

''There was a lot of encrypted data on the disk,'' Kurtzman said, ''and it was in Serbo-Croat. Ridivic had lost some data. He may have had to make his copy in a hurry. We got enough to prove the theory that the FAP had been breaking into UN systems and siphoning off information.''

''In the notes he made, Ridivic mentioned he had heard about the FAP having plans for some kind of strike against the U.S. and her allies. The UK was one of them. Right now we don't know what they intend, but I'd like to find out. There were also a few names that didn't mean much until Aaron linked them with other incoming items,'' Brognola said.

A new image came up on the screen—mortuary shots of a dead man and woman.

''Here we have Constantine Dupre. He was found

dead in his Paris apartment with the body of a woman beside him. They had both been subjected to physical abuse before having their throats cut. Dupre was with the UN. He was on extended leave so he wasn't missed at first. It was only when the caretaker at his apartment building alerted the police that he was found. According to the medical report, he and the woman had been dead for nearly three days.''

"What was his job with the UN?" McCarter asked.

"Dupre was in the IT section. He had access to a lot of the UN computer systems used for controlling UN deployment. It was tied in to the military networks.''

"Dupre either worked for the FAP because he wanted to or they had something on him?" James queried.

"Pass on that for the moment," Brognola said.

"Who was the woman found with Dupre?" Hawkins asked.

"Papers found in the apartment have her down as Ilyana Petrocovich, a Russian biochemist. I'll come back to her shortly.''

"Next up is Paul Weller," Kurtzman said as another image filled the screen. "He was found dead a few days back. Apparent suicide.''

"And another connection?" Lyons asked, stirring restlessly in his seat.

"The FBI had been keeping watch on Weller on another matter. He was suspected of running a highly sophisticated forgery operation. The FBI had been closing in for a while, and when they intercepted one of his couriers it gave them the evidence they needed. When they entered Weller's home, they found him dead. He had a gun in his hand and a hole in his skull. After they'd confiscated all his paperwork and computer, they had one of their experts check it out. Weller had a sophisticated encryption net set up. The FBI guy almost lost the data a couple of times. He finally broke the code and extracted Weller's hidden files. The man was good. He had a program going that could produce official paperwork so exact even the FBI couldn't fault it—visas, medical histories, passports. He even had a supply of nearly perfect paper stock to print it on. And photographs for identification purposes. We found these in his files.''

A double set of passport pages came on-screen.

The detail on the left showed the face of the woman found in Dupre's apartment—dark hair, high cheekbones, full face. According to the passport, she was Ilyana Petrocovich. The right-hand image was of a different woman—blond hair, a similar shape to the face. Her name was Ludmilla Karpov, and she was a Russian freelance journalist.

''What we do know,'' Katz said, ''is that the woman on the right, calling herself Karpov, is actually Ilyana Petrocovich. Information passed to us by Russian security after the end of the cold war included databases on a number of their people who no longer work for them. Petrocovich was one of those people. The dead woman is unknown to us. Our guess is she was hired to impersonate Petrocovich and collect the passports. Unfortunately in doing that, she set herself up as a victim.''

Lyons leaned forward and studied the images.

"This unknown woman goes to Weller, posing as Petrocovich. She asks for a new identity, goes back and collects the forged documents, then returns to Europe. Now we have Ilyana Petrocovich being impersonated by someone else. The twist is that the fake Petrocovich gets herself killed. Deliberate?"

"Could be," Katz said. "In the eyes of the world, Petrocovich is dead and gone. Out of the picture. People stop looking for her, so she can go where she likes and not be bothered."

"This impostor provides a body and an ID, and all she would have signed up for was the trip to America and a nice payoff."

"Surely Petrocovich would have known the switch would be picked up sooner or later," Manning said.

"I'm sure she knew that," Katz agreed. "But during the time the deception went unnoticed, Petrocovich would have been setting up her new identity and staying out of the light."

"So what is going on?" James asked. "Disruption of UN peacekeeping in Kosovo. Dead people connected in one way or another with the same. Big why coming up."

"You're the people to answer that," Brognola said. "As of now, it's priority."

"I've sketched out mission briefs," Price stated. "Details are in your files. If anyone has other ideas, let me hear them ASAP. We need to get things rolling."

Brognola turned to Katz. "Do you have anything to add?"

"Bloody hell," McCarter said. "I thought he'd nodded off again."

Katz was the first to smile at the Briton's remark. There was no hiding McCarter's respect for Yakov Katzenelenbogen. They had fought together from Phoenix Force's inception, through long years and countless missions. They had saved each other from death on many occasions and had shared laughter and grief along the way. It had been Katz who kept McCarter in check when his rebellious nature had got the better of him, and he had been a strong champion when it came to considering McCarter for the job of Phoenix Force's new commander on Katz's retirement.

In McCarter's eyes there was no better man than Katz, and he would have walked through fire if the Israeli had asked him to.

Waiting for the banter to subside, Katz tapped the documents on the table in front of him.

"I've had a chance to go through the intel that's been coming in from various sources. In isolation the data has little impact, but once you start to link the items there does seem to be a common thread. They all come back to Kosovo in one form or another. Now we all know the problems there—political, military, ethnic. We have a fragmented country with numerous groups vying for power and recognition. Throw in resentment that has been simmering away for decades and you have one hell of a brew. It's a time for getting even, settling old scores, imaginary as well as real. The poorer strata wants a share of the wealth, while the ones who hold power and money have no intention of letting go. We are left with a complex set of issues that are going to take a lot of sorting out. And while that is taking place, individuals, or groups, are just waiting their chance to reach out for the brass ring.''

"You believe that's what we have here?" Price asked.

Katz shrugged. "I'm postulating at the moment, illustrating scenarios that might come true all based on the sketchy information we have. What we don't know is how or why they connect. We have no names, no personalities the finger can be pointed at.''

"What we do know is the situation out there," Brognola reminded them. "And the FAP is in there somewhere. We need to find out what their intentions are now that they seem to be threatening the U.S. If that's true, is it in Europe or here on the mainland? We also need to know whether they're in bed with some outside agency. The possibility of upcoming talks aimed at promoting some kind of lasting peace deal is on thin ice. It wouldn't take much to shut them down. Keep that in mind.

"All right, people, we have our information. The need here is to go in and assess the situation. If this particular balloon does go up, the U.S. is going to get dragged in. We have our NATO commitments, political entanglements and a lot of our people on the spot. This could get nasty. Too many people on the sidelines waiting to jump in and stir the pot.''

He paused, clearing his throat. "One other thing. Remember that we have both Greece and Turkey on the fringes of this. Any hard fighting might spill over the borders, and then we'll have a destabilizing situation that could push either of those countries into a defensive stand. It's happened before. And don't forget the Russians. Small fires can turn into damn big ones given the right ingredients.''

Price pushed to her feet.

''Able Team, you have the files on the people we've already identified. Find out what else is going on we don't know about.''

Lyons nodded. He gestured at Blancanales and Schwarz, and the three-man team left the room without another word, already engrossed in the upcoming task.

''David, Phoenix Force is booked to fly to London. That's where you can start. A lot of the dissident groups from Europe make their homes in London. It could be a jumping-off point for you. We're liaising with the UN at the moment. They've admitted we have a point when we say we need to insert independent observers to look into the problem. All we have to do now is convince them it has to be done sooner than later. If the problems escalate, there's a tragedy waiting to happen over there.''

''You have such an optimistic outlook on life, Barb,'' McCarter commented.

Price gave him one of her disarming smiles.

''It's part of my mystique, David. Haven't you noticed?''

CHAPTER TWO

London, England

David McCarter turned away from the window, grimacing at his teammates.

"Wouldn't be London if it wasn't raining."

Calvin James, stretched out in a large, overstuffed armchair, raised his head to peer at the Briton.

"But every time we come?"

Rafael Encizo nodded in agreement.

"Give me a break," McCarter pleaded.

The telephone rang and McCarter grabbed the receiver, listening for a moment. "Great. So we'll see you shortly? Okay."

"Something happening at last?" Gary Manning asked. He was seated at a table, with maps and files spread out before them.

"You'd think we'd been here for a month instead of twelve hours," McCarter said. "So listen up. That was Maddox. He has the information we need. He's on his way over."

Kevin Maddox was Phoenix Force's liaison in London. He was an operative of British Intelligence and had been at RAF Upper Heyford to meet them on their arrival. Phoenix Force had flown to England on a U.S. Air Force Hercules transport. Maddox had been waiting with an unmarked car that had whisked the Stony Man team through the misty Oxfordshire countryside and into London, where they had been settled in an anonymous safe house in Cricklewood. Here they had organized themselves and made contact with the Farm while Maddox checked his department for updates on the information they had been asked to supply.

The door opened and Hawkins wandered in.

"You guys want more coffee?"

James nodded and held out his empty mug for Hawkins to fill from the steaming pot he was carrying.

"Hey, I'll have some," Manning said.

"Gary, you sorted anything from those satellite photos?" McCarter asked.

"About the only thing they confirm is it's damn rough territory where we might end up."

He indicated the images on the sheets spread out across the table.

Taken by orbiting satellites, the photographs were sharp and detailed. They had been obtained from high-clarity television cameras located in the satellites. The detail was so sharp that it was almost possible to pick out the smallest of objects on the ground. A series of overlapping shots produced a continuous panorama of the terrain.

"Here is where the bus was attacked. Over here is where the shooters must have been waiting. Shell casings were found here and here, and tracks can be seen where the ambushers came in and retreated."

Manning reached for another sheet while Mc-Carter examined the satellite images.

"Whoever they were, the shooters knew their way around. The spot they used to hide is the best piece of ground in the immediate area. Gave them a full sweep of the road. Shooters here and here. In those positions they had the bus and Land Rover in a cross fire. They would have had their targets in their sights well before they reached the kill zone. Had them covered all the way. Once they'd taken their targets, all they had to do was move back into those rocks, disperse and disappear before anyone could go after them. If there had been anyone left alive."

"The way you describe it makes it sound like they deliberately set out to hit that bus," Hawkins said.

"This was no spur of the moment hit," McCarter replied. "They knew exactly where and when that bus was due. We're not talking about a combat situation. This was deliberate. They waited for that bus, knew it was carrying unarmed people. Then they took their time and opened up."

"The same way they took out the Land Rover carrying the UN escort," James said. "One rocket straight into the vehicle."

"Pretty grim way to make your point," Manning said.

"The way they see it, Gary, they're fighting for their country. The UN and NATO will be invaders as far as they're concerned."

"From what I've read, the majority of the Albanians are ready to accept talks," Hawkins said. "Why can't these guys see it the same way?"

"The rest of the country is wrong from the standpoint of the FAP. You see what you want to see in any given situation."

McCarter popped the tab on a can of soda. "I agree that the peace talks are important. If the FAP keeps on with its harassment, the talks will go out the window and the Serbs will jump at the chance of coming down hard again on the ethnic Albanians. That will mean reprisals, more fighting and the bloody country in chaos again. And that will increase the possibility of dominoes falling all over the place."

"You believe what Katz said about others being dragged in?" Encizo asked.

"Look at Greece," McCarter said. "They don't want anything spilling over their northern border or setting off nationalistic elements in Macedonia that might expand any fighting. There's a long history of politics and deep feeling in that area that could erupt. Even if it doesn't actually come to that, the Greek government might feel justified in activating its military along the border as a precaution. In that situation anything could happen."

"Maybe that's what the FAP wants," James suggested. "To start a regional conflict and drag everyone in."

"It wouldn't necessarily mean they'd benefit from that," Hawkins said. "The Albanians might end up total losers, even worse off than they are now."

McCarter drained his soft drink.

"Hasn't stopped wars being fought before. And maybe the FAP feels it's worth the chance. From what we know of their policy, anything is better than staying under Serb control, even if it's diminished.''

"If we can't have it, nobody can?" Manning said.

"We live in a weird world."

A computer was set up in the corner of the room. It had a large monitor and was configured to receive both E-mail and fax messages. Encizo was closest to it when the screen flashed a message indicating E-mail was incoming. He activated the screen via the mouse, and watched as the message scrolled across the screen.

"David, message from Stony Man." The team gathered around the monitor and read: Able Team has made contact. Will advise on result.

"They haven't wasted any time," Hawkins observed.

"They might not have had any choice," McCarter pointed out.

New Rochelle, New York

CARL LYONS WAITED patiently while Rosario Blancanales eased the car to the curb, then opened his door and climbed out. His partners followed, and they stood for a moment scanning the empty house. Nobody expected to find anything here, since the FBI had gone over the place with a fine-tooth comb.

"Let's do it," Lyons said and walked up the drive to the front door of Paul Weller's house.

Blancanales, trailing his partners, caught a flicker of movement from a window in the house next door. As he turned his head, he saw a curtain fall back into place. He caught up to Lyons and Schwarz as they reached the door, Lyons using the key provided by the FBI.

"We're being watched," Blancanales stated.

Lyons glanced at him, his face tense.

"Only a nosy neighbor. Might be worth having a word, though."

"Go ahead," Lyons said.

Blancanales crossed the lawn and skirted a bed of neat flowers. He climbed up the steps to the porch and rang the bell. He heard movement inside, and seconds later the door opened.

Arlene Gorshin was blond and blue-eyed. She was thirty-seven years old, worked out regularly and considered herself in excellent shape for her age. She answered the door dressed in a clinging exercise leotard, gently dabbing at her flushed face with a pink towel. When she saw Rosario Blancanales she smiled at him in a way that said far more than just hello.

"Miss, may I have a few words with you?"

He flashed the Justice Department badge and ID that Stony Man provided as cover, holding it up so the woman could study it closely.

"Agent Loomis?"

"Yes, ma'am. Douglas. Doug to my friends."

"What can I help you with, Agent Loomis?"

"Please, call me Doug. I hate all the formality."

"Would you like to come inside?"

Blancanales followed her through the door, closing it behind him. The interior of the house was bright and filled with paintings and wood sculptures. The lounge had a polished wood floor and somewhere Blancanales could hear wind chimes tinkling gently.

"You have a lovely home, ma'am."

"Why, thank you." Gorshin paused and turned to smile at him. "And stop calling me ma'am. It's Arlene."

"Fine."

"Sit down, Doug. Would you like a drink?" She was fussing around a drinks cabinet.

"Not for me."

"I'll have one if you don't mind. I was just doing some exercises when you knocked."

Blancanales recalled the moving curtain as he sat on the edge of a bright orange couch that had an Indian blanket draped across the back. He slipped a small notebook from his coat pocket and took out a pen.

Gorshin perched on a low chair across from him. She had a tall glass of what looked like orange juice in one hand. When she saw the notebook she screwed up her face.

"Oh, dear, now you look all official."

"Don't you worry about this. It's mainly because I have a bad memory."

Gorshin giggled, not certain whether he was serious or just trying to put her at her ease.

"I suppose you're here because of what happened to Paul Weller?"

"That's right. My department has been handed the investigation."

"Well, at least you're a sight more polite than those FBI men."

"I'm sorry about that, Arlene. Did they talk to you?"

"Talk at you more like. When they eventually came to see me, it was like I was as guilty as Paul Weller. The way they looked around in here you would have thought I had something to hide. I mean, here I was ready to tell them what I knew and all they did was snap at me. I didn't like them."

"That couldn't have been very pleasant, Arlene. Not for someone as sensitive as you."

"Why, Doug, you are very perceptive. How did you guess?"

"All I had to do was look around in here. The pictures, sculptures. A person who fills her house with things like that has to have an artistic nature."

"Are you sure you wouldn't like a drink?"

"Honestly, I'm fine. Look, I hate to have to bring this all up again, but I would greatly appreciate any information you might be able to give me about Paul Weller. Anything at all, Arlene. It doesn't matter how silly it might sound. I really need your help."

"What can I tell you? Paul was a nice person to know. Always polite. Never caused any trouble. I knew he worked from home. He told me he was involved in some kind of financial dealings and did all his transactions with his computer. He always seemed so in control. You know what I mean? He just didn't seem the kind to kill himself. I felt so awful when I heard what had happened. I guess it's silly saying he didn't seem the type. I mean, what is a suicide supposed to look like? They're just people who have problems they can't handle."

"Arlene, did Paul have many visitors?"

"Not really. Apart from the ones who came to collect the packages. He sent them out regularly. He told me once that they came to collect correspondence connected to his work." The woman paused to take a sip of her drink, peering at the silent Blancanales over the rim of the glass. "Is that what he was doing?"

Blancanales smiled and shook his head. "I'm afraid Paul was into something illegal."

The shock on her face was genuine.

"And he was living right next door to me all the time. Oh, my, Doug, that's quite frightening."

"So, there were couriers. Anyone else? Say, in the last few weeks?"

"A man did come to see him about two days before he died. I'd never seen him before."

"Can you describe him?"

"A big man. Very heavy build. He was in the house for about ten minutes and then he left."

"Did he have a car?"

"Nothing special. A standard Dodge saloon. Mid-blue, I think. I do remember it left in a hurry. Is that any help?"

"You are doing just fine. Now was there anyone else?"

"There was a woman last week. She came late in the afternoon. Stayed about an hour. I was working in the garden, which is how I know."

"Can you describe her at all?"

"Dark hair. Striking looks. Well made-up. Very sleek. European, I'd say."

Blancanales reached inside his coat and took out an envelope. There were photographs inside that

Stony Man had provided. One of them was from the evidence taken from Paul Weller's house. It was the photo he had been using in the creation of the passport for Ilyana Petrocovich, the woman Stony Man knew as Ludmilla Karpov.

"That's her," Gorshin said without a moment's hesitation. "She's the one."

"Thank you, Arlene," Blancanales said. "That's just great."

By the time Lyons and Schwarz came out of Weller's house, Blancanales was waiting beside the car. As they climbed inside, he turned to wave to Arlene Gorshin, who was watching from the window of her house.

"Well, tell, Romeo," Schwarz said, grinning.

"That lady is very nice," Blancanales said, "so you mind your manners."

"Did she give you anything?" Schwarz continued, still smirking.

Blancanales produced the photograph.

"She identified her as a visitor to Weller's house a week ago."

Lyons took out his cell phone and called Stony Man.

"We have an ID. The dead woman made a visit to Paul Weller the week before she died."

On the other end of the line Brognola acknowledged the information.

"Okay. Keep in touch."

"Where to now?" Blancanales asked as Schwarz pulled away from the curb.

"Let's go for a cruise."

"What?" Lyons said.

"I want to see if that car is actually following us, or if I'm just getting paranoid," Schwarz replied.

Blancanales glanced in the rearview mirror. In his mind he suddenly knew what he would see before the image registered—a midblue Dodge saloon.

London, England

KEVIN MADDOX EASED his six-foot-six-inch frame into one of the large armchairs, dumped his attaché case on the floor beside him, then took the mug of black coffee T.J. Hawkins held out to him. He might have been part of British Intelligence, but his manner and dress suggested a self-sufficient cop. He had a straightforward, no-nonsense attitude that told Phoenix Force he would always be on the edge with his superiors. Maddox was good at his job, which was probably the main reason he managed to hang on to his position.

"Right," he said. "Update time."

"Free Albania Party?" McCarter queried.

"The name has cropped up a few times," Maddox said. "Not in a definite way, you understand. The talk about the FAP has it as some trigger-happy bunch of crazies. No one has a good word for them. There is a circle of what they call FAP administrators, and they tend to stay in the background. As for real action, we can't claim to have seen much here in London. The FAP is here, but most of the stories about them seem to be rumors circulating among the Albanian refugees in London."

"How strong a community is it?" Calvin James asked. "The refugee one."

"Since the Kosovo troubles the numbers have increased. London is like a magnet for refugees. Political exiles. Like any major city, it has its enclaves where the dispossessed go. There is also the fact that London and the international airports are a crossroad. You can fly in from anywhere and leave for anywhere. Being close to mainland Europe, we're never far from the action."

McCarter attracted Maddox's attention.

"Has there been any trouble from the Albanians?"

"Very little. They stay within their own groups and keep a low profile."

"No agitation? Marches? Protests?" Manning asked.

"A few, but even they were small-scale. Couple of dozen people. Homemade banners. All they wanted was to go back home."

"What about rallies? Indoor meetings? That kind of thing?"

"Special Branch from Scotland Yard has been monitoring the few meetings that have taken place. Again, nothing to get agitated about. Just some back street church hall with a couple of speakers. The usual stuff about the return of the homeland, trying to raise money so they could fund medical help for those back home. Cup of coffee and a few sandwiches afterward. Nothing overtly political. Certainly no hellfire outrage encouraging open rebellion against the government in Belgrade."

"So what's the point?" Hawkins challenged.

"Look at it like a placebo," Manning said. "Doctor gives a patient a fake pill. Patient takes it and believes it does him good. It's a way of giving the patient comfort. He feels better.''

"So these rallies are just a way of making the refugees feel like they are doing something even though the reality is the opposite?'' Hawkins shook his head.

"The Albanians here in London,'' Maddox explained, "have been forced to leave their country because of any number of reasons. Some have just given up in total despair because they've lost everything. Others may have left due to political pressure, religious persecution. At the end of the day, they can't see any definite plan for the future. Their lives have been destroyed. Whatever happens in Albania, they might never be able to go back.''

Hawkins took a moment to think about the matter.

"I guess you must be right. I never thought of it that way. There's no way I could ever imagine what it must be like to lose everything the way these people have.''

"Hell, we all grumble about where we live from time to time,'' James said. "I know I do. But when you take a real hard look we don't have it so bad after all.''

McCarter perched himself on the arm of a chair.

"Any names from this Free Albania Party? I mean, is there any hidden agenda or serious work going on behind the scenes we should know about?''

Maddox reached inside his jacket and pulled out a folded sheet of paper, which he passed to McCarter.

"One of our undercover agents has been working

on the fringes of the FAP. He's had to take things very slowly. One of his recent reports said the people at the top have become very closemouthed just lately, as if there might be something going on they don't want broadcast.''

McCarter studied the brief report. There were a few names, none of which meant anything to him.

"We can send this over the fax."

McCarter handed the sheet to Hawkins, who crossed to the computer and opened the fax center. After placing the paper on the scanner unit, Hawkins fed the image into the program and sent the document to Stony Man.

Stony Man Farm, Virginia

AARON KURTZMAN ROLLED his wheelchair away from the printer, scanning the information that had just come through from Phoenix Force. He crossed to Carmen Delahunt's station and passed her the printout.

"Check out those names. All sources. All angles. I need some answers."

Delahunt nodded and turned to her keyboard. During the next few minutes, she was occupied with the information input. Aware that the intel had come from Britain, she requested that the data search include Interpol as well as European security agencies, the British National Computer Data Base and then U.S. information banks. Once she had all the information keyed in, she asked for an all-source search, with a request that any information be collated and printed out. After hitting the access key, Delahunt turned from the console and pushed to her feet.

"Anyone want coffee?" she asked as she made her way to the ever-present pot.

"Here," Huntington Wethers called, holding up his empty mug.

Delahunt took his mug. "How's it going?"

Wethers eased away from his keyboard, flexing his shoulders.

"Slow. The problem is we don't have much to go on yet. There are few hints about leakages. A suggestion that someone has been hacking into the military net, and UN breaches of security, but nothing much in the way of identifying the people involved."

"At least we have one player—Petrocovich. From her background detail she was brilliant but not a team player. Very dedicated to her work. But why would she go freelance?"

"Someone like Petrocovich would have hated having to abandon her work. She could have spent years on a major project. Maybe she was close to perfecting it. Then the Russians about face and start to cut back on research. That could have left her pretty upset and determined not to have it all taken from her."

"She's no different from the Nazis who came to America and continued their rocket development here," Katz added as he also joined the group. "People get hooked on research, their pet project. For many of them there isn't anything else. They live for what they're doing. Deprive them of it, and they just fall apart."

"Okay," Delahunt agreed, "let's say you're correct. So Petrocovich carries on her research under various assumed names provided by this guy Weller. She makes her concoctions and sells them to the terrorist cells. How come she ends up supposedly dead in Paris with this Dupre character?"

"She could go about her business without having to keep looking over her shoulder?" Price suggested.

"Why not? Maybe she needs isolation. Breathing space."

"And Dupre?" Delahunt asked.

Katz shrugged. "A dupe to make the death look even more dramatic. Two lovers murdered by some lunatic."

"If that's true, Katz, we're dealing with some pretty cold characters," Wethers said.

"When you walk alongside the tiger don't be surprised if he ends up eating you," Katz said.

Price grinned. "Oriental wisdom?"

Katz shook his head. "Not really. It just sounds authentic when you talk like Bruce Lee."

Wethers chuckled as he made his way back to his computer.

"Let's do a little work along those lines," Kurtzman suggested. "Presume Petrocovich is still alive. Run some checks, searches. Let's go to work, people."

CHAPTER THREE

New Rochelle, New York

"Let's reel him in," Lyons said, easing his Colt Python from under his jacket and resting it on his thigh.

"Alive, too," Blancanales added.

"Wouldn't have it any other way," Lyons muttered.

Schwarz cruised along the road, turning at the first corner, which took them away from the residential area and into empty countryside.

"He's still with us," Blancanales said. "Persistent son of a bitch, isn't he?"

Schwarz tired of the slow pace. He hit the accelerator and the car surged forward. Up ahead, the side road they traveled petered out to become a narrow dirt strip that ran alongside undeveloped fields. Dirt and pebbles clattered against the underside of the vehicle. Behind them a faint dust trail partly obscured the tail car.

"See that old truck?" Lyons said. "Slow when you reach it and let me out, then make a stop."

"Here we go," Schwarz muttered.

He swung the rental car around the front of the battered, rusting hulk of the abandoned truck, touching the brake long enough to allow Lyons to kick open his door and roll out. The moment the Able Team leader hit the ground Schwarz swung the wheel, taking the car back into full view, then stomped hard on the brakes, this time bringing the vehicle to a dead stop.

The Buick closed the gap quickly, the driver slamming on his own brakes and swinging the wheel to avoid rear ending the rental car. As the Buick came to a lurching stop Lyons broke cover, coming from behind the truck. He reached the driver's door in three strides, yanked it open and made a grab for the driver.

The big, heavy man retaliated, kicking at Lyons and catching him on the hip. The ex-LAPD cop grunted, sidestepped the next kick and swung the heavy Colt Python in a short arc that made contact with the driver's head. The blow dazed the man, and Lyons dragged him out of the car, kicked his feet from under him and dropped him facedown on the ground. By the time Schwarz and Blancanales arrived, Lyons had the driver's gun out of his hip rig and was waiting for his partners.

"Typical," Blancanales grumbled. "We get the backup and you have all the fun."

"It's what being the boss is all about," Lyons said. He tossed the confiscated handgun to Schwarz, who examined it with interest.

"Looks like this has been around the block a few times," he remarked, passing the gun to Blancanales.

"Haven't seen one of these in a long time."

The autopistol was a Makarov, a functional, hard wearing gun, with few refinements but hard stopping power.

The driver of the Buick sat up, rubbing at the bloody gash on his head. He was dazed but not incapacitated. He muttered to himself and leaned back against the side of the Buick, his body starting to slump.

"Maybe you hit him too hard," Blancanales suggested.

"Damn lucky I didn't shoot him," Lyons replied.

"Well, I think we should..." Schwarz began.

The Buick driver twisted away from the side of the car, his right hand dropping to his ankle. He came up with a short-bladed knife that flashed as it cut in toward Lyons's groin. It was only the Able Team leader's swift reflexes that saved him. He half turned, felt the knife graze his trousers, and out of the corner of his eye he saw the driver shoving up off the ground with a speed that denied his bulk. Lyons's momentum bounced him off the side of the car, almost into the second slash of the knife. In the split second before it hit, Blancanales dived in close, grabbed the driver around the neck and hauled him sideways. The man yelled, his voice grating as Blancanales hugged his throat, almost cutting off his air. The driver rose to his feet, despite having Blancanales hanging on to him, and swung him around with the ease of a man lifting a child. Pain flared across Blancanales's shoulders as he crashed against the side of the car, the driver trying to shake him free.

Schwarz rushed in and planted a foot behind the

driver's knees, causing him to slump. As the man went down, Lyons clubbed him behind the ear with the Python's barrel. He hit hard and solid. This time the driver collapsed and didn't move. Blancanales rolled the man's heavy bulk off him and climbed to his feet. He dusted himself off, glancing at his partners with a look of embarrassment on his face.

"What the hell is this guy on?"

Schwarz pulled plastic cuffs from his pocket. He rolled the driver onto his side and looped the plastic around the man's wrists, securing them. Blancanales helped him get the man into the Buick's back seat.

"Let's get out of here before somebody sees us," Lyons said.

He got in the rear of the Buick to keep an eye on the captive while Blancanales drove the car. Schwarz followed them in their vehicle.

Stony Man Farm, Virginia

"HERE'S WHAT WE HAVE on the guy," Akira Tokaido said, turning in his chair.

Barbara Price took the printout, reading the data as she crossed to one of the phones. She pressed the speed-dial button that put her through to Lyons's cell phone.

"Can we talk?" she asked when he answered.

"Sure."

"We have one Georgi Khan. He's Georgian. Forty-one years old. Spent time in the Soviet military, but quit just after the collapse. Within a few months he was on the Russian Mafia's payroll. He's your basic hard man. Now he hires out as a bodyguard. He speaks good English, a little French and pretty good German. While he was in the army he was a top athlete, a bodybuilder. He's still known to frequent health clubs wherever he goes.''

"Any known associates who might be part of this deal?'' Lyons asked.

"No links yet, but we're still working on that.''

"Did you find out where he's staying?''

"A hotel in New Jersey called the Clarendon Grand.''

"As if,'' Lyons grunted.

"You going to take a look?''

"Affirmative.''

"I'll call if anything breaks.''

The Clarendon Grand Hotel, New Jersey

KHAN'S ROOM WAS BLEAK and contained the bare necessities. The only luggage Able Team found was a battered holdall. Inside were a few items of clothing, all of Russian manufacture. In the bathroom they found shaving gear and a toothbrush.

"This guy likes to travel uncomfortably,'' Blancanales said. "He's one step up from being a damned hobo.''

"Here's his passport,'' Schwarz said.

He had found the item in a drawer in the scarred clothes chest that leaned against one wall. The Russian passport showed that Khan had visited the U.S. twice within the past two weeks. Prior to that he had been in Paris. The date tallied with the time Constantine Dupre and the fake Ilyana Petrocovich had died.

"Too many coincidences," Lyons said. He turned the pages of the passport. "Here. A couple of weeks ago he was in Belgrade."

"That date shows he was in town when Paul Weller killed himself," Schwarz said.

"Gets around for a big guy," Blancanales said to no one in particular.

Lyons scooped up the assortment of papers.

"Let's get these back to the Farm."

Stony Man Farm, Virginia

"LET'S ASSESS what we have so far," Price said.

Kurtzman activated one of the War Room TV monitors, punching up images.

"We have three people dead. Paul Weller's death was taken as a suicide on the first count. There now seems some doubt as to that. It may turn out he was murdered, and the death staged to look like he shot himself. Next we have Constantine Dupre found dead in Paris, and there's no doubt that he was murdered. With him was the woman thought to be Ilyana Petrocovich. The Paris authorities are trying to ID her but no luck yet.

"If Petrocovich isn't dead, we need to find out where she is, because there could be links to the FAP. If she's involved with them, we have to establish why. Previous information told us she was a biochemist when she worked for the Soviets. Now that she's freelance, I doubt she's changed to formulating perfume. For all we know she could be working on something for the FAP."

"We also know that the FAP is an extremist

group," Katz said. "The upcoming peace talks, as much as they might be needed, are not going to satisfy their agenda. From the previous information we have, they'll keep right on doing the same thing they've been doing for the past several months."

"Why won't they talk?" Tokaido asked. "I understand they refuse to accept any kind of compromise for Kosovo. They want one hundred percent ethnic Albanian control. Okay, so how do they expect to get it by just carrying on killing and bombing? It doesn't work. All it does in the end is make everyone mad, including the people who were on their side at the beginning. Look at Ireland. Even the IRA had to sit down and talk."

Katz considered for a moment.

"Look at it this way. The FAP is driven by a number of negative ideals. People in their situation have a hard core of rage, hatred and frustration. All are fighting for control. They see their country and their heritage being taken away piece by piece. Their culture has been torn apart and is still being trampled underfoot. By now they have gone beyond compromise. All they see are outside forces taking control and dictating how their country should be divided. Strangers are telling them what to do, where to live and who their friends are. Military force is being used to control what was theirs. People who live thousands of miles away are making the choices. The FAP feels that the only way they can make a statement is by defying all that. Their acts are a way of saying we are the Albanians. Not you. And we will go on fighting you until every stranger has gone and our country is returned to us."

"But it doesn't make it right, Katz," Tokaido insisted. "It doesn't justify what they're doing."

"You're right, it doesn't. But to the FAP it's the only way their voice is ever going to be heard. If they simply sit back and allow things to happen, they believe they will be wiped out, and everything that was ever great about the Albanian people will be lost forever. Remember, too, that the ethnic Albanians are a Muslim people. Their religion is so important to them they'll die before they allow it to be defiled, which is what they see happening here. The Muslim believer has a powerful grasp of his religion. It is more important than life itself. He will defend it any way he can. If that means total sacrifice, then so be it."

Tokaido shook his head. "Man, we live in a mixed-up world."

"Amen to that," Kurtzman said.

"Our priority is to find out what the FAP intends to do," Katz said, "and what the link is between the FAP and Ilyana Petrocovich. We have to remember what we've learned about these people. They are against the U.S., Britain, NATO and the UN. We need to get to them and stop whatever they're planning."

"If the FAP has something going with Petrocovich, the results could be nasty," Delahunt commented.

Katz pushed to his feet and crossed to pour himself a mug of fresh coffee. He paced around for a moment or two, gathering his thoughts.

"The flaw in all our thinking is that we are only

theorizing. We need hard facts, proof so that we can act to stop anything that might come up.''

"Looks like it's back to you guys," Price said to Able Team.

"The FBI isn't going to be able to hold Khan for long," Lyons said. "He already has legal representation, and they're crowing about his rights being violated. There's no proof he's been involved in anything illegal. According to his lawyer, he was only driving through the area when we stopped and assaulted him.''

"So let him go but keep him under surveillance," Katz said.

"Exactly what are we going to do?" Schwarz asked. "When he leaves the FBI, he'll be tracked by a helicopter using a TV camera. Jack is almost ready to go.''

Jack Grimaldi was Stony Man's ace flyer. He was a skilled aviator, and he could fly anything from a Piper Cub to the space shuttle.

"Okay," Price said. "Once Jack is in position contact the FBI and have them release Khan. After that it's up to us.''

"The guy isn't dumb," Blancanales said. "I'm pretty sure he'll suspect his car has been bugged, so I'm betting he'll take a cab.''

"What if he decides to use the subway?" Delahunt asked. "Jack isn't going to be able to track him then.''

"We thought of that," Lyons said. "Khan will have a tail. No way we can get round that in a place like New York. This is where we'll need to wing it. We can't get too close and can't afford to lose him.

So we'll play it carefully and use Jack as the main man, but bring in foot soldiers if and when Khan goes underground.''

"The tails will be in touch with Jack via mobile communicators. They follow Khan until he leaves the subway, then relay the information to the chopper so that Jack can eyeball him when he shows aboveground.''

"The FBI has agreed to provide a tag team to follow Khan,'' Lyons explained. "Once we're back in control, they'll back off and leave the rest to us.''

"Khan's papers have been returned to him via the FBI,'' Kurtzman said. "They scanned everything and took prints, trace samples. They're running those down now. We have copies of all the documents and papers, and checks are being made on all the information.''

Lyons stood. "We'll move out. I want to be in position when Khan is released.''

The men of Able Team left to pick up their transport.

Price glanced at Katz. "There's nothing more we can do until the teams call. It's time to hand over to you, Aaron.''

Kurtzman nodded and swung his wheelchair toward the door. The meeting was over.

CHAPTER FOUR

London, England

Peering through rain-streaked windows, the men of Phoenix Force monitored the activity around the dilapidated church hall, which was located in a rundown area in East London. At the far end of the street a high corrugated iron fence hid the work of a construction company. The company notice board explained that a new multilevel car park was being built.

"Bloody hell, that's just what they need around here," McCarter had muttered. "Another car park. That'll bring plenty of jobs for the unemployed."

An hour later they were still watching the church hall. A trickle of people had moved in and out of the grimy building. None of them had looked particularly well-dressed, and their body movement had suggested a lack of spirit, a world-weary acceptance of their lot in life.

"Man, it has got to be hard for them," James observed. "In a foreign country, everything they had had gone and not much of a future ahead of them. I guess they have a right to be angry."

"I agree," McCarter said. "The majority of these people want to go home. But their case is being made more difficult by the actions of a minority of extremists. Every time the radicals do something destructive or violent they set the cause back and make it harder for these poor buggers."

"Hey, what's this?" Hawkins said.

A dark van had eased around the corner. It was cruising slowly along the street, on the opposite side to the hall. A few yards from the building it pulled to a stop. Smoke trailed from the exhaust, showing that the engine was still idling.

"I don't like the look of this," Manning said.

"Me neither," McCarter agreed.

The van lurched into motion, tires squealing against the wet tarmac, then swung in across the sidewalk. A sliding door in the side of the van rolled open, and a group of armed men spilled out. All were clad in dark pants and leather jackets, with black ski masks pulled down over their faces. Moving with practiced ease they fanned out, two of them covering the door to the hall while the rest of the group—three in all—ran inside.

"This isn't good," James said.

"David, what do we do?" Manning asked.

The sharp crackle of autofire made the decision for them.

"We don't sit on our arses and let it happen," McCarter snapped.

He kicked open his door and exited the parked car, his hand dipping under his jacket for the holstered Browning Hi-Power. The rest of Phoenix

Force followed suit, weapons out and ready as they spread apart prior to crossing the street.

ONE OF THE HIT TEAM'S spotters caught sight of Phoenix Force. He yelled to his partner, and without any hesitation the pair opened fire on the Stony Man team. The harsh crackle of autofire sent pedestrians scattering for cover. Window glass behind Phoenix Force shattered as the erratic fire missed them by inches.

Aware that the next volley could be well on target, the Phoenix Force commandos used the time to track their targets before returning fire.

McCarter and James had picked the same man. They fired almost in unison and the autogunner went down hard, his upper body taking the combined firepower. The man's partner shouted something above the firing guns inside the church hall. Screams of pain were audible above the shooting.

T.J. Hawkins, the agonized sounds ringing in his ears, dropped to one knee, fisting his pistol in both hands. He caught the remaining gunner as the man leveled his autorifle at Calvin James. Hawkins squeezed the trigger twice, his 9 mm slugs drilling the gunner in the head, spinning him. He dropped to the ground, writhing in agony before the extreme damage shut him down permanently.

"Rafe, the van," McCarter said.

Even though the van was empty, Encizo took his approach carefully. Once he had confirmed it was deserted, he put a bullet in each tire, disabling the vehicle.

Activity inside the hall's entrance warned Phoenix

Force that the other three men were on their way out. McCarter signaled for his team to spread out, clearing the door. Shadows moved in the entrance and the hit team appeared, pushing a pair of frightened men before them.

"If you try to stop us, they die," one of the masked men yelled.

His accent was strong, his English awkward, but he got his message across.

"You understand?"

McCarter stepped forward. "I hear what you're saying, but there's no way out. The police will be here very soon, then you'll be dead. The British police don't like you people bringing your bloody war to this country."

The spokesman laughed. "You think this is war? It is nothing to what will be happening soon. Then maybe you will stop interfering in our war."

One of the other men spoke, gesturing to the disabled van. The spokesman shook his head.

"Burst tires will not stop us."

McCarter shrugged, moving as if to walk away. Before anyone could realize what he was doing he swiveled slightly, raising his pistol.

McCarter aimed and fired, a snap shot that cored through the spokesman's skull just above his right eye. The man's head snapped back, blood spraying from the exit hole. He stumbled, losing his balance, and dropped like a deadweight.

Before reaction time set in, Phoenix Force moved into action.

Manning, off to one side of the main group, brought up his own handgun and triggered twice, firing slugs into the head of the gunner on Mc-Carter's left. The man went to his knees, trying to pull his autorifle on-line, but a third bullet from Manning's pistol took him out for good. He spilled over onto his back, legs twisted under his shuddering body.

The surviving gunner, after seeing his two partners go down, decided it was time to leave. He broke to the right, ducking behind the van and emerging on the far side, close to the wall of the church hall. He sprinted along the street, splashing through puddles and the trash littering the street.

"I'm after him," James said.

He followed the running man and saw him approaching the corrugated construction-site fence.

The sound of police sirens could be heard in the near distance.

The running man hit the fence full on, using his solid weight to buckle one of the metal sheets. He hit the fence a second time and it gave under the impact. The man pushed his way through, and James saw him vanish from sight.

"Damn!"

The Phoenix Force warrior didn't hesitate. He closed the gap and slid through the opening, spotting the skeletal outline of the car park rising into the gray sky. The structure was surrounded by the chaos of the site. Diggers, mixers and piles of building material were scattered around, and the churned earth had been reduced to a slippery mud by the rain. This late in the afternoon the site was deserted, the construction crew having quit early because of the rain.

James spotted his quarry immediately. The terrorist had discarded his ski mask and was skirting the edge of a deep pit no more than twenty feet away from him.

"Hey!" James yelled.

The terrorist glanced over his shoulder, eyes wide with alarm. For a moment he held his pose, unsure how to react.

Then he shouted, "No!" It was a yell of pure defiance, a challenge to anyone within earshot.

The man's autorifle shifted toward James, and a choppy stream of slugs blew muddy geysers into the air as they cut their way closer to the Phoenix Force commando.

It was no time for a debate, James decided. This confrontation would leave one of them dead, and the ex-Navy SEAL had no intention of quitting life yet.

He raised his pistol, leveled it and stroked the trigger twice.

The bullets impacted against the terrorist's chest and punched him backward, his arms thrown wide. The autorifle spun over and over as it left the man's grasp. The terrorist was allowed a brief scream as he toppled over the edge of the pit. By the time James reached the rim, the gunner was facedown in the water that had flooded the bottom of the pit, wide ripples still rolling away from his wallowing corpse.

"Damn it all to hell! Why didn't he give it up?"

James knew the answer to his own question. The terrorist mind had a single track. Surrender wasn't an option. You went into the action because you believed in the cause, and allowing yourself to be taken by the enemy was simply admitting defeat. Defeat wasn't an option. It was a simple equation—choose death before dishonor.

Movement attracted James's attention. He looked around and saw Gary Manning coming toward him. The big Canadian looked into the pit.

"You okay, Cal?"

"I wouldn't have shot him if he hadn't made a play. I gave him a chance."

Manning shrugged.

"His choice, then."

They made their way back to the street. Two police cruisers were already on the scene. Uniformed officers were moving pedestrians along while others had already started to cordon off the area. McCarter was in deep conversation with two more officers. James and Manning joined him.

McCarter glanced around, nodding briefly to his teammates.

"The others are inside checking casualties," he said.

Another couple of vehicles sped down the street, one containing an armed response unit. They spread out, weapons up and ready.

McCarter's diplomatic skills were being pushed to the limit as he dealt with the police officers. They were unsure of his credentials, questioning the authority that had allowed Phoenix Force to make life-and-death decisions on the streets of London. McCarter's role as leader of Phoenix Force was being put to the test. Whatever else he might have been, McCarter was learning to be a consummate tightrope walker. He managed to hold the officers at bay until Kevin Maddox arrived to take control, using his position in Special Branch to pacify the police and advise them to back away.

By this time Phoenix Force had assessed the damage inside the hall. They found four dead Albanians, with another five wounded. The hit had been short, sharp and brutal. The gunners had moved directly to the main hall, where a number of the refugees had been settling for the coming evening. Once inside they had simply opened fire, their targets indiscriminate. It had only been Phoenix Force's intervention that had cut the attack short. The exchange of fire outside the hall had alerted the hit team, and they had backed off instantly.

"We have something here," Encizo said, beckoning McCarter.

He led the way to a side door that opened onto a narrow, dimly lit passage.

"The dead guy I found outside had this in his belt," Encizo stated, producing a handgun from his jacket.

McCarter examined the weapon, a German-made Walther.

"The guy had a chair near the outside door. There were magazines and a couple of coffee mugs. I'd guess he was there to stop anyone coming through here."

"Let's take a look," McCarter said. "Maddox will keep the local cops out until we've checked the place."

The heavy oak door at the far end of the gloomy passage opened onto a steep flight of worn stone steps. McCarter and Encizo drew their handguns as they made their way down the steps. They found themselves in a low-ceilinged cellar. The air was chilled, musty.

"I don't think it's a hobby room," McCarter muttered.

"More like a command center," Encizo said.

He indicated a trestle table, which held a map and sheets of printed paper. Nearby, a wooden crate held weapons—a number of SMGs, handguns and grenades.

"What the hell were these guys planning?" McCarter asked.

Encizo bent over the map, tracing marks and locations.

"Embassies," he said. "London-based embassies. Here's the U.S., France, Germany. I can't make out what the papers say. I don't recognize the language."

"It would take more than what they've got here to hit three major embassies."

"Maybe they were expecting more weapons or explosives. Maybe more men."

"Bring all the paperwork. We can fax it to Stony Man and have Aaron analyze it. Maddox can have his people take this place apart."

They returned to the street and McCarter spoke to Maddox.

"You'd better get your people in there. The cellar looks like it was being used as a base for something being planned."

"The FAP?"

McCarter shrugged. "Check out the dead guy by the door. The way we read it he was there to stop people going into that area.'' McCarter showed the Special Branch man the handgun Encizo had found on the corpse. ''Not what you'd expect your run-of-the-mill refugee to be carrying.''

Maddox examined the weapon.

''So where did our hit team come from?''

''Guess? I'd say they'll turn out to be Serbian. Maybe they found out the FAP had a cell here in London and decided to take it out before it could initiate any strikes.''

''We'll do some background checks on the deceased.''

''We're going back to the house. We need to check a few things out.''

''Fine. Markham,'' Maddox said, using McCarter's current cover name, ''are we looking at an escalation of the Albanian-Serb problem here? The last thing I want is them fighting it out in London.''

''I've been wondering along those lines myself,'' McCarter replied. ''Let's hope we're both guessing wrong.''

Stony Man Farm, Virginia

HAL BROGNOLA SAT next to Hunt Wethers in the Computer Room. Katz stood behind Wethers's chair, his gaze fixed on the monitor screen. On the screen was the information recently gained from the papers faxed from Phoenix Force.

''Translation is sketchy on such short notice,'' Wethers said, ''but I figure we have the main details.''

"Sketchy or not," Brognola said, "I don't like the implications."

The data on the screen laid out a plan of operation that involved FAP cells moving to all-out action against targets in London, Paris and America. The decision had been made by the FAP council of war that the forenamed countries had colluded with the Serbian government to prevent the ethnic Albanians from regaining control of their territories. The so-called Peace Initiative had no jurisdiction over ethnic Albania. As far as the FAP was concerned they had been totally betrayed, deceived, and any concessions made had been without the true consent of the Albanian people. The Peace Accord was a mockery, ignoring the pleas of true Albanians and leaving them at the mercy of the Serbian military and police. The FAP—the voice of Albania—wouldn't rest until their needs had been met, even if it meant conducting a long-running war against the oppressors and the countries who had aided them. It would be a total war, with no exceptions made, and the guilt lay solely with the conspirators who had sat at the conference tables. Upcoming additional talks, designed to strengthen the peace plan, would be disrupted and further strikes against undisclosed targets would be made.

"If that's sketchy," Brognola said, "I'd hate to see the full text."

"It leaves us in no doubt as to what they're up to," Wethers said.

"The hard part is the where and when."

"And where does Ilyana Petrocovich fit into this?"

"That's the question that scares the hell out of me." Katz spoke up, voicing all their fears.

"What are we talking here?" Wethers asked. "Germ warfare?"

"It's what Petrocovich has been involved in since she left school," Brognola explained. "She went straight to the Soviet Germ and Biological Warfare Research Department and rose through the ranks faster than any other woman. She had her own section by the time she was twenty-three, and her team was responsible for a number of nasty breakthrough developments in toxins and delivery systems. She had her team reduced to a small number of dedicated people, and they were moved to some ultrasecret base out in the Soviet boonies. Information on her became pretty scarce after that until the breakup of the Soviet empire. It seems she'd fallen out with her masters because they were pulling the plug on her research. It was all part of the new Russian plan of cooperation and openness. That was when Petrocovich went independent and started to peddle her talent and her wares to whoever would pay enough. And there are always takers for her product."

"Correct me if I'm wrong," Wethers said, "but where does a group like the FAP come up with the finances for something like this? Albanians aren't exactly in the top ten when it comes to having a lot of money."

"He has a point," Katz observed. "Might be worthwhile checking out. See if we can get a line on who might be bankrolling the FAP. Maybe we have some outside interests here. Let's not forget that the ethnic Albanians are a Muslim culture, and we all know how they tend to back one another. There might be some sympathetic outsiders aiding the FAP, giving them cash or weapons."

"And even Ilyana Petrocovich?" Brognola mused.

Katz nodded. "Why not?"

"This deal is getting scarier by the minute," Wethers commented.

"Get the rest of the team in," Brognola said. "I'll go wake Aaron."

London, England

MCCARTER LISTENED to Brognola's short-and-to-the-point message. He didn't say a word until the big Fed had completed his rundown on the information Stony Man had extracted from the FAP documents.

"How do we play this?" McCarter asked.

"Let Maddox and his people handle the London end. I think we need to move you guys on. Go for the main chance."

"Kosovo?"

"This scenario looks like it could blow up into something really nasty," Brognola said. "We don't have time for niceties. Or the luxury of preplanning. This is going to have to be running with the ball."

"Thinking on my feet is how I operate best," McCarter said.

"We'll give you all the help we can from here. Once you get out there, it might not be smooth running, but we'll do our damnedest."

"Never thought otherwise, boss."

"I've got you a ride on an RAF supply plane. You'll be met by an SAS man, and he'll take you to a covert SAS base on the border with Macedonia. They'll help provide anything you need. Over the border in Kosovo you'll liaise with a UN mission. They've been told to cooperate. But once you initiate any action..."

"We're on our own. I understand."

"Keep in touch."

McCarter hung up. There was nothing left to discuss.

Phoenix Force was on operational alert.

Kosovo-Macedonia Border

THE ARRANGEMENT HAD been made through the U.S. and UK governments. A direct call from the President to the British prime minister had Phoenix Force flown from Britain to Macedonia where they then made the trek to a covert SAS base close to the border with Kosovo.

The SAS was in the area to scout Kosovo and gather information that might be of use to the NATO forces.

The SAS, as usual, played its presence down even though it would have an important role to fulfill if the current situation worsened. The crack special force, in the event of any NATO intervention, would be used to report on enemy movement, provide directional assistance for allied aircraft, and if the order came through they might even carry out termination strikes on designated targets.

At present they were on standby, so the opportunity to aid Phoenix Force was welcome. It relieved the long hours of inactivity for the small group of highly trained and motivated men from the camp in Hereford.

Phoenix Force arrived in the early hours. It was still dark, the gloomy weather threatening snow. The Stony Man team had been accompanied on the flight and the journey into the hidden base by a member of the squad who had come to Britain to pick them up.

Sergeant Ray Tanner was an SAS veteran, a hard-as-nails professional with a no-nonsense attitude and a sense of humor second only to McCarter's. He hadn't questioned the reason for Phoenix Force being sent to Kosovo, but he did observe, and that observation told him a lot about the men he was with.

They appeared at ease with one another and with the situation. Tanner saw that these men were specialists in whatever they did, and combat wouldn't be a stranger to them. They handled themselves with the confidence that was gained only by having to face hardship and the possibility of sudden death on numerous occasions. During the flight from the UK they had used the time to check their weapons and equipment. Once that had been done they relaxed, snatching sleep when they could, exchanging small talk, just like any men who knew tough times lay ahead.

From the landing zone Phoenix Force had followed Tanner through the darkness, loaded down with their equipment, moving with speed and silence. Tanner had led them to the SAS base, assigning them a place to store their gear and to sleep.

AT DAWN Phoenix Force joined the rest of the SAS team for breakfast, and then McCarter met with the officer in charge, Major Felix Cameron.

"We need a way to get to them," McCarter said. "Any suggestions?"

That was how Phoenix Force found themselves over the border in Kosovo, at a low-key meeting with Captain Yves Moreau. He was with UNPRO-FOR, one of the numerous UN monitoring units trying to maintain a day-to-day peace within the restrictions of the UN mandate. The problem with that was the lack of coordination between those in the field and the UN high command. It took too long for decisions to reach the people who mattered.

A few miles from the UN base, a skirmish between Serb militia and Albanian rebels was raging in full swing. Automatic gunfire mingled with the thump of incoming mortars. After some time the Serb forces opened up with 30 mm cannon, and the air trembled to the crash of exploding shells.

Since Phoenix Force had arrived at the camp less than an hour earlier, the bleak weather had taken a turn for the worse. Snow was dropping from the chill sky, drifting across the base, and the ground underfoot was wet and muddy.

Moreau tried to ignore the noise of battle. He was a tall, dark-haired man in his early thirties. His casual attitude was designed to hide the fact that he cared very little for the closeness of the conflict.

For their foray into Kosovo Phoenix Force had

outfitted themselves in UN uniforms, blending in with Moreau's group.

"I understand that your presence here is something of a mystery?" he said in perfect English.

"I don't know how much you've been told," McCarter replied.

"Enough to understand I should not question you."

"Captain Moreau," Manning said, "we're here to investigate certain incidents that have compromised UN missions. There was also the tragic incident not long ago where a bus was attacked and a number of people killed."

"Tragic is not the word I would use," the captain said. "That attack was nothing short of murder. If you are here to hunt down those bastards then you have my support. I had friends on that bus."

"Is there anything you can tell us that might help?"

"The rumors are that the FAP was responsible. It's not the first time we have heard the stories about those damned terrorists. Believe me, that is what they are."

"Our problem is where to start."

"I may be able to help you. I have a contact. He is a local Albanian, and I will try to get hold of him. If I can, I will let you know."

The subdued whistle of an incoming 30 mm shell terminated their conversation. Way off target, the shell landed uncomfortably close to the base camp. It threw up a shower of muddy earth that rained on the perimeter of the camp. Before the smoke from the shell had drifted away, a Serbian police 4x4 appeared, swinging into the middle of the base camp. An armed officer climbed out, dragging on a heavy topcoat. He spotted Moreau and intercepted the Frenchman.

"You should not be here," the Serbian yelled. "We will not guarantee your safety."

"No one is asking you to," Moreau told him calmly. "This is a United Nations base. My orders are to remain so that we continue to monitor the situation as we have been doing for the past months."

"Interfering with our business. You should go home and leave us to do our work."

"Protecting the peace?"

"Yes. Our peace. Our policies. Not those forced on us by foreigners."

"Which policies are those, Milisivic?" Moreau asked quietly.

The officer stiffened. For a moment it looked as if he might strike Moreau. After a few seconds he relaxed and stepped away from the French captain, a little smile playing around the edges of his mouth.

"Clever, clever," Milisivic said. "Do not become too clever, Captain. It is not wise."

Moreau watched the police officer return to his vehicle. Once inside Milisivic spoke harshly to his driver and the 4x4 spun around and drove off, trailing sprays of mud.

"Friendly local cop or what?" Manning asked.

"Not the kind you'd want to meet on a dark night," McCarter answered.

BACK AT THE SAS base again, McCarter sought out Major Cameron and relayed what Moreau had offered.

"The danger is not having full intel on the situation," Cameron explained. "We're trying to upgrade our information all the time. A maverick group like the FAP doesn't make it easy. They hit and run, come and go. It's hard to get a line on them."

"Moreau?"

"Nice enough bloke. I like him, but I don't think he understands the complexity of the situation. I don't like using the word but naive springs to mind when Moreau is mentioned."

MCCARTER RETURNED to his teammates.

"Buggered if I can get a handle on this place. Everyone's heard of the FAP, but no one can point the finger in its direction. Looks like we're going to have to figure it out for ourselves. Gary, let's have another look at those satellite photos."

They were poring over the images when McCarter received a radio message. It was from Moreau, asking to meet the Phoenix Force commander again.

"I HAVE SPOKEN to my contact, who lives in a village a few miles away. He tries to sell me information from time to time for food and medical supplies. Nothing very exciting. However, he has come to me with information regarding an arms shipment that is to be flown in and collected by the FAP. The plane will land in the foothills up-country."

"Who is this contact?"

"I promised him I would not give away his identity," Moreau said.

"Captain Moreau, I don't take my men into any situation, especially in hostile territory, on the word of someone I don't know."

"This places me in a difficult position."

"Not to put too fine a point on it, Captain, but it puts me in a bloody dangerous position. All you have to worry about is your conscience. I have the lives of my men to look out for."

Moreau hesitated, torn between his inner feelings and the harsher realities of life.

"If this arms drop succeeds," McCarter said, "the FAP will have more weapons to kill with. More dead people to stack up against your conscience. Maybe more of your friends."

Moreau recalled the dead and dying in the ambushed bus.

"Very well. His name is Ciric Brako. As I said before, he lives in the village along the road."

McCarter nodded. "Thanks for that. Okay, so this Brako says he can furnish us with details about the drop? When and where is it?"

"He wants to meet me later this morning. Then he will give me the information."

"He only meets you?"

Moreau nodded. "He does not trust anyone else. He has to be careful. It is a risky thing he does."

"Remind him we're not exactly in Disneyland ourselves."

"I will pass you the information the moment I have it."

IT WAS A LITTLE after midday when McCarter was able to share the information with his team.

"We go into this with ears and eyes wide open."

"Do I detect a slight lack of trust here?" James asked.

"In this case more than usual. I can't quite make up my mind about this bloke Brako, which is why I passed his name back to Stony Man."

"We're still going to put ourselves in the hands of an informant?" Hawkins asked. "He'd better be good."

"Moreau seems to have confidence in him. He could give us something useful."

"Or it could blow up in our faces."

"Sometimes there's no other way to kick start things," McCarter explained. "I don't relish the idea, but where else do we go? Sometimes a risk is the only option."

"There's not much else we can do," James admitted. "Taking out an ad in the local paper will be too slow."

By late afternoon, when it was time for Phoenix Force to return to the UN base, no word had come back from Stony Man about Brako. McCarter didn't like it, but there was no time left for waiting.

MOREAU MET THEM when they arrived at the base, and he provided them with a UN Land Rover. McCarter oversaw their weapons being hidden under the emergency equipment in the lockers at the rear of the vehicle.

"You're taking a big risk," Moreau said, watching the preparations. "If the local police or the military find them, you could be in big trouble. And I don't know what I could do to help you out."

"If my people are reading things right, any risks we take are nothing compared to what the FAP is planning," McCarter replied. "I don't like it any more than you, but we don't have any other options. If we run into trouble, we'll handle it as it comes."

ALONE FOR A MOMENT McCarter found himself continuing to consider just what Phoenix Force was doing. They were about to walk into an extremely unstable zone, where armed conflict continued to blow hot and cold. No one could foresee what might happen, even in the next few hours, and the team had no jurisdiction within that war zone. He knew without having to ask that his people would follow wherever he led. It wouldn't be the first time Phoenix Force had placed itself directly in the firing line, and most probably it wouldn't be the last. Despite that background, McCarter felt an obligation to his men. It was the same obligation Katz had shouldered for many years, and he'd come through every time. McCarter had inherited that responsibility now. Times like these it weighed heavy.

"Hey, boss, you look serious."

McCarter glanced around and saw Hawkins watching him. The younger man, huddled in his thick coat, had a slight smile on his lips. His image reminded McCarter of himself when he'd been younger, and for a fleeting moment he envied Hawkins his youth. It was true that with youth came a brashness, a cocky belief in individual immortality. As if nothing, no one, could do them any harm.

McCarter knew that feeling. It had been his creed for years.

McCarter brushed at snow clinging to his face as he joined Hawkins.

"Bloody cold," he said. He was aware of Hawkins's continued scrutiny. "I was thinking about the mission. What we might be getting into."

"Thinking about the guys?" Hawkins observed. "Don't. We accepted the risks when we signed on. Anyhow, aren't the good guys supposed to win?"

"Those were in the days when it was white hats against black hats. Now it's bloody hard to figure which is which."

"No worries, boss. Now come on inside. There's hot food and drink waiting."

McCarter followed him inside the UN hut.

Hot food and drink now, but what would be waiting for them out in the combat zone?

CHAPTER FIVE

Southwest Kosovo

"Explain it to me slowly," Lec Pavlic said. "I don't want to miss a single word of this."

"Don't treat me like an idiot, Lec," Drago said angrily. "The fact that something has gone wrong is not my doing. So don't play high and mighty with me."

Pavlic fought to control his temper. He really wanted to hurt someone, to strike at them with fists and feet until they were bloody and cringing on the floor. He didn't care who was responsible. He just wanted to strike out, to make someone, anyone, suffer.

"What happened?"

"The London base was hit. Only two of our unit were killed. The rest were away at the time. Some of the refugees using the hall were killed."

"Who did it? The British police? Military?"

"From what we've heard they believe it was a Serbian strike team."

Pavlic rose to his feet with such force his chair

was thrown aside. He banged his fist on the table, wild, unreasoning rage flaring in his eyes.

"Serbian? Can't we make a damned move without those bastards following us? Drago, how did they find out we had people in London? Is our security so bad we are unable to hide anything?"

Drago shrugged in desperation. "I don't have any answer to that. We will try to find out. But these are difficult times, Lec. You know our situation. We have enemies on all sides. Not just the Serbs. Some of our own people disagree with the way we operate. For all we know, it may have been one of them who gave the information to the Serbs."

"So! Are we wasting our time, Drago? If the people we're fighting for can't believe in us, what then? Should we just surrender to the Serbs? Or walk into a UN base and give up?"

"I wasn't suggesting that, Lec, and you know it. All I'm saying is things are hard. Our policy doesn't go down with some of the liberals. They're ready to give away our heritage just to end the fighting. You don't have to ask twice to know I for one would never even consider that. This is a fight to the end. We win or we die. I understand that, and I am willing to make the sacrifice. Others may not. So we have to be very careful."

Pavlic picked up his chair and sat down, his head in his hands.

"I thought things were going well for us, Drago. Then we find we have a spy in our midst."

"Yes, and now he is dead. But he did meet his contact before he died. What we can't be sure of is how much information he took with him."

"Don't worry. Ridivic was not as clever as he imagined. Some of the data he took with him was false, planted so he would take it and pass it to his friends from America. If they take the information as true, it will take their attention away from us for a while. Long enough for us to complete our work."

"He might also have taken real information. Lec, I've said it before. We're becoming too dependent on these damned machines. There's too much information inside them, and it is far too accessible."

"We've done as much as we can to limit the damage. Weller is dead, and so is Dupre. And Ilyana Petrocovich has done what she can to eliminate her identity. All we need is a little more time. If Petrocovich keeps to her deadline, we will have everything we need."

"What about the bombing campaign?"

"Still on schedule. However this goes, Drago, we will be heard."

Lec Pavlic looked up. His face was gaunt, and dark rings circled his eyes. He was neglecting himself badly. He ate little, worked tirelessly and refused to ease off. He was a driven man, filling his empty life with dark plans for vengeance against a world conspiring to destroy his nation. Since that bleak day beside the mass grave, when he had seen his slaughtered family, Pavlic's existence had been channeled toward the coming holocaust. He had a single vision, a sole purpose—to bring his beloved country back from the brink of fragmentation. There would be no compromise, no wavering over territorial rights. Albania had to be autonomous, fully, one hundred percent, with not the slightest deviation from that criterion. Pavlic's intentions were to use the very stuff of nightmares to achieve that victory, and he didn't care how many died to enable him to reach that goal. He refused to acknowledge the foreign presence in his country, the so-called peacekeepers who gave away the rights of others and then patted themselves on the back for their good results. While these invaders smiled into the TV cameras and made speeches on their progress and the concessions they had gained, thousands were suffering, many dying because even during the peace talks the killing went on. The attacks. The artillery bombardments. The nighttime terrors when people were dragged from their homes to be murdered. The peacemakers sat around tables, eating and drinking, smiling into the faces of the very people behind the killings, and all the time this was going on no one listened to the real people, the ones who mattered. They were simply pawns to be moved around the board until someone could call checkmate and the game was over. Over for them. Once they had finished their talks, they would jet off back to their comfortable homes in their own countries where they would give little thought to the suffering they had left behind. That suffering didn't end because of a signature on a piece of paper. Hunger, lack of medical attention, homelessness. None of those things magically vanished. They still existed and would remain for a long time. Society destroyed by conflict took a long time to rebuild itself. Shattered lives were never the same again. Intolerance and bigotry, the deep-seated hatreds remained, too. They might slip beneath the surface, yet though they might be out of sight they remained, festering slowly, the smoldering rage filling the empty voids of destroyed ambitions. The loss of life, of loved ones, which could never be replaced, these were the embers that would one day erupt into flame again.

As far as Lec Pavlic was concerned, those things would never be allowed to be forgotten. His devotion to his cause had been fueled initially by desperation. The slaughter of his village, and especially his family, had been the nucleus of his rage. The unspeakable loss, consumed now by the fire of his overwhelming need to have his voice heard, still remained at the very heart of his being. His personal loss had been materialized into Albania's loss, and Lec Pavlic wouldn't step away from his responsibility.

He wouldn't rest until he had made his pledge come true, and make it he would, because the ones who had allowed his people to suffer were about to become victims themselves. The streets of America and her allies would be littered with the debris of war. They would soon be counting the cost to their people as had the Albanians. Death would stalk the peaceful lives of the innocent, as it still did to his own nation. As the echoes of their suffering were heard across the land of plenty, the governments might take time to reflect on the price of interference and injustice.

Pavlic's yet-to-be-launched campaign would highlight the plight of his country. Perhaps when the Americans went to bed and slept like the rest of the terrified, then they might begin to understand what it was like to be unsure. Unsure when the next bomb might explode. Or where. Indiscriminate strikes were the most difficult to live with because of the uncertainty.

Pavlic envisaged his campaign as a prolonged and relentless series of totally indiscriminate bombings, where every area of existence was a legitimate target. There would be no exceptions.

A great deal remained to be done yet, people to be placed, equipment to be smuggled in. America especially was a big country, vast and ever-changing, but that was also one of its weaknesses. Such a large country, with a mobile population, America was an easy target. The people the FAP already had there, established as citizens, would ease the burden of entry. Once they had their teams in place, it would be easy to hide them. America had no internal borders. Its people moved from one side of the nation to the other with little to challenge them as long as they stayed within the law. There were many places where a person could hide—vast cities, great tracts of land. It was a country where money could buy you a safe place, and the people were friendly and always ready to help. They made it so simple.

Pavlic's teams would use America's freedom to their advantage. They would allow the country to conceal them until they were ready to do their work, and then they would show the Americans what it felt like to have that friendship thrown back in their faces.

There was going to be a great deal of personal satisfaction for Lec Pavlic when that did happen, when the gullibility of the American masses became the fuse of their self-destruction, the day America would no longer be the safe home her people had always believed it to be. The shattering of that great American ideal would go a long way to easing the pain in Lec Pavlic's heart. Not the complete eradication, because it was going to take a great deal more to wipe that away. He had realized he wasn't going to achieve his goal quickly, or even in the short term. That didn't matter to him. His aim was total vindication for his country, but at his price and on his terms. The destruction of a single American building wouldn't achieve his aim. It would be many buildings and many people over a long time.

"Lec! Lec!"

He glanced up to see Drago staring at him.

"Lec, Malik is here. I was only informed a few minutes ago."

Pavlic smiled for the first time in many days.

"Perhaps we will have good news for a change. Bring him to me, then ask someone to make fresh coffee."

Drago nodded, glad of the opportunity to get away from Pavlic for a while. As much as he admired the man, Pavlic frightened him. His intensity seemed to devour him, leaving only a walking, talking shell. There was no doubting Lec Pavlic's loyalty to the cause, his single-minded intent, but there were times when it blotted out everything else. Pavlic's demands were hard. He pushed his people to the limit, then showed them how he was prepared to go beyond that limit. It had to be admitted, Drago thought, that he often wondered if there was anything Pavlic wouldn't do in the name of the cause.

He made his way through the mountain stronghold. The FAP base was located in natural caves, worked on by Yugoslav partisans during World War II. They had constructed rooms and added to the caverns, using the isolated place to launch their attacks on the Germans. Now the FAP had taken over the forgotten base and brought it back to life as their own stronghold. He passed through one of the caverns, which now resembled a communications center. Everything had been cleared to make room for the mass of electronic equipment that had been installed. Computer stations dotted the area; cables snaked across the floor; monitor screens flickered and hunched figures labored over keyboards. Satellite uplinks allowed access to information and communications. It might have been impressive if the purpose of the setup had been less sinister.

Pavlic's command center was there for one purpose only: to assist in his acts of terrorism and the advancement of his retribution against the destroyers of his country and its people.

Drago immediately saw Malik's tall, imposing figure. He was dressed in black, from his clothing to his shoes, all of it topped off with a long leather coat. Sensing Drago's presence Malik turned, a smile exposing his even white teeth. He held out his arms and embraced Drago.

"Greetings, my brother, it is good to see you again."

"And you," Drago answered. "We did not expect you so soon."

"Time is not our ally at the moment," Malik said. "When I heard of the incident in London, I decided it might be an opportune time to look at our time-table and perhaps make some adjustments.''

Drago's hesitation alerted Malik, and he put a comforting hand on Drago's shoulder.

"Lec is anxious, perhaps?"

"Anxious? Angry. Frustrated. Determined to show the world we will not be forgotten.''

"My brother, we must make allowances for him. I understand and sympathize for your plight. Lec is a hard taskmaster, but never forget his intentions. He has given us the chance to achieve a great victory over our enemies. The plan to break apart the solidarity of Albania is a strike at our existence. Already your people have given too much. Over the many years they have sacrificed much. Now there is the opportunity for a real home and what happens? A conspiracy designed by the Americans and fermented in the weak minds of the United Nations to deprive true Albanians of their homeland. To help establish their plan the Americans have involved their lapdog NATO to police the divisions. If we do not make our stand now, it will be too late.''

In Drago's mind there was agreement with Malik, but deep in his heart he still felt a concern for Pavlic. And it was that concern that still left him with a feeling of unease.

When Malik joined Pavlic they embraced and greeted each other as true believers. Malik, his physical presence overwhelming even Pavlic's, took the man aside and gave him gentle words of counsel. He saw Pavlic as a worried man, concerned for the smooth running of their complicated schemes, and he sought to allay those concerns.

"Listen to my words, and I believe you will be comforted. Our contract with Ilyana Petrocovich will shortly be concluded. She is close to completing her final tests, and soon the reinforcements will arrive from Libya. Then we will be able to proceed."

Pavlic poured himself a second cup of the rich, strong coffee they had been brought. He was aware of Malik's intense stare and knew he should respond.

"There will be no problems?"

"Of course not. Lec, it is permissible to smile. The path to everlasting glory does not have be traveled in perpetual gloom."

"The incident in London, and the near-escape of that traitor Ridivic. They concern me. For all we know the Americans may have gained information from them both."

"Also they may not have learned anything of value. It is a risk we have to accept. In any conflict there will be some kind of security breach. It is inevitable. But you do not fold up your tents and sneak away at the first disappointment. Of all people I would not expect it from you."

"You misinterpret me, Malik. I have no intention of sneaking away. I was merely suggesting we remain cautious."

"Of course, and you are right. Perhaps I was allowing myself the luxury of playing counselor."

"Malik, you are my counselor. My strong right arm. If it hadn't been for you, we would not be in such a position as we are now. Your backing has given us the means to carry this fight..."

"Enough, Lec. Have you forgotten our pledge?

The money would never be mentioned again. Or the weapons. What you are doing is beyond those things. They have to be used because we live in a materialistic world. They do not have to become a thing that binds us."

Pavlic fell silent, realizing he had almost insulted Malik. Everything else apart, that wouldn't be something he would do. Malik had become more than just a supporter of his cause. He had become part of it, showing Pavlic that in the world of the just and the true believer, anything was possible. That even a group as small as the FAP could make their mark, could make the world sit up and take notice.

"Forgive me, Malik. My heart sometimes rules my thoughts and makes me speak foolish words."

"It is forgotten. Now, tell me if you have heard from the ship."

Pavlic nodded. He turned to the scarred desk where he kept his work and searched for a chart. Malik joined him and they studied the chart.

"The ship left on schedule. It altered course as planned and waited off the Libyan coast for the reinforcements to be brought out and taken on board. From the rendezvous they sailed out past the Italian coastline and up into the Adriatic. According to the message we received early this morning, they should make the dropping off point the day after tomorrow. We will have people waiting to guide them in and then bring them here."

"Are your people in place to meet the plane tonight?"

"It's all arranged. By tomorrow we'll have

enough weapons to keep fighting for as long as we need to."

"Good. Then we are still on schedule." Malik straightened. "Drago told me that there would be food ready soon. Shall we go and eat? I have a feeling I'm going to enjoy a good meal."

"First I must tell you something else. We suspected that the group that wiped out the hit squad in London might be some special team sent by the Americans. It appears we could be right. A group of five. The same number as in London have shown up at the UN base near the border. Our source cannot tell us more at this point. I believe they are looking into our activities, so I have arranged for our man in the area to feed his UN military contact information regarding the arms shipment flying in tonight."

"Isn't that risky?"

"Malik, every day is a risk for us at present. Our people will be in place to meet the plane. They will also be waiting to deal with this team of specialists. If the Americans want to play cat and mouse with us, then tonight they will be the mice."

Malik inclined his head. "You are becoming even more devious than I, my friend. I will have to keep an eye on you. Now let us go and eat."

UN Base Camp

FULL DARK HID the rising contours of the terrain beyond the base camp. It was still snowing, and the weather had become more intense during the past half hour. David McCarter viewed the inclement weather with a satisfied expression on his face.

"I'm glad somebody thinks this is funny," Calvin James said. He was standing beside McCarter, watching the snowfall with a definite scowl on his face.

"I would have expected someone from Chicago to appreciate snow," McCarter said.

"In your dreams, man. Snow looks good on cards. Even looked good on *White Christmas* but that was only a damn movie. In the real world snow is wet, snow is cold and it sucks. Come to that, I can't even hide in the stuff."

"Never thought of that, Cal."

"So why the grin?"

"A good snowfall will help to hide us when we go in. With any luck our FAP friends will have their hands full guiding the plane in, so they won't notice us."

"Let's hope you're right."

Sergeant Tanner crossed from the far side of the room. He was carrying a mug of hot coffee.

"I'd prefer tea," he grumbled. "Everything's ready. All your kit. Weapons checked in the Land Rover. Plenty of spare ammo. Stun and frag grenades. Smoke canisters. Communication gear. Rations."

"Hear that?" McCarter said to James.

He glanced at Tanner. "Marry me, Sarge."

"Not bloody likely, sir. You're not my type. Too pushy."

James grinned. "He's seen right through you, man."

Manning, Encizo and Hawkins were already preparing for departure. They pulled on night clothing, complete with thick parkas with fur-lined hoods. Gloves were provided, too. A combat harness, holding ammunition and a sheathed knife, went over the coats, and each man carried a compact transceiver that would enable him to communicate with the others. In backpacks they carried spare dry clothing and rations. Each man had a full canteen of fresh water. In addition to his normal gear James, as the unit's medic, carried a comprehensive medical kit.

The lead weapon for this mission was the Heckler & Koch MP-5 submachine gun. In addition, each man carried a 9 mm Beretta autopistol, except McCarter who still favored his Browning Hi-Power. Extra clips for each man's weapons were carried in the combat harness. Pouches held other equipment, such as garrotes and plastic riot cuffs. McCarter wore a money belt under his shirt, which held a quantity of notes in U.S. dollars as well as the local currency.

After donning their own clothing, McCarter and James took the mugs of coffee Tanner handed them.

"Remember how cold it can get out there," Tanner warned. "Don't let yourselves lose body heat. Keep air circulating inside your clothing and stay dry. If you get wet, try to change to your spare gear. And watch your skin. Don't let sweat freeze on it. It's a good idea to exercise the face muscles. Helps to prevent frostbite. Same with the hands. Gloves stay on. If they get wet inside, you could be in trouble. If things get really bad out there, find cover. Stay together for warmth."

"Thanks, Sarge," Hawkins said. "And thanks for the assist."

"I know what it feels like being out there on your own," Tanner said. "I was cut off during the Gulf War. I was out in that desert for two days before I got picked up. And by a bloody Yank, too. So go easy, lads."

"No worries there, Sarge," Manning assured him. "We all figure on coming back."

The door opened and Moreau leaned in.

"It is time to go."

The surprise of the day had been Moreau's decision to guide them into the Kosovo countryside. The UN captain had considered his conversation with McCarter long and hard, and his decision had been based on his innate sense of what was right. The frustration of his position, coupled with the anger at the unnecessary deaths of the UN people in the bus and the escort Land Rover, had been festering inside ever since it had happened. The arrival of Phoenix Force, willing to put themselves on the firing line, had been the catalyst that had pushed him into action. Even McCarter's objections had been countered when Moreau had pointed out that they were strangers to the area, while he, Moreau, knew it well.

"You would not get far on your own," he had said. "In this weather it is easy to get lost. I can drive you for a good part of the way and direct you from a drop-off point. Then I will return to base and we await your signal."

The look in his eyes told McCarter the Frenchman wouldn't back down. He was willing to take the chance, and McCarter had to admit he had spoken the truth.

"What's behind all this, Moreau?" McCarter asked when he had the man on his own.

"How would you feel if you were in my position? Here I am in charge of fighting men not allowed to fight. We know what is going on in this damn place. So do the commanders back at HQ. Yet we do nothing. We see people die every day, and all we can do is help the wounded. Politics demand that we stay neutral, that we do nothing in case we upset people. For God's sake, we are letting people die! We stand about wringing our hands while the damned negotiators back at the UN refuse to make any kind of hard commitment. That is what is behind this, my friend."

"I'd hate to see you when you're mad, Moreau."

"I am plenty mad. At the stupidity of all this. By the time anything gets done, it will be too late. Saving a country that has no people left in it does not seem too clever to me. Better to do something while there are people around to save."

"I can't argue with that," McCarter said. "Just don't let yourself get into something that might turn against you. Know what I'm saying?"

"It does not stop you and your men."

"We play by different rules, Moreau. Our accountability is to people who understand and facilitate what we get involved in. If you get caught, the UN isn't going to be very happy."

Moreau smiled. "Allow me to take that risk, my friend, and I will sleep a little better at night."

"You're a hell of a guy, Moreau."

"That has yet to be proved."

Phoenix Force moved out, leaving the scant comfort of the hut behind. They all climbed into the UN Land Rover, and Moreau slid in behind the wheel. He fired up the engine and swung the vehicle away from the base, picking up the rough track that served as a road. He drove slowly, negotiating the rutted way with care. Wet snow clung to the wiper blades as he tried to keep the windshield clear.

After a half mile, Moreau turned the Rover across a shallow stream and eased it into the comparative cover of a wooded area. The track wound its way in and around the trees and shrubbery, Moreau driving with the ease of someone who knew his terrain well. When they emerged from the wooded area, the track was no longer visible. They were in rugged, undulating terrain, the land rising now. Ahead of them lay the dark hills, and farther on the snow-shrouded mountains. The peacekeeper drove steadily, negotiating any obstacles that stood in their way.

Two hours later Moreau drove the Land Rover into the shadows of a crumbling bank of earth. He cut the engine, reached for a map clipped to the dash, unfolded it and indicated their location.

"We are here. Now you will have to make your way on foot to this ridge to the north." He indicated the direction they would have to travel. "If you make good time, you will be there just after midnight. The landing strip is situated on a plateau, here, that will protect it from drifting snow. The plane is supposed to be touching down at around one a.m.

There are no guarantees now that the weather has changed. It is the best chance I can offer you.''

"Let's just hope your informant didn't get his facts mixed up. We'll look bloody silly if we sit out all night on the wrong hill.''

"I trust him,'' Moreau said. "That is all I can say.''

Moreau folded the map and slid it into a plastic cover. He passed it to McCarter, who tucked it inside his coat.

The Briton checked his watch. He satisfied himself the time was correct and had his team synchronize their own watches. Nodding to his teammates, he watched them exit the rear of the Land Rover and melt into the shadows.

"Thanks for your help, Moreau.''

"Good luck, my friend. If you do meet up with these FAP terrorists, be warned. They will not hesitate to kill you.''

McCarter patted the man on the shoulder.

"Be seeing you.''

"I hope so.''

McCarter was gone then, closing the door behind him. The French soldier started the Land Rover and turned it. He began the return journey to the distant base camp, his thoughts with the group of men he had just left behind. He hoped their mission would prove successful and that the FAP terrorists might receive a taste of what they had been dishing out over the past months. Like most professional soldiers Moreau hated and despised terrorists. They were, in his opinion, nothing more than heartless murderers who used their political rhetoric as justification for mindless slaughter. Real soldiers fought out in the open, face to face, and had no qualms about confronting their enemies. These terrorists slunk about in the darkness and vented their twisted logic on the innocent—women and children, civilian targets where the victims weren't even given the opportunity to fight back. Bombs in shops and shots in the back. These were the terrorists' credentials, and they did little to enhance the reputations of the craven killers who flaunted them.

Moreau had been driving for a couple of hours. The snowfall had increased. He dropped down a gear, bringing the Land Rover almost to a halt. Peering through the smeared windshield, he blinked his aching eyes. Flitting shadows moved across his field of vision, and the peacekeeper couldn't be sure what he was seeing. More than once he almost convinced himself he had seen the blurred outline of a man standing to the side of the slow-moving Land Rover, but then he laughed at his own foolishness. It was the night and the swirling snow playing tricks with him.

Or so he thought until a vague shape materialized no more than four or five feet in front of him. Moreau knew he wasn't seeing things this time. He slammed on the brakes and the Land Rover stalled, jerking to a dead stop.

The man blocking his path was solid enough, and so was the Kalashnikov AK-74 he held.

Morcau swore under his breath. He reached for the autopistol holstered on his belt, fingers touching the butt a second before the waiting gunman opened fire. The stream of 5.45 mm slugs shattered the windshield and ripped into the French soldier's upper chest. The impact drove the breath from his lungs as he was slammed against the seat back. Moreau made another attempt to claw his pistol free, despite the horrendous injuries. He could barely see due to the blood streaming into his eyes from the gashes caused by splinters of broken glass from the windshield.

He sensed movement off to his left—another man, also wielding an AK-74.

Moreau roared out his final defiance, expressing his contempt for the terrorists. Then both weapons opened up again, raking the Land Rover with a steady stream of withering autofire. Moreau's shredded body was thrown back and forth, flesh spurting blood as the powerful slugs ended his life and left him slumped across the seat of the riddled Land Rover.

The gunners vanished as quickly as they had appeared. Silence returned, broken only by the soft clicks as the stalled Land Rover engine began to cool. Snow drifted in through the shattered windshield frame and settled on the blood-spattered interior of the cab. Flakes dropped on Moreau's body, the still warm blood staining the white crystals pink.

McCARTER RAISED HIS ARM and brought the team to a stop, beckoning them to move in close. The snowfall had increased, and while it wasn't extreme it was slowing their progress to a degree.

"I estimate we're about ten minutes behind schedule," he said. "I'd like to speed up, but I'm not going to risk anyone being injured."

"Give the word," Hawkins said. "We'll manage."

"No sweat," Encizo agreed. "The sooner we get out of this, I'll be happy."

"Okay, we'll notch it up a little. But no risks." McCarter checked the terrain. "If this weather holds, that plane isn't going to be having any more luck than we are."

He moved off, with the rest of the team following. They fell back into the formation they had traveled before, Hawkins at the rear, watching their back trail.

The weather closed in. Visibility was reduced with a vengeance. The snow clung to them, frosting their clothing and sticking to skin. The desire to brush it away from their faces had to be tempered with caution in case the exposed skin became chafed. On McCarter's instructions they closed ranks, maintaining eye contact with the man in front. They all knew how easy it would be to become separated in this kind of weather. A hesitant step, a simple pause might open the distance between individuals. A sudden flurry of snow, even in close-quarter file, could create the situation where one or the other might step out of line. In those scant moments, a man could become lost. If that happened, the loss could turn fatal if the errant man wasn't returned to the file quickly.

Heavy snowfall was a great leveler. It changed terrain, flattened and softened the topography until landmarks vanished. The most experienced tracker, on familiar ground, could lose his way in a snowstorm. Once swallowed by the whiteout, a man could quickly become disoriented. Turning this way and that, he'd become even more confused until he had no idea where he was. Confusion became fear and fear turned to panic. The harder he tried to re-locate himself, the deeper into trouble he got.

Phoenix Force, well aware of such possibilities, made certain they stayed in tight formation. They had survived too long against too much to let natural hazards threaten them.

As they moved to higher ground a wind began to buffet them, driving the snow down from the slopes. The discomfort of the driven, icy snow was in-creased by the chill factor. The teammates huddled inside their protective clothing, bending their heads against the blast, and trudged on, instinct and trust making them follow McCarter. The continuous snowfall had layered the ground but had yet to build to a depth that would hamper their progress. While the way was still passable they kept moving, push-ing forward without complaint. They kept their weapons close to their bodies, shielding them from the cold. After almost forty minutes of hard slog-ging, they emerged onto a flat plateau and McCarter brought them to a halt. They gathered in close, pro-tected to a degree by eroded rock formations that edged the plateau.

McCarter pulled out the plastic-covered map he'd kept inside his coat. He peered at the contours, checking them with their surroundings, and indi-cated to the others where map and terrain matched.

"Unless we've found an exact duplicate, this should be the place," he said.

"I think this is it," Encizo stated, drawing their attention.

Across the plateau they could see hazy lights. Someone was laying out twin rows, well spaced apart.

"Marking out a strip for someone to land," Manning said.

"Yes," McCarter agreed, "and he's on his bloody way."

Faintly at first and then rising over the undulating moan of the wind came the drone of aircraft engines. It was a distant sound that approached rapidly, echoing as it bounced back and forth between the hills.

Calvin James eased back from the cleft in the rocks he was using for cover and made a silencing motion with his hand.

Damn, McCarter thought, that was all they needed. Bloody visitors.

He crept alongside James.

"Two of them," James whispered, "both carrying AK-74s. Moving from left to right."

McCarter nodded and flattened against the rock, peering out carefully so he was able to see the approaching men. He watched the pair trudge through the snow, almost up to the rock that concealed him. They paused, pulling out packs of cigarettes and lighting up. They stood close together, conversing in low, grumbling tones. It was obvious they didn't think much of being out in that kind of weather.

The noise from the aircraft increased. It was coming in from the far end of the plateau. Peering into the swirl of snow, McCarter spotted the winking lights on the wing tips of the aircraft. It was coming in low, the pilot having made the decision to try to land. The weather would make it difficult, and it was likely that the pilot had realized he might get only the one chance.

"We wait," McCarter said. "Once the plane's down we let them start unloading. It should distract them and give us a better chance to move in close."

The team huddled close to the rocks where they were at least sheltered from the wind to a degree.

The incoming plane sank lower, veering a little as the wind caught it. The pilot corrected quickly, adjusted his flaps and made a perfect landing. The moment he was down he reversed the pitch of the propellers, using the power of the engines to slow the aircraft. Snow was dragged into the air by the whirling blades of the propellers, creating a white fog around the dark bulk of the aircraft. Easing onto the brake pedal, the pilot brought the plane to a stop some forty feet from the end of the plateau. He cut the engines and the heavy roar was lost in seconds.

"Heads up, lads," McCarter whispered.

The moment the aircraft had come to a stop, dark figures emerged from the shadows and converged on the machine. A number of them hurried directly to the aircraft while others seemed to hang back, some of them acting oddly in the way they began to cast about.

McCarter watched them, a creeping suspicion forming in his mind. Being cautious was one thing, but the men out there were playacting, and not being very convincing about it.

"Something odd's going on out there," he warned the others.

At his side, James and Manning observed the stilted performance of some of the FAP terrorists.

"What the hell are they up to?"

"Something we don't really want to know about," McCarter said. "I think the buggers are waiting for us to show."

"You certain?" Encizo asked.

"Certain enough that I'm bloody well keeping us out of it."

"Hey!"

The warning yell came from T.J. Hawkins.

As his teammates turned to check out what was happening, they were met by the sight of four armed figures emerging from the surrounding shadows.

McCarter brought up his H&K, cursing under his breath.

The trap they had walked into was being well and truly sprung.

Stony Man Farm, Virginia

"I THINK I HAVE something," Akira Tokaido called out.

Aaron Kurtzman finished refilling his mug with the rich, black concoction that passed for coffee, then rolled his wheelchair back to his station, meeting Tokaido as the young man reached the same spot.

"Tell me," Kurtzman said.

"Hunt gave me the disk Gregor Ridivic smuggled out. There didn't seem to be much of interest on it. Ridivic must have snatched it because he figured it might be helpful."

"All we managed to pull were some details about proposed campaigns. the ideas the FAP had on furthering their cause," Wethers said. "It was stuff they were going to put out over the Internet to drum up sympathy for their cause—contact names for ethnic Albanians who had moved to the U.S. and made a new life, begging letters, that type of thing. Touting for funds and solidarity. Not exactly top secret information."

"Right," Tokaido said. "On the surface that was all there was. But I did some playing around."

"And?"

"I found some hidden files, and I had to break an encryption code." He grinned at Kurtzman. "I tried that program you showed me the other day. I had to juggle it around a little, but I broke through and uncovered a lot of stuff in the background."

Tokaido leaned over and tapped the keyboard, transferring the information from his computer to Kurtzman's.

"These guys have some hard agendas. Look at this. And this. It looks like a master plan of what their intentions are over the next few weeks. It's pretty hot stuff. So why put it on disk and risk it being found? And why in English?"

Kurtzman studied the information.

"Maybe it's what they intended. For it to be found, I mean. It could be something to put us off the track. We go looking for all these sites, and the FAP hits elsewhere."

"You think so?"

"It wouldn't be the first time a bluff had been played out," Katz said from behind Kurtzman and

Tokaido. They hadn't heard him come in. "Plant false information to put the enemy off the scent. It leaves you time to go for your real targets without having someone on your tail."

"That leaves a nasty thought," Tokaido said.

"What?"

"Maybe Ridivic thought he was getting away with genuine information while all the time the FAP was using him, sending him out to pass this phony data and then killing him as a show of intent."

Katz touched the young man's shoulder.

"I hate to say it, Akira, but welcome to the real world. It's the way the game is played. Using the death of a man to make their deception authentic is nothing new, and it won't be the last time it ever happens."

"So we haven't really got anything worthwhile after all," Tokaido said. "Just useless data."

"Not exactly. At least we know the FAP is up to something it needs to divert us from. So false leads are planted, hoping to keep us off their backs for a time. They wouldn't go to all this trouble for nothing."

One of telephones rang. Katz picked it up and answered.

"How's it going with Khan?"

On the other end of the line Carl Lyons grunted his reply.

"At least you haven't lost him. He could be prolonging his journey just to put off any tails. The man's no fool. Remember he worked for the Soviets. They don't mess around."

Again a short reply came through to Katz. Lyons

was showing his frustration. Able Team was having a hard time pinning down the Russian. He was playing it cool, probably taking his time trying to lose them. It begged the question, why? If he was so desperate to get Able Team out of his hair, what exactly was Khan up to?

CHAPTER SIX

Kosovo

The first shots crackled in the night, muzzle flashes identifying the shooters. The impact of the 5.45 mm slugs against the rocks that had concealed Phoenix Force threw sparks into the air.

The intended targets had already moved. The teammates split apart, without command, and with the natural reactions of men who had faced hostile gunfire too many times not to respond swiftly.

McCarter had dropped to the ground, rolling away from the shelter of the rocks. James, almost shadowing him, did the same. They came to rest, pulling themselves to their knees, bringing up the MP-5s to lock on to the dark outlines of the men advancing on them.

The first short burst from McCarter's weapon hit the lead attacker, putting the man down instantly. The impact of the 9 mm slugs toppled the terrorist onto his back, the barrel of his own weapon turning to the night sky and sending an uncoordinated blast into the snowy darkness.

James, on bended knee, took out one gunner and

clipped the side of the man next to him. As the second terrorist hesitated in reaction to the pain, James made a slight correction to his aim and touched the trigger again. This time the attacker dropped, kicking briefly against the pain.

"Move out!" McCarter snapped to James. "You're covered."

James broke to the right, moving away from the rocks and toward the dispersing attackers. McCarter was close on his heels, using his subgun to clear a path for them through the scattering ranks of the terrorists.

Nearby, Manning, Encizo and Hawkins had adopted a similar strike back, having put two men down in the first seconds. Now they broke for the trees that lined the slope ahead of them, aware that there were more of the terrorists at their backs, and once they had cleared the rocks Phoenix Force would be open to their fire.

On the run McCarter plucked one of the smoke grenades from his harness. He pulled the pin, half turned and lobbed the canister in the direction of the rocks. It fell just short and moments later began to issue thick coils of dense smoke. The wind caught it, pushing it back and forth in the area around the rocks.

An angry face behind an AK-74 rose out of the snow almost in McCarter's path. The terrorist angled his Kalashnikov in the Briton's direction. The Phoenix Force team leader ducked low, under the muzzle, then swung his MP-5 in a brutal arc. The hard steel of the barrel clipped the FAP terrorist's jaw, opening a gash that blossomed red. The man grunted, feeling the rush of blood down his chin and the sharp pain that followed. He also felt the jab of the MP-5's muzzle in his side a fraction of a moment before McCarter pulled the trigger and blew a burst of 9 mm slugs into his body. The man screamed, the sound cut off as he fell to the ground, his blood spattering the snow.

"Go! Go! Go!"

McCarter's order kept his teammates on the move. They slogged through the snow. Bullets zipped past, drilling into the snow, and clipping the trees as Phoenix Force stumbled into the scant cover and dropped to the ground. They positioned themselves, weapons aiming back the way they had come, and waited for the expected rush.

The dark shapes converged on the rock formation, vanishing in the smoke, then coming out the other side. As soon as they moved into the open the FAP terrorists opened fire, sending a scattering of shots into the tree line where Phoenix Force had taken cover. Someone lobbed a fragmentation grenade that fell well short of its target. The resultant blast lit up the scene for an instant, giving the team something to shoot back at, and the well-placed volley took out two of the terrorists and sent the rest seeking cover.

"Let's move," McCarter said, taking advantage of the hiatus.

His men melted deeper into the trees, using the tangled growth as excellent cover.

"Move around," the Briton ordered. "I want to take a closer look at that plane."

Encizo and Manning took the rear, falling slightly behind the others to watch out for any of the terrorists. McCarter led the others in a wide loop that curved back in the direction of the landing site. They reached it by emerging on a slight bluff that overlooked the plateau. The aircraft lay below them, a number of figures busy unloading crates. A medium-size truck with a canvas top had reversed up to the open cargo door.

"These boys are well-organized," Hawkins said.

"Time we threw a spanner in the works then," McCarter suggested.

"Make it fast," Encizo said, emerging from the gloom behind them. "In a couple of minutes we'll be having company through the back door."

As he finished speaking, the crackle of Manning's MP-5 added emphasis to his words.

"Rafe, take T.J. with you and back up Gary," McCarter said. "Cal, you're with me."

The Briton plucked a grenade from his webbing and crawled to the lip of the bluff. Below, alerted by the gunfire, the unloading crew had stopped. The terrorists abandoned the boxes and retrieved their weapons, turning in the direction of the shooting. McCarter didn't wait. He pulled the pin and lobbed the grenade in the direction of the parked truck. James's grenade followed, arcing through the night to land in the snow only feet from the starboard landing wheel of the aircraft. The twin blasts were followed by yells of rage and pain.

The truck lurched sideways as McCarter's grenade exploded. The blast was followed by a boiling flood of orange flame as the gas tank blew, sending tendrils of fire in all directions. One shadowy figure was engulfed, becoming a flailing human torch running mindlessly through the snow.

James's grenade ripped the landing wheel from its seating. The starboard wing of the aircraft sank, the tip hitting the ground.

The scattered terrorists turned in the direction of the bluff, firing wildly as they converged on the snowy slope. In their reckless action they left themselves open to become easy targets, and McCarter and James had no difficulty in driving them back. The FAP rebels tried to scale the slope twice before the relentless fire from their enemies' position dissuaded them from further action. By then five bodies were sprawled at the base of the slope. The others, realizing the futility of further retaliations, melted away into the surrounding terrain, leaving the crippled aircraft and the burning truck behind.

McCarter stood, ejecting the spent magazine from the MP-5. He reloaded, turning away from the edge of the bluff.

The crackle of distant gunfire in the trees had faded, too, leaving an uneasy silence.

"Welcome to hell night," James murmured softly as he snapped a fresh magazine into his own weapon.

Manning, Encizo and Hawkins came into view.

"Clear," Manning reported.

McCarter nodded.

"Any survivors?"

Manning shook his head.

"Let's take a look at that aircraft," McCarter stated. "But stay alert. There may be wounded down there, and the others might still be close by."

They took their time descending the slope, checking the bodies as they went. None of the terrorists were alive. The burning truck threw a baleful glow across the scene around the aircraft. The dead lay in the wreckage strewed around the area after the explosions. Discarded weapons littered the ground. The crates in transit between plane and truck had been hurriedly dropped at the outset of the firefight.

"I've seen boxes like those before," James said. He brushed snow aside, pointing to the markings on the top. "Russian AK-74s."

"Same here," Encizo added. "Rocket launchers in this one."

"We've got grenades in this one. Packs of plastic explosives and detonators," Hawkins announced.

Manning had climbed inside the aircraft and checked out the remaining boxes.

"Look at this," he said, hauling a sealed box to the cargo door.

McCarter examined the plastic container. He broke the seals and freed the snap fasteners. Inside were sealed plastic bags. The Briton used his knife to slit open the plastic. Inside was a bright orange plastic suit with a visored hood.

"What are they," Hawkins asked, "decontamination suits?"

James shook his head. "Chemical protection suits, more like. To protect someone dealing with toxic materials probably."

"Or biological agents," McCarter said. "Don't forget we have Ilyana Petrocovich involved somewhere in this mess."

"There's a comforting reminder," James muttered.

"We should check and make sure only the suits are on board," Encizo said.

"Right," McCarter agreed.

Manning and James remained outside to keep watch while McCarter led the others inside the aircraft.

They checked the cargo area. There was little else of interest except a couple more cases of weapons. McCarter went to the flight deck, where he found the two-man flight crew dead in their seats. Each man had been killed by a bullet through the back of the skull. Whoever had executed the men hadn't been thorough enough because McCarter found a wallet in the back pocket of the pilot. There was also a flight manifest, in Italian, detailing the cargo. McCarter pocketed that, as well.

"Someone didn't want the flight crew talking to anyone," Encizo said when he joined McCarter on the flight deck.

McCarter led the way outside.

"Put all the crates back inside," McCarter ordered.

"Gary, use whatever you can to rig a detonation. Destroy as much of this stuff as possible."

Manning nodded and went looking for the explosive compound.

"What I want to know is why we were set up," James said.

"And by who."

"We can ask Moreau when we get back."

"Talking about getting back," Hawkins said.

"Everybody in the mood for a long walk?"

If they were, no one actually admitted the fact.

Base Camp

SERGEANT RAY TANNER heard about Moreau's death from an UNPROFOR patrol. They had come across the Land Rover and the French soldier's body midmorning of the following day, acting on a report from a patrolling helicopter. Tanner's immediate reaction was concern for the five men who had gone out with Moreau. As far as Tanner was concerned, the team had been left out in the field without any kind of backup. He didn't doubt their skill at surviving in the hostile climate. What did concern him was the obvious.

Someone had betrayed them and Captain Moreau.

In Tanner's opinion there could only be one suspect—the informant who had given Moreau the information about the weapons drop. Tanner took no more than a few seconds to figure his options.

He made his way from the hut and crossed to the motor pool where he had a quick conversation with the French sergeant in charge. It took him no time at all to persuade the man that he needed a vehicle in order to check out something connected with Moreau's death. The French soldier, angry at his captain's death, and unable to react due to the UNPROFOR protocol, turned his back while Tanner took one of the parked Land Rovers.

Tanner drove away from the base camp and followed the route of the narrow road heading west. He took his time due to the snow that still covered the road. It was quiet that morning. There was no more firing from the Serb artillery. Reports had informed UNPROFOR that negotiations had resulted in the Serb forces withdrawing to positions agreed to during one of the recent UN discussions with the government in Belgrade. With the knowledge that the situation could change quickly Tanner made his trip with as much speed as possible, parking and concealing the Land Rover in a clump of trees about half a mile from the small village where Moreau's informant lived.

Armed with only his Browning Hi-Power pistol but using the skills acquired through his years with the SAS, Tanner closed in on the village and took cover in the burned-out shell of a house overlooking the east side of the village.

There was little activity, as only a few people remained in the village. The majority had fled during recent hostilities and when Serbian troops had made a hit-and-run strike on the place. Tanner saw smoke rising from three houses. One of them, he knew, belonged to Ciric Brako, the informant Moreau had used a number of times. Brako had visited Moreau the day the five men had arrived at the base camp, and it had been shortly after that Moreau had passed the information to them.

Working his way down to the rear of Brako's house, Tanner spotted a car parked outside. The trunk was open and the engine running. Moments later Brako emerged with suitcases in his hands. He stowed them in the trunk, closed the lid and returned to the house. It seemed apparent that the man was leaving the area.

Tanner slipped around the side of the house. He

slid his combat knife from its sheath, moved to the front of the idling car and thrust the keen blade into the tire, which deflated with a soft hiss. He repeated the action on the rear tire, resheathed the knife, then ran to the front door of the house and eased himself inside.

The chill inside wrapped itself around Tanner as he made his way along the passage. He could hear a voice, and a partly open door revealed its source. Peering around the edge of the door, Tanner spotted Brako. He was using a cellular phone and was engaged in a heated debate with someone on the other end. Tanner couldn't tell what was being said because Brako was using his native tongue.

The man cut the conversation, banged the phone onto the table, then scrubbed a big hand through his tangled mass of black hair. The result of whatever he had been discussing had left him angry. Tanner took the opportunity to move into the room, pushing the door shut and leaning against it.

"What's wrong, pal? They decided not to pay you?"

Brako spun, his face showing the surprise he was feeling. He stared at Tanner, trying to recognize him and failing.

"Who are you? What is it you want in my house?"

"Seeing as you're leaving I thought I'd drop in to say goodbye."

"What? Are you crazy?"

Tanner moved his right hand so that Brako could see the Browning Hi-Power.

"Not crazy, you miserable son of bitch. Just good

and mad because a brave man is dead because of you.''

The expression in Brako's eyes told Tanner he'd hit the spot.

"I...I do not know what you mean."

"Lying bastard!" Tanner growled. "Captain Moreau is dead. Shot to pieces by the miserable terrorists you run errands for. You were with him yesterday, passing him information about the weapons drop coming in last night. Some people went out to intercept it. I'm guessing your people were waiting for them, too. What was it, Brako? A show of strength by the back-shooting little bastards calling themselves the Free Albania Party?''

"I have nothing to do with the FAP."

"Wrong answer. If I was you, Brako, I'd choose my next words with a lot more care.''

Tanner closed in on the man, who was starting to sweat. His eyes flicked back and forth across the room, seeking a way out.

"Don't even think about it,'' Tanner whispered. "Just stand there and sweat. Funny thing. I've seen you everywhere I go. Tough until the shit hits the fan, then you crumble. You're all the same. Real hard when you're shooting someone in the back. Planting bombs to kill women and kids. And always hiding behind something.''

Tanner could feel his anger rising. He was aware he was baiting Brako and he also knew that what he was doing was against all the training the SAS had put him through. The aim was to stay objective, not to allow emotions to direct his feelings or dictate his actions. But this time it was different. This time it was for him, for Ray Tanner and all the brave men who put their lives on the line to deal with scum like Brako. He had lost a lot of friends over the years. Men he had come to respect. From his own SAS mates to the American Delta Force commandos he'd worked with. The Navy SEALs and the GSG-9. How many had laid down their lives in clandestine operations that meant their bravery would never be recognized by the masses they fought for? Tanner knew the answer. Too many had died. Far too many.

"You and I have some talking to do, Brako. I need information, and by God I'm going to get it."

"Never! I will never betray them."

Brako's response was delivered with all the energy he could muster. Following his shout, he launched himself at Tanner, closing the brief gap with surprising speed, his large hands clawing at the Briton's face. They collided with a thump, Tanner briefly knocked off balance. He countered Brako's push with a savage knee jab that slammed into the man's testicles with crushing force. Brako screamed, doubling over, and Tanner slammed the barrel of the Browning across the back of his adversary's skull. Brako went down hard, his body twisting as he hit the floor. He drew in a ragged snort of air, lashed out with a foot and caught Tanner behind the knee. The sergeant stumbled and nearly went down. He regained his balance, half turning so he could keep the Serb in his sight, and saw the man had a stubby handgun in his fist, pulled from beneath his coat.

Brako's finger snapped the trigger back too fast, jerking the autopistol so that the 9 mm slug tore through the fleshy part of Tanner's left arm instead of impacting with his chest.

The Briton held his fire for a long few seconds. He deliberately made certain he had target acquisition before he eased back the Browning's trigger and fired twice. The 9 mm rounds cored through Brako's skull, tearing into his brain and emerging from the back of his head along with a section of bloody bone and hair. The Serb toppled over, heels drumming against the scuffed floorboards before he died.

Tanner swore in frustration, condemning himself for getting dragged into a shootout like some half-witted trainee. He knew he had to get out of the house quickly in case someone came to investigate. He was about to leave the room when he suddenly remembered the cell phone Brako had placed on the table. He picked it up and pushed it into one of the pockets in his combat jacket. Jamming his pistol back in its holster under his jacket, he made his way to the front door, checked that the way was clear and eased around the side of the house. Tanner retraced his steps back into the trees, and from there to the hidden Land Rover. He spent a few minutes rifling items from the Land Rover's first-aid kit, doing what he could to bind up his bloody arm. Then he started the engine and began the return journey to the base camp.

Base Camp

PHOENIX FORCE RETURNED to the base early in the afternoon. They were tired and cold, still angry at being set up, but that anger had at least been dissipated by their victory over the FAP terrorists.

Any enthusiasm they might have had was dampened when they heard about Moreau. The news was given to them by Tanner. The SAS sergeant reported his own involvement, culminating in the death of Ciric Brako.

"Sounds like the bastard got what he deserved," McCarter said. "It doesn't bring Moreau back, though."

"It makes me feel a little better," Tanner replied. "The only disappointment was that Brako died too bloody easy."

McCarter smiled. "Sergeant, that isn't a nice thing to say."

"No, sir? Then tough shit."

"How's the arm, Sarge?" James asked.

"Sore. But I was lucky." Tanner reached into his tunic pocket and pulled out the cell phone he'd picked up in Brako's house. "I thought this might be of use to you. Brako was on it when I went into his house. Maybe you can trace his calls. Get some locations?"

"Bloody right we can," McCarter said.

It was time to contact Stony Man.

Stony Man Farm, Virginia

"NO CASUALTIES?" Barbara Price asked.

McCarter's voice reached her over the secure line.

"Not in the team. But one of the UN military who helped us was killed. He was betrayed by the informant who gave us the information about the plane flight.''

"Ciric Brako?''

"Yes. The one who owned the cell phone.''

"Aaron's got his team working on that now. They're going to access the network and pull out the call details Brako logged recently.''

"Not try and access them?''

"You lost me.''

"You said access as if it's a definite conclusion.''

Price laughed. "I see what you mean. Well, would you suggest Aaron couldn't do something when he's in the same room and sitting no more than ten feet away?''

"I should have more faith, you mean?''

"Precisely.''

"Our flight out will be leaving tomorrow afternoon. Straight into Aviano. I'll talk to you then.''

"We may have some details on the charter company who rented out the plane. And the phone information.''

"Okay.''

Brognola took the phone and spoke to McCarter.

"Any problems with the UN?''

"No. There's enough confusion about the general situation to smoke screen our involvement. We can keep a low profile until we fly out. Do something for me.''

"What?''

"See to it that Sergeant Tanner is left in the clear over his involvement. He deserves our help. I don't want any flak coming his way.''

"Consider it done. Why the afternoon flight? Nothing sooner for you?"

"In the morning I'm getting one of the UN chopper pilots to fly a couple of us to check out the landing site to see if we can spot any trail left by the FAP when they moved out. It's a long shot, I know, but worth a go. We're still running on guesswork out here. The sooner I can get a fix on this group the better. So any chance is better than nothing."

"If you need any official string pulling give me a yell."

Brognola put down the phone and turned back to check on Kurtzman.

"Aaron, I need an update. You got the time?"

Kurtzman swung his chair away from his monitor.

"No, but I'll create some especially for you."

CHAPTER SEVEN

Kosovo

The pilot of the UNPROFOR helicopter eased the cruising machine on a parallel course with the ridge below. Behind him James and Hawkins checked the terrain through opposite sides. James had the map McCarter had used on his knee, pinpointing landmarks as they flew.

They had been in the air for almost half an hour when the pilot turned on his throat mike.

"Below and to the left. We're coming up to where they found Captain Moreau."

He angled the chopper around so that James and Hawkins could see the spot. It had been marked by red and yellow flags stuck into the ground around the Land Rover. A UN vehicle was parked close by with a five-man squad guarding the Land Rover for the arrival of the UN incident investigators.

The area fell behind them as the pilot resumed his course, keeping the chopper just above tree height. The snow had stopped falling sometime in the early morning. The fall during the night had eliminated the tire tracks of Moreau's return journey from leaving Phoenix Force.

"Not likely we're going to find anything," Hawkins said. "Let's face it. That snowfall last night wiped out everything."

"Let's wait until we reach the plateau," James stated.

The pilot took the chopper higher as the terrain began to climb, the undulating hills giving way to outcroppings and near-invisible ravines. Checking his map coordinates the pilot swung the helicopter in a wide arc, then leveled off as he spotted the plateau ahead.

"This what you're looking for?"

James studied the white expanse below. For a while he wasn't sure, then he made out the softened outline of the aircraft. A single tail fin was all that showed through the layer of snow. Close by was the gutted skeleton of the burned-out truck, again mostly covered by snow.

"This is it. We were over there behind those rocks. We came in through those trees."

"Plane came in from that direction," Hawkins said. "And the truck showed from there. Must be a trail there somewhere."

The pilot swooped in lower, overflying the truck, and eased the chopper in as close as he could to the ground. Powdery snow swirled up in a twisting spiral as the rotor wash snatched it from the ground.

"That can be the only way," the pilot said, indicating a gap in the rocky terrain.

"Let's see," James urged.

The chopper slid forward, nose down to give them

a clearer view of the terrain. Despite crosswinds, the pilot held the chopper on an even course. He flew along the faintly etched line of the trail as it wound its way to and fro across the hilly landscape, changing course as it was confronted by some natural object that dictated a change in direction.

"Ahead," the pilot said after a while. Peering over his shoulder James saw the dark outline of low mountains straddling the skyline.

"What do you think?" James asked.

The pilot shrugged. "If it was me, I'd use the mountains. The height gives an advantage when it comes to defense. There is a better view all around. What can I say? These Albanians know this country. Maybe they're on the other side, down in some valley. They could have dispersed to one of a dozen villages."

James put a hand on the pilot's shoulder.

"I guess you're right. I was just hoping we might find something. Give it another fifteen minutes then we'll go back."

"No problem."

"Hey, don't worry," Hawkins said. "We tried."

The pilot swung around a high cliff. Before them lay a rocky escarpment, where the crumbling stone lay exposed to the extreme weather. It swept back from the edge to reveal a broken maze of rock, still white with snow.

"I see movement," Hawkins said, twisting in his seat as the chopper overshot the area.

The pilot eased back on the controls, bringing the chopper around in a tight curve, heading back for the spot Hawkins had indicated.

"There! See the son of a bitch," Hawkins demanded.

Leaning across his partner, James followed Hawkins's finger and saw a dark figure dashing across the escarpment. Sharp sunlight bounced off the metal of a rifle he was carrying.

"I see him now!" the pilot exclaimed and brought the chopper in lower, following the running figure.

James keyed in the transmit button for the chopper's radio. For security reasons it had been decided that no contact would be made with Phoenix Force back at the UN base unless it became strictly necessary. Waiting for a response, James scanned the map on his knee, identifying the grid reference for the area they were in.

Manning's voice came through James's headset.

"Flyer One from Base. Acknowledge. Any message. Over."

"Base from Flyer One. Take down this reference. We might have gotten lucky," James reported and quoted the map reference. "Going in for a closer look. Over."

"Flyer One from Base. Information received. Take it easy. Over."

"Base from Flyer One. We will. Talk to you later. Over and out."

As James cut the contact he heard the pilot swear just before the chopper made a sharp sweep away from the escarpment.

The sharp ping of bullets impacting against the chopper made James sit up straight.

"Jesus Christ!"

The pilot's exclamation emphasized their predicament. Both James and Hawkins saw that the lone figure had been joined by others. All except one were firing off autorifles. The remaining man had stepped close to the edge of the escarpment where he stood motionless, a slim tube resting on one shoulder.

"Rocket launcher," Hawkins said.

The tube belched smoke, and a brief blossom of flame burst from the front of the launcher. Trailing a pale stream of vapor, the launched rocket curved its deadly arc across the open sky, racing toward the chopper. The pilot made the right maneuvers, desperately trying to take the chopper out of the rocket's path. His attempt was too little too late.

The rocket struck just forward of the tail rotor, exploding with enough force to rip the aft section off. The stricken chopper lurched across the sky, losing height with terrifying speed. The pilot struggled with the controls, doing what he could to minimize his lost command. There was little he could do to maintain any kind of steady flight. The chopper began to spin, spiraling out of the sky. If it hadn't been for the hardy tree line on the slope of the escarpment the chopper would have smashed into the rock face. Instead it crashed through the thick foliage, tumbling in a graceless descent, splintering branches and tree trunks as it fell in a series of lurches that cushioned its descent to a degree.

James and Hawkins, strapped in the center of the cabin, were protected to a greater degree than the pilot. When the canopy of the chopper was shattered by a splintered tree trunk, the jagged wood tore through his body, ending his life in a brutal moment. There was little either of the Phoenix Force warriors could have done to prevent the length of wood from doing the same to them if the crippled chopper hadn't chosen that moment to roll over, sliding away from the broken tree. It slithered the last twenty feet to the ground down a loose shale slope, coming to rest against a heavy boulder. After the racket caused by the crash, the silence that followed was almost unreal and it stayed that way for some time.

The silence was finally broken by the creak of disturbed metal from within the shattered body of the chopper.

James lifted his head and gazed around the wrecked cabin. He concentrated on the mess, trying to detach himself from the pain that seemed to have taken over his entire being. He could feel the slick wetness of blood on the left side of his face. Some had run into the corner of his eye, and he raised his hand to brush it away. The action made him groan. For a moment he thought he had broken his arm, but realized it was only bruised. Even so it hurt like hell. James stayed where he was as he assessed his condition. The pain across his ribs had been caused by his seat harness pulling tight during the crash. It would leave some heavy bruising, but at least it had done its job. He moved his legs. No problem there apart from a gash in his right thigh, in the upper area. It had already stopped bleeding. He began to feel the cold, which meant he needed to get out of the chopper and move around to get his circulation going.

James turned to check Hawkins. The younger

man lay slumped forward, supported by his seat harness. Leaning across him, James freed the harness belt so he could move. He checked Hawkins's pulse and found it was strong. Grabbing hold of the man, he sat him upright. As he slumped back in his seat Hawkins stirred suddenly, eyes snapping wide open. He stared around wildly, then recognized James.

"What the hell happened?"

"We got hit by a rocket and we crashed."

"Dammit, I remember." Hawkins cleared his head. "Cal, the pilot...?"

"He's gone," James said. "He tried to get us down in one piece, but he didn't make it."

Hawkins rubbed his chest and ribs. "Damn, I'm sore."

"Seat harness. That's what saved us, T.J."

"Hey, you smell something hot?" Hawkins asked.

"I do now. It's time we got out of here."

They scrambled out of the wrecked chopper. Ignoring the aches of their bodies, they put distance between themselves and the smoldering helicopter. The two men were still in the open when the chopper burst into flame. Leaked fuel from ruptured tanks had ignited, probably coming into contact with live electrical wiring that had shorted against metal. The combination of fuel vapor, oxygen and hot wire came together and created fire. It spread quickly, seeking more of the spilled fluid, expanding and abruptly flash burning, sending a raw burst of flame out and up, engulfing the shattered chopper and anything within proximity.

"That's all we need," James muttered. "Maybe

we should just send out a damned laser display just so they know exactly where we are.''

''I've got a better idea, Cal. Let's get the hell out of here in case those old boys come lookin' for us.''

They moved off without further discussion, both realizing the difficult position they were in: down in hostile territory, with little chance of rescue in the immediate future. Although their last contact with the other members of Phoenix Force had given their map reference, it would be some time before any concern would be raised. Unless someone tried to contact the chopper. In the meantime, James and Hawkins needed to keep moving in case of pursuit by the FAP terrorists. That meant they would be abandoning their reported position, which would make it that much harder for any rescue attempt to reach them quickly.

James allowed all the negative aspects of their position to run through his head, then cast them aside. There was no profit in allowing himself to get depressed. It was down to him and Hawkins to stay ahead of the game and by some means or other let their teammates know they were down—but not out.

They maintained their course for a half hour, following the natural descent of the terrain. On these lower slopes there was still plenty of cover—rock falls and fissures, clumps of foliage and the occasional stand of windswept trees. Even so, the landscape was unknown to them whereas the FAP were on home ground. For all they knew, the terrorists might have roving patrols.

In a shallow depression, shielded by overhanging trees, James and Hawkins took a break. A clear, icy stream ran along the bed of the depression and they were at least able to take a drink and rest.

James did what he could to clean the gash in his leg, tearing off a strip of the T-shirt he wore under his camou gear. He flushed the gash with fresh water, then bound another strip around his thigh.

While they rested they took stock of their belongings. Both men were dressed in winter camouflage fatigues. Each man carried his handgun in a shoulder rig, with extra magazines in pouches on their belts. Both had knives tucked into belt sheaths. Neither man had been able to recover their autorifles, which had been stowed in weapon racks in the chopper's cabin. James still had the map with him, stuffed inside his jacket. He took it out now and spread it out.

"Here's where we were. Since we came down, we've been moving roughly east. So I figure by now we should be about here."

Scanning the map, Hawkins followed the route they had flown to get to the FAP stronghold.

"We need to be here," he said, jabbing a finger on the map at the point where the UN base was located near the border. "Cal, my man, that is some stroll."

"Tell me about it."

"Pity we can't call for a taxi."

James took another quick drink from the stream. Sitting back, he took out his handgun, checked the magazine and made certain the action was clear. Returning the pistol to his holster, he watched as Hawkins went through the same routine.

"You ready?"

"As I'll ever be."

"Let's go."

They set off, following the drift of the land and trying to maintain the course they had set for themselves.

James had the feeling they wouldn't be on their own for long.

His assumption was correct. The Phoenix Force pair had only been on the move for thirty minutes when Hawkins, checking their back trail, spotted figures on the higher slopes near where the chopper had come down. Hawkins paused to take a rough count and made out at least four, maybe five, in pursuit.

"Company coming up from behind," he said.

James took a look, watching the oncoming group.

"Can't say we weren't expecting them."

They moved on, stepping up the pace. With snow still on the ground, James and Hawkins were leaving a clear trail but there wasn't a thing they could do about that. Their aim was to stay well ahead of the FAP terrorists, lose them if possible even though that was a slight possibility.

Twice the two men were stalled by icy, tumbling streams, the water level raised by the snow. They forded the streams, enduring the crippling cold, and emerged on the far side drenched to midthigh and shivering with the cold. All they could do was keep moving, which at least kept the circulation going.

"Damn, that water is cold," Hawkins muttered as they breached the second watercourse.

Toward noon they reached a dense stand of timber. There was no way around it they could see. It stretched out in both directions, creating a thick green barrier. Pausing as they entered, James and Hawkins turned to see their pursuers still in evidence, and closer now.

"They on damned horses or what?" James asked.

"No. They just know the country better than we do, Cal."

The thump of a heavy bullet hitting one of the trees close by caught their immediate attention. Bark and wood chips flew into the air. The trailing sound of the shot reached them a split second later. James and Hawkins ducked for cover, pulling quickly back into the shadow provided by the timber and foliage.

"They also have bigger guns," James commented.

"Long range," Hawkins said. "Could be a sniper rifle."

"This gets better every time you speak."

They eased back into the timber, allowing the natural wrap of low branches and foliage to close around them. It helped conceal their movements as they kept on moving, their need still to distance themselves from the men on their trail.

Pushing deeper into the trees, and attempting to keep the noise of their passing to a minimum, they had reached midway through when James threw up a hand, halting Hawkins.

"Off to the left," James whispered. "Movement. Reflection, too. Light on a gun barrel."

"Let me get between you and him," Hawkins said, "so you can block me when I turn his way. Soon as I spot him, you go down."

"Most likely I will," James remarked, but he

showed his faith in Hawkins by doing what the younger man had asked.

As James deliberately turned his back on the fleeting shadow Hawkins peered across his shoulder, watching the distant shrubbery. His patience was rewarded moments later when he made out the rising shape of a dark-clad figure. The distant man lifted a long-barreled rifle to his shoulder and leveled it. Hawkins took a sharp breath, held it and brought up his Beretta in a single fluid movement. His target acquisition was swift and certain. Hawkins held for scant seconds, then pumped three fast shots at the motionless figure. He saw the man turn aside, the muzzle of the rifle jerking skyward, then the target went down.

"Go!" Hawkins said.

Together he and James broke into a run, ducking deeper into the trees. They brushed against low branches, sending powdery snow flying. Stumbling, slipping, they increased their pace, forgetting caution in their race to gain some distance. More than once they went to their knees as they hit some concealed object, each man pausing to help his partner when the other stumbled.

And all the while they were moving they constantly checked their surroundings, knowing that just because they couldn't see their pursuers didn't mean they weren't still nearby.

Ahead of them the tree line began to thin out. The terrain was low-lying, almost flat, which meant the loss of cover the trees were offering. Despite that, James and Hawkins kept running, because there was no other option open to them.

The rattle of autofire reached their ears. Bullets began to chop into the trees, spitting bark and splinters. Shredded leaves blew into the air. Both Phoenix Force warriors felt the tug of bullets snapping at their clothing.

They broke from cover, the trees falling behind. The bleak, snowy terrain stretched before them, offering little in the way of decent cover.

James felt the earth slip from under his boot as he stepped into a hole. He went down on one knee, the impact dragging breath from his lungs. Immediately Hawkins spun, covering his partner. He faced back the way they had come, his Beretta gripped in both hands. Hawkins's keen eyes spotted movement just inside the tree line. He triggered a 3-round burst, spacing his shots, and saw dark figures move back into the shadows. He fired another burst, and bark flew off the tree trunks.

"Okay," James yelled. "Let's go."

Hawkins turned and saw that his partner was back on his feet. Without another word they moved on.

"There," Hawkins said, indicating the dark shadow of a deep depression ahead of them. They angled toward it, sliding awkwardly down the steep bank until they hit bottom. A tangle of shrubbery grew at the base of the depression. James and Hawkins went straight for it, pushing into the dense thicket. They ignored the slashing branches and the sticking thorns. The ground underfoot was soft with a mix of snow and mud and pools of cold water. Its only saving grace was the fact that it would provide them with cover while they tried to maintain the lead they still had over the pursuing FAP terrorists.

The one chance they would have of possibly shedding their pursuers was the onset of darkness. It lay a few hours ahead, unfortunately. But if James and Hawkins could evade capture until nightfall, their chance of evasion would increase.

James and Hawkins pushed into the depths of the defile, each taking a side of the depression to watch over. The tracks they were leaving would draw their pursuers to them like a landing beacon.

The constant pursuit was draining their reserves. Fit as they were the Phoenix Force warriors were beginning to slow down. Reactions, dulled by the ceaseless movement and the tension of their situation, weren't helped by the cold. They were wet, starting to feel the pangs of hunger, and neither of them dared even imagine what a mug of hot coffee might do for their morale.

"This is crazy," Hawkins muttered, shrugging aside the lash of thorny branches. He felt them snagging his clothes, impeding his progress.

Distant voices yelled to one another. The FAP terrorists were getting closer. Hawkins glanced to his right, searching for the source of those nearest his position. He caught a glimpse of a dark-clad, armed man running parallel to the edge of the depression, trying to bring his weapon on-line. The man fired in frustration, snapping off a short burst that hit the ground well away from Hawkins. The Phoenix Force commando turned on his heel, committing himself to standing fast as he brought up his Beretta two-handed. He tracked the running man, eased back on the trigger, fired twice and saw the target go down. The FAP man hit the ground face first, his momentum carrying him forward. He slid over the edge of the depression and cartwheeled down the slope.

As Hawkins moved on, he heard firing from up ahead and saw James firing up at the rim of the depression on his side. His target faltered, swaying as he tried to complete a move he had started before James shot him. His right arm had been pulled back, something grasped in his hand.

"Grenade!" James yelled.

The hit man sank to his knees, weakened by the bullet wound, and despite his efforts he was unable to rid himself of the grenade in time. It detonated still in his hand, the blast shredding the man's upper body. His headless torso remained in a kneeling position for long seconds, the body going into spasm, and it remained so until gravity took over and pulled it to the ground.

The unexpected event took the FAP terrorists by surprise, and during their inaction, James and Hawkins plunged deeper into the heavy thickets, worming their way into what turned out to be a maze of bushes, stunted trees and tangled foliage. The ground underfoot turned into a quagmire of pooled water and greasy mud. It slowed their progress but didn't stop them. Enduring the nightmarish conditions and the wet and cold, up to their knees in muddy water, the Phoenix Force pair continued their flight. They had by this time become disoriented, all claim to knowing which way they were going cast aside. Their destination became secondary to staying alive. Survival was the name of the game now.

As James and Hawkins negotiated the hostile terrain, conscious of the FAP terrorists somewhere behind them, they were both acutely aware that exhaustion would eventually take its toll and they would be forced to slow down. Sooner or later the falling numbers would reach zero, and when that happened they would have to make a decision.

Neither man wanted to admit to that just yet, but the nagging thought remained on hold at the back of their minds.

James went down, slithering on his stomach in the cold, slick mud. A hand gripped his arm, and James looked up into Hawkins's face.

"Let's go, buddy," Hawkins said, hauling the man upright.

"Thanks."

"Hey, no problem. I might need the same any time now."

They pushed on, slogging through the undergrowth, the soft ground dragging at their boots.

"I can just hear David yelling at us for being lazy sods," Hawkins said.

"Yeah, and telling us he could do this all bloody day and not even raise a sweat."

"You know what sucks?"

"What?"

"He probably could."

Stony Man Farm, Virginia

AARON KURTZMAN HIT the key and sent the data stored in his computer onto the large monitor screen in front of him. He sat for a while, examining the information, his big right hand gripping a mug of steaming coffee. Kurtzman had been in front of his screen most of the night. He was tired but refused to allow himself to give in. He had stuck with the current problem until it had been resolved, and now he was getting results.

The cell phone liberated by Ray Tanner from Ciric Brako had provided Kurtzman with a starting point. The phone's personal number had given him access to the network that provided service to the phone users. The computerized network provider, linked by the satellite system, held data on the calls received and made from the phone. Kurtzman's initial problem had been getting into the network. The challenge was what made Kurtzman come alive. As far as he was concerned, it wasn't a case of if he could get in, it was how long it would take him. This time it took him a few hours of creative computing, but he eventually broke through the network's barriers and logged in on Brako's account. Once he had done that, Kurtzman was able to download the call details and bring them to his own computer. With the data transfer completed and saved, he exited the phone system.

Only then did Kurtzman relax. He pushed his chair back, taking a long drink of coffee before swinging it around so he could grab one of the phones and call Barbara Price, asking her to join him in the Annex and to bring along Hal Brognola.

While he waited for their arrival, Kurtzman scanned the data. There had been a lot of calls over the past few days. Even more during the preceding weeks. Brako had called the same numbers over and over again. Sipping his coffee, Kurtzman isolated one of the numbers and set a trace on it. The powerful Stony Man system began its search, scanning and retrieving.

The detail on the first number had just flashed up when the door opened and Price hurried in. The first thing she did was help herself to a cup of coffee. Taking large gulps from the mug, she joined Kurtzman and peered at his monitor through sleepy eyes.

"Sorry, did I get you up?" Kurtzman asked dryly.

"You're a funny guy, Aaron. Remind me to laugh at you one day," Price grumbled.

Chuckling, Kurtzman tapped his keyboard and ran a full ID check on the name the computer had delivered.

"I got into the phone system and extracted all the numbers Brako had been speaking to over the past few weeks. This is the expanded information on one of those numbers. And it's interesting reading too."

Price digested the data. She muttered something under her breath that sounded fairly rude to Kurtzman, but he didn't ask for a translation.

"What have we got?" Hal Brognola asked as he joined them.

Kurtzman explained, then indicated what he'd got from his number check.

It didn't take more than a few seconds for Brognola to grasp the significance of the information onscreen. He reached for a phone, tapping the speed-dial button that would connect him with his UN contact. Over Kurtzman's broad shoulder he could still see the data on screen:

Name: KARL DESARTE
Status: NATO COMMUNICATIONS OFFI-
CER
WITH UNITED NATIONS MISSION
CURRENTLY LOCATED IN MACEDONIA
Responsibility: LIAISON WITH UNPROFOR
MILITARY COMMAND

"That's the bare bones of it," Kurtzman explained to Price. "There's plenty more, but I figured
this was what Hal would be interested in."

"I'd say so," Price agreed.

Kurtzman printed the data on Desarte and handed
it to Brognola, who was in conversation with his UN
contact. Turning back to his screen, Kurtzman called
up the next number and asked for a search.

"Time to bring in the rest of the team," he said,
reaching for the phone. He spoke to Wethers and
Delahunt, asking them to report to the Computer
Room. Tokaido was on an extended break due to
being the last on duty.

Kurtzman began to split the telephone numbers
and transfer them to Wethers's and Delahunt's stations ready for their arrival.

Brognola put down the phone.

"Desarte will be taken off-station within the next
few minutes. The security people will take him for
questioning. I'm confident we have our NATO
mole. Good work, Aaron."

"Tell me when we have this all ticd down."

Kurtzman went back to his screen and highlighted
one of the numbers he'd kept for himself. He
worked silently, lost in his cyberworld.

Price and Brognola distanced themselves from Kurtzman so they could assess the current situation.

"Phoenix is checking out the firefight area to see if they can pick up anything on the FAP terrorists. Even David thinks it's a long shot, but worth the time," Price said. "We don't seem to be having much luck here at home since Able lost Khan in New York, but they haven't given up yet."

"My last update from Aaron concerning Ilyana Petrocovich was still zero. The fact we know she tried to pass herself off as dead hasn't made it any easier to locate her current whereabouts."

"Maybe something will flag up from this list of phone numbers," Brognola said, hope in his voice.

"Maybe," Price answered.

"By the way, what's Katz up to?"

Price smiled. "He's locked himself away with a telephone and a laptop. He said he wanted to contact some old friends."

Brognola knew what she was referring to. Katz still maintained contact with people in intelligence networks, and old adversaries who had changed sides due to the relaxation of the cold war. People who had done their best to kill the Israeli were now trading information with him. It was an odd situation born out of necessity. A major threat might have diminished, but others, and often with far more sinister agendas, had taken its place. Katz, being a pragmatist, had seen the advantage of using former enemies as allies albeit with a keen eye and ear for any ulterior motives they might have. He played the game to his advantage, only giving when he decided what he might receive was worthy of the exchange.

"Let's hope he hasn't lost his touch," Brognola said.

THE PHONE HAD RUNG a number of times before it was picked up. The line was perfectly clear, a tribute to the excellence of the state-of-the-art satellite communications setup. Katz heard the gentle breathing of the person on the other end of the line.

"Yuri, how are you?"

There was a distinct pause, followed by a soft, almost mocking chuckle.

"My God, I thought you would be dead by now."

"No. I'm too stubborn to die. You should know that."

"What do I call you today? Whenever our paths crossed before you always had a different name."

"Well, I'm still in the same business but nowadays I'm not in the field."

"Thank goodness for that."

"Call me Joseph."

"So, how can I help you? I know very well that you have not called to ask about my interest in gardening. Or how my grandchildren are growing."

"As much as I would like to I'm afraid the reason for my call is serious, Yuri."

"Then ask."

"Ilyana Petrocovich."

"You are serious. That name never trips lightly off the tongue."

"Where would I look for her?"

"You have not heard that she is dead?"

"Yuri, we both know that is not true."

"The difficulty is knowing who she is working

for. Since she became freelance there have been many rumors. First it was the Chinese, then there was a suggestion she had taken up a contract with the North Koreans working on a biological warhead for their No Dong missiles.''

"You said suggestion?"

"Our intelligence reports proved that the deal had gone no further than in-depth discussions. It appears that Ilyana's demands were too much for the Koreans. She is a dedicated worker who insists on being left completely alone. She demands total control and will not allow anyone to interfere with her projects. The Koreans refused to accept that. They expected access at all stages. So the negotiations were broken off. Ilyana stayed in Paris, and her Korean negotiators returned home.''

"Was it the same when she worked for the department?"

"Of course. Ilyana was a brilliant biochemist, but she placed herself above all her co-workers and refused to become just another worker. She had her own small team, and she was allowed to set her own agenda. There was a great deal of aggravation within the department at the time, but she got her way because of her talent. She was the youngest person ever to join the department. Right from the first day she showed promise."

"Talent is hardly the word for the kind of horrors she created," Katz observed.

"A bad choice of words, my friend. But you will appreciate that in those days we were engaged in an ideological war, the East and the West both hoping to become masters of the world. To do it we thought we needed to have the biggest weapons. The most destructive. The vilest biological weapons." Yuri paused. "Joseph, we were all so stupid. In my declining years I can look back on it and see the way we were going, how close we all came to wiping ourselves off the face of the earth. I see my grandchildren playing in the sun, and I realize I might have been responsible for their deaths."

"While the Ilyana Petrocoviches of this world are still on the loose, Yuri, none of us are completely safe. Which is why I need to locate her."

"There are some people I could talk to. Call me back in an hour, Joseph. I will try to have an answer for you."

CHAPTER EIGHT

New York

"If this son of a bitch doesn't quit running us around soon, I'm personally going to take him out."

Carl Lyons glanced up at the speaker. It wasn't often that Rosario Blancanales lost his temper, but when he did it was a sight to see.

"Ease off," Lyons said. "The way I see it, we've got him running scared."

Blancanales stared at Lyons. For a moment it looked as if he might blow, but then he smiled.

"We've got him running scared?"

"Yeah."

"We've been following him so long it's like being married to the guy," Schwarz said testily.

"Don't you start," Lyons warned.

They were in a diner across the street from a seedy hotel where Khan had spent the night. The man showed no sign that he had a destination. His routine had been uneventful. Since leaving FBI custody Khan had wandered the city, seemingly taking in the sights, but Lyons, suspicious as ever, had stuck with the man. It had been a relief for Able

Team when the FBI had allowed them to take over. Brognola had stepped in and suggested his people carry the surveillance, giving the FBI time to work on the forensic evidence they were building. It was a suggestion the Bureau accepted quickly enough. They had already put in a great deal of time on the case prior to Weller's death and had collected a great deal of evidence. Khan was a loose cannon, having come out of left field, and his involvement in the affair appeared tenuous.

Brognola promised that if his people came up with anything of significance the FBI would be informed. It was little short of a good PR job devised by the big Fed, but Brognola was becoming extremely adept at the political ploys and counterploys needed to play the interagency game. He also knew that agencies like the FBI operated on procedures and that meant there could be delays in getting operations on the road. They might be short delays but often that was enough for things to fall apart. Stony Man went for the instant cure to problems, initiated by the men in the field. There were occasions and situations where there was no time to wait for departmental approval.

"So where is our boy going today?" Schwarz asked. "Another trip to the movies? Or back to that strip show?"

"If I knew that I wouldn't be here," Lyons said. "I'd have a booth on the Atlantic City boardwalk and tell fortunes."

"Ouch!" Blancanales whispered.

Khan stepped out of his hotel at that point. He went to one of the cabs parked nearby and climbed in. Blancanales started the rental car and trailed three vehicles behind the cab. It was a long ride, and it took them through the Holland Tunnel into New Jersey and an industrial strip.

"Looks better all the time," Schwarz said.

The cab dropped Khan outside a medium-size electronics unit, and he went straight inside. Blancanales pulled the car to a stop across the access road and cut the engine.

Lyons took out his cell phone and keyed in the number that would connect him to Stony Man. He waited while the signal was sent up to the communications satellite, then bounced back to the Farm.

"I need a check on a company," Lyons said when he got through to Kurtzman. "It's called Sonilab 2000. The address is Avenue 23, Franklin Park, New Jersey. We're parked across the road from it and our man is inside, so we need the info fast."

"I'll get back to you," Kurtzman said.

"What if Khan leaves before we get the intel?" Schwarz asked.

"Good question," Blancanales agreed.

"That's why I asked."

"Will you two quit before I throw up?" Lyons snapped. His impatience showed as he fell right into the trap his partners had sprung. Lyons scowled at them, more angry with himself for actually falling than because they had conned him. "Pair of clowns."

"Praise indeed coming from Ironman," Schwarz said.

They settled back, the moment of levity gone. It had been nothing more than a tension breaker, something to ease the boredom brought on by the eternal waiting that assignments often entailed.

Less than ten minutes had elapsed before Lyons's phone shrilled. He accessed the line and identified himself.

"Sonilab 2000 manufactures all kinds of electronic switches and relays. Not exactly in your one hundred best companies, but it manages to keep itself just about solvent. I did a background check and this is where it started to get interesting. Phoenix Force sent in a list of phone numbers for us to check. One of them led us to a holding company managing a group of organizations, some of which are in the U.S. We'd already done the groundwork, so I was able to cross-reference Sonilab against those organizations. We have a connection. Sonilab, way down on the list, is part of a group run by Millennium. The board comprises a half dozen individuals who all have ethnic Albanian backgrounds. They've all lived here for years, long before the troubles started, but family ties are never broken."

"Sonilab could be providing equipment or money," Lyons said.

"Probably both. There are a hell of a lot of Albanians in the U.S. Fund-raising has become high-profile lately. A lot of cash has been raised for Albania."

"Thanks," Lyons said. "We'll take it from here."

"Sounded fruitful," Schwarz said.

Lyons put away his phone. "You could say that."

"We wait for Khan to come out?"

"We wait. No telling what we might find if we go barreling in there."

Lyons settled back and relayed the information he'd received from Kurtzman to his partners.

It was only a short wait after that. A black BMW came into sight from somewhere in back of the unit. It rolled to a stop beside the entrance. Khan appeared, flanked by a couple of men who, though dressed casually, carried themselves in a manner suggesting they were in a combat situation. Khan was carrying an aluminum case.

"And then there were three," Blancanales murmured. "Four if you count the driver."

"Yeah. I'm counting," Lyons said.

Blancanales started the car and watched the BMW ease onto the road and make a left. He allowed the BMW to reach the far end of the road before he set off in pursuit. Lyons used his cell phone to call in the BMW registration to Stony Man. It might not mean anything but there was always the chance they might get something on the owner, or who had rented it.

The BMW turned in the direction of the Holland Tunnel.

"Great, he's going back to that fleabag hotel for lunch," Blancanales commented.

"Can I interrupt?" Schwarz asked from the rear seat.

"Tell me we've picked up a tail," Lyons said.

"Correct."

"Damn!" Lyons snapped.

He glanced back over his shoulder and saw a dark panel truck coming up fast behind them. The driver had his eyes fixed on the rear of the rental car and by the rate he was closing in, he had his foot to the floor.

Blancanales swung the car to the right, hoping to lose the panel truck. The vehicle followed.

The BMW had already taken the curve ahead and was accelerating fast.

"Pol, we can't waste time with this joker," Lyons said, sliding his Colt Python from its shoulder rig under his jacket. He clambered over the seat into the rear, dropping beside Schwarz.

The panel truck shot forward, the crash bar mounted on the front slamming into the rear of the lighter car. Blancanales had to fight the wheel to prevent the car from fishtailing out of control. A second nudge from the truck sent the vehicle lurching forward.

"This mother is serious," Schwarz yelled.

"Yeah? Well, so am I," Lyons replied.

He hammered the rear window glass with the Python's barrel, shattering it. As the fragments fell away, Lyons stuck the big handgun through the opening and triggered a pair of shots into one of the front tires. The rubber blew apart and the truck began to swerve violently. He fired again, taking out the other tire. This time the veering truck spun in a half circle before coming to a shuddering halt.

"We got problems, guys," Blancanales said.

The car had developed a list to one side, and Blancanales was having trouble keeping the vehicle on a straight course. He jammed on the brakes, bringing it to a grinding halt.

The rattle of autofire and the thud of bullets slamming into the rear of their vehicle drew Able Team's full attention. In unison they kicked open their respective doors and exited the car, dropping behind it for cover.

Three figures had emerged from the panel truck. Each was armed with a stubby Uzi, and they were advancing on the stalled rental.

"I have that urge to shoot back," Schwarz stated, pulling his handgun.

"Give in to it," Lyons said. He leaned around the rear of the car and pulled down on one of the gunners, triggering a single shot that knocked the man's leg from under him. As he went down, Lyons put a second shot through his skull, pitching him over on his back.

The gunner closest to the rental dropped to one knee, angling his Uzi in the direction of the car's underside. His first volley sent sparks arcing up from the roadway, while more of his shots rapped against the rear axle.

Blancanales realized the gunner's strategy. He was going for the lower shots in the hope of getting some of his bullets to ricochet off the road or the underside of the car and find targets in Able Team as they crouched behind the vehicle. It was a good idea.

Blancanales scooted to the front of the car, crawling around the front so that he had a clearer shot of the resourceful gunner. Resting against the side of the car, using his knee as a steady for his gun hand, the Able Team commando took steady aim and fired twice.

His target dropped with the sudden looseness of death, both slugs having cored deep into his skull.

The surviving gunner paused in midstride, seeing his partners going down. For a second it looked as if he were about to quit. His Uzi wavered, then leveled again as the man uttered a harsh yell of defiance and opened up. His blast of 9 mm slugs raked the rear of the car, sending sparks into the air before he was cut down by the combined power of shots from Lyons and Schwarz. He crashed to the ground hard, his legs kicking briefly in a denial of death.

Carl Lyons ditched the empty casings from the Python's cylinder and used a speed loader to replenish his weapon. Only then did he stand and join Blancanales and Schwarz.

Able Team moved in on the downed men, kicking aside discarded weapons. They checked the three men, who were all dead.

"We might have got some information if we'd kept them alive," Schwarz said.

"Their choice," Lyons snapped. "They dealt themselves in."

"Well, while they were doing it our mark got away," Schwarz stated.

"Don't remind me."

Lyons took out his phone and punched in the Stony Man number.

It was still ringing when they heard the approaching wail of police sirens.

"Plan B?" Blancanales asked.

"Plan B," Schwarz agreed.

Price came on the phone in answer to Lyons's call.

"Hi," Lyons said. "I think we have a problem."

Stony Man Farm, Virginia

"YOUR NEGOTIATING skills are required," Price said as Brognola caught her gaze.

The big Fed shook a couple of antacid tablets from the pack he held and swallowed them.

"Now what?"

Price explained Able Team's problem. Brognola listened, shrugging briefly. It wasn't as bad as it could have been. He would only be dealing with the local police. He would need to go to the local top cop and stress the need for cooperation in a matter of national security, which of course he couldn't elaborate on because of protocol. However, he would appreciate the help of the home ground force in helping to track down a group suspected of being involved in an international conspiracy. It sounded pretty good to Brognola. He hoped he found himself dealing with someone who would be equally impressed.

"Aaron, I need you to flag the head cop in the area Able Team is operating. Name and phone number."

"I got it."

Brognola took the phone from Price and brought it to his ear.

"Carl, talk to me."

Before Lyons began to speak Brognola picked up the wail of sirens in the background. The local cops were already on the scene.

Price glanced around the room. Along with Kurtzman, Carmen Delahunt was on duty. Price made her way across to her.

"How's it going, Carmen?"

Delahunt leaned back, brushing strands of hair from her face. She indicated the screen.

"I've been checking some of the numbers Aaron gave me. The ones from Brako's phone. I'm starting to pull in some interesting results. Aaron's trace program means we can follow on and pick out individual numbers the number we got from the original list has contacted. Kind of like a chain link. One gets you another, then others, and so on. Take this number here. Brako called it. I follow through and check that number and find it has called other numbers. Now when I pick up on those, I find they've also contacted Brako and other numbers in the circuit."

"So these people are all talking among themselves?"

"In spades," Delahunt said. "These guys have been busy. Especially during the past couple of weeks."

"What about numbers out of the circle?"

"A few. The system is listing them right now. We should have addresses to go with them if everything works like it should."

"How did we do things before all this stuff?" Price wondered out loud.

Delahunt smiled at the thought.

"Card files, telephone calls and lots of footwork."

"Amen for the silicon chip."

Delahunt's printer began to disgorge paper. As it slid into the tray, the woman lifted it out.

"Here we go," she said.

She split the list and handed some to Price who sat in an empty seat. The pair set to the task of checking the numbers.

"We have a shipping line working out of New York," Price said.

Delahunt took the details and keyed them in. The data flashed up on screen.

"Charter company. They freight anything to anywhere."

Delahunt keyed in instructions and set the computer searching. In the meantime, she and Price went through the list of numbers.

"Got some calls to that electronic company Able Team just checked out."

"Sonilab?" Kurtzman asked.

"That's the one."

Kurtzman made a note of the connection, then went back to his on-screen task. His monitor had just flashed up the registration of the BMW Lyons had phoned in. He studied the data, nodding to himself.

"What have you got?" Brognola asked, cutting the connection as he finished speaking to Lyons.

"That BMW belongs to a guy called Mark Slamen. I'm running a background check on him now."

"What's his involvement in this particular deal?" Brognola wondered.

"I'll try and find out. While I do that, here's your

contact in the NYPD. Talk to this guy and maybe Able Team can stay out of jail.''

Brognola took the printed sheet and went off to do his PR job.

Kurtzman returned to his keyboard. He began to set up a cross-reference program that would highlight and detail any and all connections between Mark Slamen and phone connections they had unearthed. Setting the search parameters, he tapped the Start key and let the computer do its work. Knowing that even with a setup as powerful as his it was going to take some time to come up with the answers, Kurtzman rolled his chair away from his station and headed for the coffeepot.

Price glanced up from her own work as Kurtzman rolled across the com room. She saw him fill his mug and take a long drink. Kurtzman flexed his big, powerful shoulders, then spun his chair and moved across to stare up at one of the large video screens. It showed an aerial view of the Kosovo region and had come from one of the roving satellites Stony Man could access. The image was sharp and clear.

Looking at the screen, Price found herself wondering just what Phoenix Force was up to at this particular moment in time.

Kosovo

"SOMETHING'S GONE wrong," McCarter said. "I can bloody well feel it."

Encizo went to the radio and checked it again. He shook his head.

"Still no signal. Staying off-air to avoid being

tracked is one thing. But not for this long. Not when it's Cal on the other end.''

"Could be he's having trouble getting through," Manning suggested. "The weather's still bad out there. The closer he gets to the mountains, the worse it'll be.''

"I'm not convinced, Gary," McCarter said, checking his watch. "It's been too long. We have to do something. Now.''

"I agree," Manning said, "but what?"

"We get Stony Man to look for them," the Briton stated.

"Say what?" Encizo asked.

"They can scan the area with one of the satellite cameras. See if they can spot anything. Those things can pick out a pimple on a bloody orange. It shouldn't be hard to locate a chopper.''

"It might work," Manning agreed. "We can give them the last map coordinates.''

"Better than sitting on our hands.''

Encizo sat at the comm unit and logged in, connecting to Stony Man via the satellite link. He asked for and got Aaron Kurtzman, who listened in silence as McCarter outlined his idea, sending the map bearings for Kurtzman to use when he directed the satellite.

"It'll be at least forty minutes before I can access," Kurtzman said. "It'll give me time to work out a detailed scanning grid for the satellite to work to.''

Price came on the uplink.

"You guys okay?"

"We'll be better once we know where Cal and

T.J. are,'' McCarter said. ''In the meantime, do you have anything for us to go at over here? It's frustrating just cooling our heels.''

''We're working on the information we got from the phone numbers. One good thing is that we identified the guy responsible for passing on NATO-UN information. He was on Brako's phone list. They had a lot to say to each other according to the number of calls. This guy Desarte has been picked up, so at least the FAP doesn't have his input any longer. We're still working on the other info. Things are a little cloudy at the moment, but there are strands coming together. We should have something for you soon.''

''Okay,'' McCarter said, unconvinced.

Kurtzman's voice rumbled out of the speaker. ''I'll be back to you as soon as I have anything. Same with any intel we get on this end. Take it easy, guys.''

Encizo put the comm set on standby, so that if anything was fed through from Stony Man there wouldn't be any delay in receiving it.

McCarter began to pace, a sure sign that he was agitated. Watching him, Manning knew that the Briton's concern was nothing to do with having to wait. He was worried about James and Hawkins. More than he would ever admit.

The door to the hut crashed open. A figured clad in a black leather coat filled the opening, snow swirling in around him. McCarter stopped his pacing and confronted the man.

''What the bloody hell do you want?''

The man stepped into the hut, heeling the door

shut behind him. His keen gaze scanned the interior of the hut, acknowledging the setup. He turned back to McCarter.

"We need to talk," said Janic Milisivic, the Serbian police officer whom they had last seen arguing with the late Captain Moreau.

CHAPTER NINE

Stony Man Farm, Virginia

Yakov Katzenelenbogen sat absently rubbing the stump of his arm. He wasn't wearing his prosthesis, and lately when he was feeling tired, whether imagined or not, the stump ached. In truth it was simply a manifestation of his weariness. Long hours of concentrated analysis, brief snatches of rest, often disturbed due to some crisis—they all added up, and every so often they caught up with Katz and he went into a slump.

"Here we go," Barbara Price said, placing a steaming mug of coffee before him.

She perched her hip on the edge of the table and studied Katz intently. Concern showed in her eyes.

"Don't tell me I need to ease up," Katz said, picking up the mug and taking a long drink. "Hal is always doing that."

"Katz, you need to ease up," Price said firmly.

Katz scowled at her, aware she was fooling with him, and he wished he had the energy to respond in kind. This time she was right. He did feel weary. He had spent his last working period on the phone, speaking endlessly with various people, to little end. None of them had much to give him where Ilyana Petrocovich was concerned. The woman was certainly elusive. She had obviously chosen to stay out of sight. Where was she?

Katz had almost reached the end of the line with his checking when he had received a call from Yuri Danko. The ex-Soviet Intelligence major had some welcome news for Katz.

"My sources tell me Petrocovich has allied herself to the man who calls himself Malik. You have heard of him?

"Unfortunately, yes."

"Then I do not need to elaborate, my friend. If this alliance exists, and my sources are genuine, then there could be trouble ahead for all of us. Malik has the finances and the organization to give Petrocovich exactly what she wants—the right equipment and, above all, the privacy she needs to carry on her research."

"How recent is your information?"

"Within the past few days."

Katz didn't comment. His mind was racing ahead, trying to see this information within the context of the current Stony Man operation.

"Joseph? Are you still there?"

"Sorry, Yuri. I was putting things straight in my head. I'm grateful for your help. If you hear anything else, please let me know."

"Of course. I will make sure my contacts know this is important. Unfortunately, it is difficult to make them realize just how important. Joseph, if your people ever locate this woman, the order of the day should be to terminate with extreme prejudice.''

''Understood. Thanks again, Yuri. Keep in touch.''

''And you.''

Price listened in silence as Katz related his conversation with Yuri Danko.

''Is this the Malik we've been hearing about?''

Katz nodded. ''Extremist. He's willing to help any Muslim terrorist group with anti-Western policies. His file has him down as extremely wealthy. Good connections within the terrorist network. Links to Libya. Iraq. He's even been tied in to the Russian Mafia, using them and their drug routes to move his people and arms. Russia is a good market for his business. Plenty of weapons on the market. Signing on Ilyana Petrocovich would be a big feather in his cap. If she can come up with the goods, Malik will have one hell of a bargaining chip.''

''If she's as good as I seem to hear everyone claim, we could have something really scary coming up,'' Price stated.

''From what I know about this Malik, he doesn't waste his time on no-hopers. Bankrolling Petrocovich suggests she has something valuable to sell. And if Malik is interested we need to find out. His anti-U.S. stance is on a par with his anti-NATO, UN and every other organization.''

''Aligning himself with the FAP keeps up his ratings with other Muslim factions?''

''Malik is no fool, Barbara. He knows a good alliance when he sees it. Keeping the faith with the downtrodden ethnic Albanians is a way of gaining himself a foothold in Europe. If the FAP remains strong, so does the Muslim presence, and it opens a gateway to mainland Europe.''

"The crazy part of this, Katz, is that the majority of ethnic Albanians don't want the FAP. The things they've done are only weakening the case for the moderates. The FAP is the face of Albanians across the world. It's all they ever see or hear.''

"Good news doesn't do much for the ratings.''

"Cynical or what, Katz?''

The Israeli shrugged. "Maybe. But when was the last time you read anything uplifting from a war zone?''

"So we need to focus on two things—finding where Malik has this Petrocovich woman hidden away, and doing something about the power base of the FAP.''

"Yes. I don't think those two items are going to have too much distance between them,'' Katz said. "Right now they're pretty close. Malik has the FAP in his court as well as Petrocovich. He's using them both.''

"Using?''

Brognola had entered the room quietly, standing behind Katz and Price, listening to their conversation.

"I meant using. Malik is a manipulator. It's true he's doing what he can to aid the FAP because they are a Muslim group and therefore by definition a worthy cause for the brotherhood. But he will also be viewing the long-term picture. If the FAP and the ethnic Albanians get what they want, namely a completely autonomous Albanian state, Malik will have a base from where he can launch his terrorist groups into Europe. I agree with Barbara's comment about the FAP not being in favor with many Albanians. But there will be a strong group who want the FAP to win through, hard-liners who see the only way of retaining a grip on their culture is by having a tough leadership. Not a token one who might still bend the knee to Belgrade.''

''I understand the logic of that argument, Katz, but what if the price of that is allowing the FAP to spread its poison farther afield? We already have them killing Americans working for the UN. They've interfered with UN procedures by infiltrating the communications setup. What else are they going to do?''

''That's what we need to find out.''

The telephone rang. Katz picked it up and spoke.

''Okay. I'll tell him.'' He replaced the receiver. ''That was Aaron. He has the satellite on-line.''

''We'd better get over there,'' Brognola said.

KURTZMAN HAD TRANSFERRED the image to the big screen. The resolution was good despite the prevailing poor weather in Kosovo. The time there was about an hour after dawn. The picture image, collected and digested by the military satellite, came through with muted colors and some disruption by the clouds. With his innate skill at manipulating computer images, Kurtzman had filtered out as much of the interference as possible. At the time Brognola, Price and Katz entered the computer room, he had the satellite on its first major scan.

"General scan at the moment," he said. "The bearings I got from Phoenix Force should narrow things down, but we're still covering a lot of ground out there."

Kurtzman's fingers were moving constantly across his keyboard, his eyes never straying from the screen as he monitored the satellite's progress.

Price turned aside to check out the room and saw that the entire team was on duty, all busy at their keyboards. She crossed to have a word with each one, updating herself on their information gains.

"This guy Able Team has been involved with," Carmen Delahunt said, "Georgi Khan. The license plate check of the car he was in when he lost the team provided some interesting data. The car is owned by a man named Mark Slamen. The name kind of stuck in my mind. Like it was made up? So I checked with immigration. Mark Slamen came to this country about eight years ago from Yugoslavia. Only his name then was Marik Slavenivic. He's an ethnic Albanian who came here because he wanted better opportunities for his entrepreneurial skills. He had a small fleet of rust-bucket cargo freighters, and within three years he had built that up to double in size and treble the value.

"The guy is a multimillionaire now and trades all over. His company, by the way, is registered in Indonesia. From what I've been able to come up with, our friend Slamen is well received by a number of suspect regimes. It would be interesting to find out the kind of cargo his ships have been carrying. Slamen also seems to have a knack for finding niche markets and creaming off the profits before anyone else can move in.''

''I feel a big *but* coming out of the corner.''

''Over the past couple of years he has been getting himself involved in fund-raising for his old home country. There's no reason why he shouldn't. Only there have been some suggestions his motives are less than pure.''

''How so?''

''Complaints from some of the other fund-raisers that his contributions have been finding their way to the wrong quarter.''

''The FAP?''

Delahunt nodded. ''There's no absolute proof, but the feeling is there. It seems that rival groups have tried to cause trouble at some of his fund-raising events. Now when that did happen, Slamen had his security people come down hard. There was a bad scene at one event in L.A. Some guy almost died when Slamen's people beat him up. It showed another side to the man. His lawyers did a good job, and Slamen came out clean. Checking some police files, I pulled this.''

Price watched a file come up on Delahunt's monitor. It was a rap sheet on a man named Tony Darber. According to his sheet, Darber was no stranger to trouble. He had a reputation for violence, and had several arrests.

''Darber worked for Slamen up to the time of his death,'' Delahunt explained.

''He's dead? Where's the connection, Carmen?''

''Darber was one of the men Able Team clashed with outside Sonilab 2000.''

"Kind of puts Slamen into the frame."

"That's not all," Delahunt added. "We dug deep into Sonilab's background. It took some doing, but we chased it down and finally made a connection. Millennium, the group that has Sonilab on its list, is itself part of a larger conglomerate owned by an offshore company called Tutulani Inc."

"Carmen, just tell me. Quit being so damned smug."

Delahunt grinned, enjoying her small triumph.

"Okay. In Tirana the highway called Rruga Margarita Tutulani runs adjacent to the city's university. Tirana University was where the former Marik Slavenivic attended classes and gained his credentials in business studies."

Price squeezed Delahunt's shoulder.

"Okay, you can crow."

"I have Akira running a check on Slavenivic's former classmates. I figured we might as well see if any names come up that might connect."

"It's worth a try," Price said. She crossed over to Akira Tokaido's station and leaned over his shoulder. "Anything?"

"The database is running a search now."

"Let me know as soon as you have any results."

Huntington Wethers had just cross the room to refill his coffee mug. Price glanced at his screen. She was studying the mass of information when Wethers returned.

"It's a list of all of Slamen's ships. Where they are, where they're going and so forth. I went back about six months to give a general overview."

"Anything we should know?"

Wethers tapped his keyboard, isolating some of the data.

"This is one of Slamen's cargo freighters, the *Levantine*. She left Lisbon and sailed into the Mediterranean. According to the cargo manifest, she was carrying cargo to Israel. She was sighted off the Libyan coast one night, stopped for a few hours close in to shore then set sail again. It was more good luck than anything else. The ship was picked up by one of the satellites keeping an eye on the Libyan training camps during its sweep."

"I'm sure they weren't picking up oranges."

Wethers grinned. He tapped his keyboard again and brought up a satellite picture.

"This was taken by one of the birds on a routine scan of the training camps. Plenty of activity here in this one. Now look at this. Same camp two days later. Guess the connection between the two pictures?"

"The *Levantine*?"

"Yes. She passed by and waited the night before the second picture was taken. And before you ask, the freighter has been tracked since she left Libyan waters. According to the latest information, that freighter is a little off course. Unless they moved Israel and didn't tell us."

"Let me make a prediction," Price said. "If she stays on her present course, she's going to make another unscheduled stop off the Albanian coast."

Wethers brought up another image. This was from the INMARSAT satellite. The scanned images overlaid on the relief map showed the course of the freighter.

"The *Levantine* should be somewhere here by now," Wethers explained. "Instead she's changed to a northerly course, up through the Ionian Sea and into the Strait of Otranto. Next the Adriatic Sea and the Albanian coastline."

"Print all this out, Hunt," Price said. "I need to sit down with Hal and decide what we need to do."

"You got it."

Price had started to move away when Delahunt caught her attention.

"I've picked up some information about Khan. He took a flight from Newark. Destination Nassau."

"What's in the Bahamas that would interest Khan?"

Wethers turned from his monitor as his printer began to slide out sheets of data.

"I think I might be able to answer that."

All eyes locked on to him.

"While I was digging into Slamen's business dealings, I came across details of a deal he did a couple of months back. It didn't seem important until I gained more information.

"Slamen purchased a new vessel, paying cash for it. Financial statements show he had a substantial payment made into his business account days before the purchase of this vessel. The money was paid to Slamen via a banking organization based in Hong Kong. I traced it back through the usual smoke screens until I located a finance broker in London who is apparently being investigated by Scotland Yard's Special Branch. They suspect he's Malik's paymaster."

Wethers consulted his monitor as he brought up the results of his searching.

"The money transfer would fit the purchase time of the vessel."

"Are we saying Slamen purchased a ship on behalf of Malik?" Brognola asked.

"I'd have to say yes," Wethers stated. "The interesting part is the ship was purchased from the Japanese. Sell-off from a bankrupt company." He brought the image of a ship on-screen. "The marine research vessel was formally known as *Tomari Maru*, and is now called *Millennium Explorer*. She's capable of carrying out long-term deep-sea exploration and is completely self-contained. She even has her own fully equipped laboratory and is fitted with state-of-the-art electronics and computers. She can stay at sea for months."

"It could be we have our elusive research facility for Ilyana Petrocovich. Privacy. No distractions. A fully contained environment where she could carry out her bioexperiments and development without hindrance. It wouldn't have taken much to raise the lab isolation to the standard Petrocovich needs."

"A floating biolab?" Brognola asked.

"Why not?" Wethers said. "It's easy to keep secure and there'd be no unwelcome visitors. No one would pay much attention to a big ship. Remember the old adage. If you want to hide, stay out in wide open spaces."

"Clever," Price agreed.

"And here's the clincher," Wethers added. "Right now the *Millennium Explorer* is operating just off Nassau."

"Contact Able Team," Brognola said. "Tell them to pack for warm weather."

"Might be wise to send along some air support," Price said. "Jack's on standby. I can arrange for him to take a chopper to Nassau as backup."

"I'll leave you to arrange that," Brognola said.

He was still caught up in the Phoenix Force problem. Two of the team down in hostile territory didn't sit well with the big Fed. His main concern was their safety. The well-being of his combat teams was high on Brognola's list. He would do whatever was required to get them back.

"How's the scan coming on?" he asked Kurtzman.

"I'm getting there," the computer expert answered curtly, the sharpness in his tone revealing his own personal concern.

Price attracted Brognola's attention.

"Call for you, Hal."

Brognola took the offered telephone, recognizing the voice instantly.

"I need to see you," the President said. "Right away. It concerns the current situation."

"I'm on my way, sir."

Washington, D.C.

"THIS HAS TO BE said face-to-face, Hal," the President said.

He sat across from Brognola, behind the big desk in the Oval Office. They were alone. The big Fed sat awkwardly in his chair, unsure what was coming, but knowing he wasn't going to like it.

"I hate having to tell you this," the President began. The concern in his eyes was tangible. "I take it you haven't pulled off any rescue bid yet?"

"No, sir. We're still scanning for our MIAs."

"How hopeful are you?"

"Until I see the bodies they're still alive as far as I'm concerned."

"If you locate them alive?"

"The rest of Phoenix Force will go in and pull them out."

"No doubt in your mind about that?"

"The Stony Man teams have an unequaled record in survival, sir. I don't see any reason to think otherwise."

"Which makes it all the harder for me to have to tell you what's happening."

The President leaned forward, hands clasped together in front of him.

"No doubt you are aware of the serious escalation in the province?"

"I understand that talks have broken down again. That the Serbian government is digging in and rebuffing everything presented to them."

"Ethnic cleansing has started again," the President said, failing to repress the anger in his voice. "There are people dying every day over there, Hal. Up to now we've tried all avenues—talks, more talks, offers, conciliation. Nothing moves that government. It bends. We think we've made progress, then it shuts the door in our faces. It's happening all the time. In fact it's happened too many times. Their time is up. We have to stop the carnage one way or another."

Brognola watched the President as he formed his next words.

"About forty minutes ago I finished speaking to the British PM. We made our final commitment to the operation that has been in the planning stages for some time. Along with other members of NATO, who have all voted positive, it has been decided to take punitive action against the Serbian government in an attempt to force acceptance of the agenda we have presented to them."

"That being?"

"The withdrawl of Serbian forces from Albanian territory. The cessation of hostile acts against unarmed civilians. A complete stop to the killing of those same civilians and the forced evacuation from their homes. They also have to accept a long-term NATO peacekeeping force in Kosovo. Before we can put our ground troops in we have to destabilize the Serbian military structure."

Realization dawned on Brognola. He groaned inwardly because he knew now what was coming, why the President had called him to the White House for a face-to-face talk.

"It's starting up again. Very shortly NATO will start a high-saturation bombing campaign over Kosovo—military targets, bases, fuel dumps. Tracking and communication sites. Power supplies. Anything and everything that feeds the Serbian military. It's going to be an all-out operation. Bombing runs round the clock, and it will go on until the Serbian government backs down. The only way to end it is in their hands."

"I take it this is on a need-to-know basis?"

The President nodded. "Under wraps until we're ready to go." He sighed. "This is where it gets hard. Assuming your people locate the missing men and go in for them, we can't warn them what's coming. I understand you communicate over secure links, but we all know nothing is one hundred percent safe. We cannot afford for anything to get out before the campaign starts."

"So my people have to go in under threat of a bombing strike? Into hostile territory not knowing what's on its way?"

"That's it, Hal."

"If they get caught after the bombing starts, they'll fall into the hands of people who aren't going to be too charitable toward them."

"Understand my position on this, Hal. I don't like having to hold back information from our own people, especially when it directly concerns their safety, but I have no other choice."

"I accept that, sir. And so will the guys. But it leaves them holding the shitty end of the stick, if you'll pardon my language."

The President smiled. "From what I know about Phoenix Force this is the kind of situation that brings out their best. I just wish I didn't have to place them in such a position."

"That makes two of us." Brognola hesitated. "Do I have your permission to use a little license when I talk to them?"

"Exactly what did you have in mind?"

"No direct message about what's coming. Just a little off-the-cuff remark that might give them a hint about stormy weather."

The President considered. "Think about it hard, Hal. If the Serbians pick up any hint, we lose our advantage."

"Trust me, Mr. President. I've played this game for a long time. Long enough to know my people and how to lay a suggestion that won't mean a thing to anyone but them."

"All right, Hal. Just remember this conversation never took place. I hope your people come through okay. We need them back home. If you can give them something that might cut them some slack, you have my blessing. Just remember if the day of reckoning comes you are in this as deep as me."

Brognola stood. He took the President's hand.

"Thank you for understanding, sir. I have to do something for my men."

The President wagged a finger at the Fed.

"Correction, Hal. Our men."

Kosovo

"BETTER BLOODY WELL get on with it then," McCarter snapped.

Milisivic glanced around the room, aware of the hostility emanating from every man present.

"What comes out of Belgrade does not sit comfortably with every Serbian," he said. "The central government has a great deal of opposition. I understand your resentment, but allow me to explain and then you can judge."

"Go ahead," Encizo said.

"I belong to an opposition group myself. We would like to see the present government go and be replaced by a more open-minded regime. One willing to accede to the peace talks. That may or may not happen. Until the problem is solved either way, we are all caught up in this madness.''

"Okay, so you say you want to overthrow the government," Encizo said. "You won't be the last man to say that."

Milisivic shrugged. "Until a few months ago I believed it would happen easily. Now I'm not so sure. We are in the same position others find themselves. Those in power surround themselves with strong protection. Security squads. The military. Even the police. They have many informants. Excellent communications. We have little. We are always on the move to avoid being discovered. It is hard to raise strong opposition in such circumstances.''

"How does all this concern us?" McCarter asked impatiently.

"You saw what happened to Captain Moreau. He was a good man but naive, and he was betrayed by the man who gave him the information about the weapons drop. That is why he died and you were almost wiped out.''

"After the event doesn't make things right," Manning said.

"If I had known earlier, I could have warned you all. Ciric Brako was known to us as an informer for the FAP.''

"How do we know whether you're telling the truth?" McCarter said. "This bloody country lives on lies.''

"That is not true for all of us," Milisivic replied.

"I came here to warn you to be careful. I tried warning Moreau off without exposing myself, but he was a proud, stubborn man. I understand I cannot make you believe me. I accept that, but I still insist you remain wary."

"Right now I'm more concerned about two of my men out there," McCarter said. "We need to find them before the FAP."

"Then let me help you."

McCarter waited, allowing the silence to drag on. He wanted to believe Milisivic. At the same time his natural caution held him back until he could be more certain about the man.

"Show me," he said. "Convince me, Milisivic. But listen good. Don't play me for a damn fool. If I think for one minute you're setting me up, I'll put a bloody bullet in you myself."

"That goes for all of us," Manning said. "No more tricks. One wrong step and you're a dead man."

"I will try to give you support when you need it," Milisivic said. "But I will be honest from the start. Any help I offer will be unofficial. You must understand that. If I overstep myself, I risk exposing my own undercover people as well as putting you in danger."

"Don't worry about that," McCarter said. "Two of my people are lost out there somewhere. Until I get them back personal danger doesn't even come into it."

"You are going to go in and try to rescue them? But that is crazy. You realize that you could walk right into Serbian military hands? Or KLA rebels?

As I told Moreau, once you leave the protection of this UN base there is no more protection for you.''

"We understand," Manning said. "Even so, we have to try to save our people. Wouldn't you do the same?"

Milisivic glanced at the Canadian. A weary smile touched the corners of his mouth. "Yes. Of course I would."

"Then understand we have to go," McCarter said.

"Tell me what I can do to help."

"Getting into the area isn't going to be the problem. Getting out is," McCarter explained. "If everything goes the way we hope and we locate our people and get them away from the FAP, there's only going to be one way out for us. We'll have to walk. Try to get back over the border."

"The FAP will not give in easily," Milisivic pointed out.

"Neither will we," Encizo told him.

"Let us assume you find your people and get them away. Do you realize the distance you might have to cover? And what if your people are injured? Will you be able to carry them all the way back across the border? With the best will in the world, my friend, I think not. You are going to need assistance."

"Can you provide it?"

Milisivic glanced at Manning. "I will do what I can. It will not be easy and I give no guarantees. But I will do what I can. I know the country well. If you are out there, I will find you. It will have to be done covertly. No radios. No contact between us of any kind. There are too many listeners. If anyone picked up even a whisper, the whole Serbian army would be waiting for us."

Milisivic waited, watching as the Phoenix Force warriors exchanged silent glances. It was as if they were communicating on a mental level. The Serbian realized he was in the presence of a group of men who survived because they lived on trust between themselves. An invisible bond that had been forged in the fire of battle and adversity. If anyone could pull off what they were intending, it was this group.

"We'll take you on trust, Milisivic," McCarter said. "But if you screw me around, I'll see you in bloody hell."

THE WEARINESS that had been threatening to drop them in their tracks hadn't lessened its grip during the long afternoon. James and Hawkins, fired by their desire to maintain the freedom they had clung to, kept on the move. They had gained some distance on their pursuers because of the onset of more snow. A thin fall had increased during the late afternoon, buffeted by the wind swirling down from the higher ground until it had became an obscuring blanket. It restricted vision in all directions, not only for the Phoenix Force pair but also for the FAP terrorists.

Although they couldn't be seen, James and Hawkins knew the rebels were still on their trail. It had become an obsession for all concerned.

James and Hawkins wanted to escape; the FAP wanted to capture them.

The equation was simple in the extreme, but the reality was far from being simple.

Toward dusk, James and Hawkins spotted their pursuers once more. The Phoenix Force commandos were at the head of a narrow defile that cut through the bleak terrain in an easterly direction. They decided to make use of the defile for a number of reasons. It would provide them with cover from the rising chill of the wind and the snow that was showing no inclination to ease off. There was always the chance that the tumbled rock and thick vegetation at the bottom of the defile might hide them from the armed figures they had spotted. Both men had been expecting their pursuers to show eventually, even though they had managed to evade them during the long daylight hours. It had been a cat-and-mouse game—James and Hawkins in hostile, unknown territory, being tracked by men who knew the terrain like the back of their hand.

The two men expected little mercy from the terrorists following them. It was in the nature of such things that those involved in terrorist acts carried little humanity. It was why they bore their terrorist label. Terrorism, by definition, was coercion by threat and violence. Terrorist rhetoric wasn't peaceful. They wanted their way by force of arms. By sheer terror. The terrorist way was linked with death and destruction, so anyone coming within arm's reach of them had to be aware that sense and reason didn't apply.

Phoenix Force, as part of Stony Man, existed to counter the threat raised by terrorism. So they accepted that by the fall of the cards, they might at some time during their careers come into close contact with the terror mongers. And here and now, stranded in enemy territory, Calvin James and T.J. Hawkins were as close to that moment as they had ever been.

As they ducked down the loose slope of the defile and began to follow its winding course, both knew time was running out for them. Although they had only seen their pursuers coming in from behind them it was possible, and probable, that there were more of the same coming in from other directions. If so, James and Hawkins were in trouble. They had no easy way out. Nowhere to go.

Pushing deeper into the undergrowth, James and Hawkins took alternate sides of the defile to watch out for their pursuers. With the onset of dusk and the spread of shadows, spotting movement on the rim of the defile became increasingly difficult.

Hawkins had taken out his Beretta and eased off the safety. He noticed that James had done the same. The show of weapons took their position to the next stage. The two men were now in combat mode, aware that they could be fighting for their very lives within a few minutes. Whichever way it went, they wouldn't go down easily. The FAP terrorists were going to find out that Phoenix Force carried one hell of a sting.

Hawkins saw the first dark figure appear on the rim. The man, clad in dark clothing, was carrying an AK-74 and he angled the weapon in Hawkins's direction, triggering a short burst that peppered the rocks nearby. Hawkins turned, the Beretta held two-handed. He tracked and held, triggering a swift pair of 9 mm rounds that caught the shooter in the upper chest. The man went down hard, slithering over the edge of the slope and rolling for a few feet before his body became wedged between two outcroppings.

James heard the exchange of fire. He had already engaged his own targets, seeing a number of men on his side of the defile. He brought up his Beretta and drove the terrorists back with a volley of shots.

The crackle of autofire reached James's ears and he saw the impact of the slugs as they struck the earth near his feet. Turning aside, he dropped behind a jagged rock, pulling back under cover as more shots pounded against his cover. Behind him the rattle of loose shale indicated the approach of more of the terrorists. James rolled around, his Beretta tracking ahead of him, and spotted two armed men dropping the last few feet to the base of the slope and fired at the closer one. The man went down with a 9 mm slug through his upper thigh. The backup man kept coming, firing on the run.

James felt the sudden pain of a bullet burn across his left upper arm. He pumped a double shot into the shooter's chest and saw him go down without a sound. And then he saw the half-dozen armed figures emerging from the shadows around him.

Close by, Hawkins was having his own problems. He had taken out one of the armed men advancing through the gloom and then found he was surrounded by three more who had slithered down the side of the defile. They came at him in a rush, making target acquisition. Hawkins leveled the Beretta, determined to take out as many as he could before they killed him. He was concentrating on the men in front of him and failed to hear the gunner who came up behind him. All he remembered from that moment was something hard impacting against the back of his skull, knocking him off balance and dropping him facedown in the dirt and snow.

"Make your decision," someone said in accented English.

James glanced at the speaker, a dark-haired, heavyset man dressed in combat gear. He was brandishing a large autopistol.

"You can die here. The choice is yours."

James considered the man's words. If he did resist, it was all over. If he was taken prisoner there was always the possibility, however remote, that he might survive. Staying alive was the intention. Being in the hands of the enemy wouldn't be pleasant, but it wouldn't be the first time it had happened. Like it or not, James realized he didn't have much of a choice.

Pushing to his feet, James held out his Beretta to his captor. It was snatched from his grasp. The man gave an order in his own tongue. Hands grabbed him, searching his clothing for additional weapons, then pushing him back along the defile the way they had come in. As they turned, James saw Hawkins, unconscious, being hauled roughly across the rocky ground. He refrained from saying anything. Right now he didn't want to antagonize their captors.

As they moved out of the defile, back onto open ground, James heard the sound of a truck. It appeared moments later, bumping across the earth. The diesel engine rumbled noisily, smoke trailing from the exhaust. Hawkins was dragged to the tailgate and manhandled into the open rear of the vehicle, with armed men watching over him.

"You can get in by yourself," the English-speaking man ordered.

James clambered over the tailgate. He was almost in when hands grabbed his clothing, pulling him off balance. He crashed to the dirty floor of the truck. A heavy boot thudded against the side of his face. Another struck him in the side. James lay where he'd fallen, offering no resistance. More men climbed into the rear of the truck. James heard the engine growl and felt the vehicle jerk as gears ground together. The truck moved off slowly, bouncing its way over the rough ground.

To where?

James asked himself the question but wasn't sure he wanted the answer.

CHAPTER TEN

Stony Man Farm, Virginia

"We're losing the image," Kurtzman said.

The large-screen picture was starting to break up as the satellite's orbit took it out of range.

"How long?" Price asked.

"A couple of minutes. I can't guarantee more. And it's starting to get dark over there, as well. All I can—"

"Is that them?" Price crossed the room to stare at the fuzzy image on the screen that Kurtzman had captured. "Aaron?"

Kurtzman did his best to sharpen the image.

"I'll be damned if it isn't."

The others had joined Price now, and the entire group, Brognola and Katz included, watched in silence as the silent scenario was played out in front of them. They watched a group of armed figures converge from a shallow ravine. Among them, one man was escorted on foot while a second was dragged along the ground. With the picture deteriorating rapidly they saw a truck roll to a stop. The man being dragged was hauled into the back of the truck. The single figure climbed in himself until hands pulled him to the floor of the vehicle. Kurtzman tried desperately to maintain the image. He was unable to hold it any longer, and the large-screen picture broke up, the satellite drifting along its orbit and losing the signal.

"Tell me you got pictures," Brognola said.

Kurtzman nodded. Whenever satellite pictures were obtained, he captured every moment on digital imagery for possible verification and analysis. The retained information, once logged, could be checked over, even enhanced. It was often during these sessions that specific information was obtained.

"Okay, let's call them up, Aaron. I want positive ID on those two men and a location. As soon as possible so we can send the details to Phoenix Force. The way the game is going out there right now, all hell could break loose in Kosovo any damn minute."

Kurtzman swung his chair around. "Listen up, people. We have a situation. T.J. and Calvin are in hostile territory. The satellite scan has shown us a possible location for them. We need to analyze the pictures and get a match for T.J. and Calvin. If it is our boys, Phoenix Force needs to know so they can effect a rescue. So let's hit the screens. Nobody goes home until we have this locked up tight."

"No problem, boss," Tokaido said over his shoulder as he ditched his headset. The youngest member of Kurtzman's cyberteam was seldom seen without his CD player plugged into his ears. It said a lot that he was committed to the job if he was prepared to go without his beloved music.

Leaving them to it, Brognola drew Price and Katz to his side.

"This has to work," he said. "I didn't want to say anything to put them under any more pressure, but I talked to the Man a short time ago. Time is something we don't have in excess."

"Meaning?" Katz asked.

"The peace talks have gone down. NATO is ready to go in hard to make the Serbians realize they can't talk on the one hand and go on killing their enemies on the other."

"Go in hard?" Price asked.

"Sooner rather than later NATO is initializing bombing raids over Kosovo. They'll go for strategic targets—military installations, airfields, ammunition dumps, communications. The plan is to weaken the Serbs' ability to mount offensive strikes.

Katz didn't appear convinced it was a good idea. "Bombing isn't going to stop localized killing," he replied. "Pushing the Serb leadership into a climb down is going to take time. With no guarantees."

Brognola fumbled in his pocket for a roll of antacid tablets and popped a couple into his mouth.

"I don't make the policy decisions, Katz, I just try to work within the frame."

"I just hope they know what they're doing," Katz said softly.

"Right or wrong, we have to get our guys out," Price stated, "and settle this damned FAP business."

Brognola glanced at his watch. "We should be getting an update from Able Team anytime. You want to check that out, Barbara?"

She nodded and walked away.

Nassau Town

"THIS IS NO PLACE for bad things to happen," Blancanales said, peering out the hotel window.

Below him the panorama of Nassau stretched out like a scene from some Hollywood glossy movie. Everything looked sunny and clean. The people wore their wealth like others wore a tan. Beyond the hotel the bay lay calm and blue, sunlight glinting on the water. Barely a cloud could be seen in the clear sky.

"I've decided," Blancanales went on, "this is where I'm going to retire."

"Right," Lyons muttered.

"Take that attitude and I might just up and quit today."

"Do that and you'll have to hand your luncheon vouchers back," Schwarz said.

"Yeah? Well, that's another dream shattered."

Lyons shook his head as he listened to the banter between Schwarz and Blancanales. It was an integral part of their makeup. It often annoyed Lyons but he admitted, if only to himself, that he would miss it if the banter stopped.

"Listen, you comedians," Lyons said. "How about taking a walk around town with eyes and ears open to see if you can pick up anything about the *Millennium Explorer*."

Blancanales nodded and reached for the light jacket he'd draped over the back of a chair.

"Let's go, partner, the boss wants to put his feet up."

"I'll hang around until Jack checks in," Lyons told him. "Somebody has to do it."

Minutes after Blancanales and Schwarz had left, Lyons's cell phone rang. Barbara Price was on the line.

"How is it down there?"

"Doing our best to cope."

"Your flyboy should be touching down at a charter airstrip next to Nassau International in about thirty minutes. You can meet him there. You won't miss him. Not the way he's dressed. He has all your gear on board. Okay?"

"Fine. Anything from our people abroad?"

"We think we've found our two MIAs. If we have, they appear to have got mixed up with a tough crowd. Looks like we'll need to send in the Marines."

"Wish the guys luck from me."

"Keep in touch."

Lyons disconnected. He pulled on his leather jacket and made certain his Colt Python was snug in its holster before he zipped up, pocketed the cell phone and left the room. Outside he went to the parking lot and got into the blue Ford rental car. Just before he left the lot he called Blancanales and told him he was going to the airport.

The Able Team leader eased into traffic and made a left. He followed the busy road until the town slipped behind him. The traffic dropped off, so he made the trip to the airstrip with time to spare. Passing through the gate, he slid the Ford into an empty parking space and climbed out. Crossing to the small aircraft hangar, he looked around for Jack Grimaldi—Tex Mason—and spotted the Stony Man flyer in conversation with an attractive young woman dressed in snug-fitting coveralls and a baseball cap that was pushed to the back of her blond head. Grimaldi spotted Lyons and put on a wide grin.

Grimaldi was playing his cover act to the limit. He wore denim jeans, over polished Western boots, a loud check shirt and a buckskin jacket. In his hands was a cream-colored Stetson hat.

"I'd like you to meet my boss man, Jess," Grimaldi said in a loud drawl. "This here is Mark Garrison. He's the feller who'll be doing all the filming while I just sit back and fly him around this here pretty island."

The woman, Jess, nodded in Lyons's direction.

"Jess Buchanan. I run a small charter service. Fly the tourists around."

Lyons smiled. "Good to meet you, Jess. Could you excuse us a minute? There's something I need to discuss with Tex."

"Sure." Jess turned to Grimaldi. "Maybe I'll see you later."

"If I have anything to do with it, honey." Grimaldi grinned.

They waited until she was out of earshot.

"Jack, why didn't you just recite the ballad of the Alamo while you were at it?" Lyons asked.

"Carl, are you mad at me?" Grimaldi asked, a faint mocking tone to his words. "I'd hate it if you were upset."

Lyons backed off. If it wasn't Blancanales and Schwarz, it was Grimaldi. Lyons's life seemed to be forever plagued by people trying to get a rise out of him. If it wouldn't have got him pegged as paranoid, Lyons would have thought they were ganging up on him.

"Where's the chopper?"

Grimaldi turned Lyons and pointed to a brightly decorated Bell JetRanger standing on one of the pads. Emblazoned on the side was the legend LifeForce Films and a depiction of the world encircled in a loop of 35 mm film.

"Stony Man came up with the idea. The company actually exists on paper. Accredited, fully equipped and ready to go. Any calls made to the phone number are rerouted directly to Stony Man where all queries are handled by the staff."

"What next?" Lyons asked. "A fast-food franchise?"

"It's a pretty good idea," Grimaldi said. "With a chopper like that, we can fly pretty well anywhere. If anyone asks, we're filming for a new show."

"All right, Tex, you'd better show me how to be a film director."

Aboard the Millennium Explorer.

MALIK LEANED against the rail, eyes narrowed against the glare of the sun reflecting off the water. Though he would have never admitted it to anyone, he was concerned with the way matters had been progressing with the FAP. He didn't see the problems as insurmountable. There was always a solution. His main concern was with the way Lec Pavlic was conducting the affairs of the breakaway party.

When he had first become involved with Pavlic, he had been impressed by the man's total dedication to his cause. Pavlic's inner rage, his unswerving, single-minded course had seemed to Malik the perfect one to become aligned to. Pavlic, still hurting from the slaughter of his family, his friends and his home, had blamed everyone for the crime. Not just the Serbians who had carried out the actual slaughter, but the UN, NATO, the British and of course the Americans. In Pavlic's eyes, they were all guilty of carrying out the crime—the Serbians who were intent on destroying the very fabric of ethnic Albanian society; the UN, NATO, the U.S. and its close ally, Britain, were all guilty of the crime of indifference. Instead of dealing with the Serbians in a practical way by using their superior strength, they had pandered to the Serbian ploy of holding peace talks. Nothing had come from those talks, as Pavlic had predicted. The West stood by and allowed wholesale killing and destruction.

Pavlic's consuming rage had driven him day and night to claw his way to the top of the FAP hierarchy. He used every emotional and psychological trick he could muster, drawing into the ranks a faithful mass of supporters who held similar views to his own. The moderates in the party were swiftly ousted. Pavlic fought every step of the way, uniting his followers by the tangible power of his arguments. His radical, powerful aims. Pavlic refused to listen to anyone who spoke about talks. Of negotiating for peace. He held those people in contempt, and showed that contempt by embarking on a campaign of violence and destruction aimed at disrupting the Serbians and the UN monitors who, as far as he was concerned, simply stood around and did nothing.

Unlike any of the other Albanian freedom fighter groups, Pavlic threw his net wide. He refused to simply maintain his position by restricting his attacks at home. He began to draw up plans to strike out at the NATO-U.S.-UK conspiracy, as he called it. He saw those groups as being allied with the Serbians. Their efforts were minimal, short-term and appeared to be doing everything to allow the Serbians to simply carry on with what they were already doing with impunity. Talk of sanctions, of bringing to trial the war criminals from the Serbian camp were a joke. There was no way the named criminals were going to be taken. How could they be? They were safe within their own borders, away from the ineffectual hands of the so-called security agencies. When the West made its solemn statements about arresting the Serbian killers, those they named simply laughed and carried on, secure in the knowledge that no one could get to them.

The policy of the FAP was simplistic. If the ethnic Albanians wanted their territory back, they were going to have to fight for it. They needed to create unrest and disruption among all the interested parties, to hamper and alienate the interfering agencies camping out in the disputed areas. And one of the weapons they could use was widespread terror. Pavlic wanted his people to see that the so-called hard-line Western powers were of no use to them.

He wanted to extend his war to the streets of the U.S.A. and the UK, to make them feel the pain the ethnic Albanians were feeling. He wanted them to pay for the death and destruction visited on his home village and its people. It was a debt that needed to be paid in blood. And more blood. By the time Pavlic had full, unchallenged control of the FAP, it had become a rogue party, pushing the term freedom fighters to the very edge.

The FAP became terrorists. They demanded; they threatened. Killing and destruction became the reason for their existence. They were, in fact, exactly what Malik needed—a rogue group willing to go that last mile and beyond. They had become out of control, ready for the push that would take them over the edge. And Malik knew exactly what he needed to do for them to fall into his hands.

His offer of unlimited funds struck the right chord with the money-starved FAP. He provided them with modern weapons, electronic equipment for communication, the means by which they could break into UN and NATO computer systems and disrupt logistical files. The enticements of money and drugs, even women, were also used to buy employees of the agencies monitoring the Kosovo situation. For Malik it was old hat, something he had been doing for years as he built his network of terrorist cells, contacts, weapons caches. His organization, dedicated to international terrorism, was funded by his own personal fortune, inherited from the family empire of businesses he had taken over on the death of his father. Malik had been into radical causes all his adult life, and they had become an obsession. It was his mission, one he undertook willingly because it was for his faith. He was privileged because his wealth helped him to maintain the battle everlasting against the enemies of Islam. His successes drew others to the cause. Money flowed in without pause, increasing Malik's ability to spread his work. He had supporters worldwide, people of his faith who were willing to donate huge sums to his organization.

The FAP had been an opportunity for Malik to plan the trial of his new weapon, the one that Ilyana Petrocovich had been working on for the past few months. She had been making the final tests within her new floating biolab on board *Millennium Explorer*.

Malik stirred restlessly. Why was he feeling unsure about Pavlik and the FAP?

He knew the answer. Pavlic's recent spate of mistakes had undermined Malik's confidence in the man. First he had allowed Ridivic to gain entry into the ranks. He had then let the man escape with a computer disk holding information, albeit misleading information. That wasn't the point in question. Pavlic had exposed his organization—and that meant Malik—to possible danger. A weakness such as infiltration had to be viewed with concern. And then there was the attack in London. Pavlic's poor security had allowed the raid to take place, effectively destroying the safe house previously established for the FAP. That had happened due to pure negligence on Pavlic's part. He had judged the London cell to be the safest they had because he thought London to be a peaceful city. The irony was that although a Serbian hit squad had been sent in to eliminate the FAP, they themselves had been confronted by an unknown team of armed men who had effectively taken out the Serbians. Malik's suspicions about the team had been increased when Pavlic's local informer had told him a similar group had appeared in the UN camp just inside the Macedonian border.

The five-man group had rung a bell in Malik's mind. He recalled other occasions, in various locations, when a mysterious combat team had appeared to take on some terrorist threat. Rumor had it they were a special force who belonged to some ultrasecret U.S. agency. Whoever they were, Malik had great respect for them. They had proved to be formidable adversaries, facing any odds thrown at them, and always seemed to survive.

The appearance of this group alerted Malik to the fact that possibly the U.S. government, seeing the damage being done to peace negotiations, had sent in their specialists to deal with the FAP. Malik's memory recycled the information he had on the earlier reports about these men. They were known for their fighting skills, but more so for their zero toleration. When they attacked they went in very hard, with little time for taking prisoners. If these were the people now on the tail of the FAP, Pavlic was going to have to tread very carefully.

When the attempt to trap the American team at the site of the weapon-plane landing had been turned around and FAP men had died, Malik became further convinced that this was the team he had recalled. Their presence in Kosovo could mean trouble

for Pavlic. The finale of the episode was when
Pavlic's contact, the one who had set up the supposed trap at the landing sight, had been found dead
in his own home. His death had served as a timely
warning to Malik. He would need to step carefully
now.

His first move had been to leave Kosovo and fly
back to Nassau. He decided to let Pavlic handle the
internal affair. Oddly, the next thing he heard was
that Pavlic's people had two of the strike team in
their hands. They were going to be taken back to
Pavlic's mountain stronghold for questioning. Malik
had seen what Pavlic meant by questioning. He was
glad he was away from the place if that was going
to happen. Lec Pavlic had little finesse. He depended
on physical violence when it came to getting prisoners to talk. It obviously satisfied his need for personal revenge against...what? When he really
thought about it, Malik realized he saw Pavlic's vengeance being directed at the whole world. He didn't
seem to have a good word for anyone. The hate that
festered inside the man had eaten away his humanity. Lec Pavlic was a dead man walking in many
respects—perhaps even a lost cause, although if Malik engineered things the way he wanted Pavlic
might yet serve a useful purpose.

It was something he would have to consider, and
consider very carefully.

Using someone like Pavlic could become a dou-
ble-edged sword that might very well injure the one
wielding it.

Malik would have to juggle his relationship with
the FAP leader very skillfully. He had to make full

use of Pavlic and his group in order to foment unease and terror in the ranks of the UN and NATO.
Into that meld came a number of other causes Malik
had designs on. The Americans and the British. Both
Washington and London would feel the crushing fist
of retribution once the campaign moved into higher
gear. The governments of both those countries, well-
documented as relentless in their interference in the
business of other nations, would be among the first
to suffer.

London was an easy target. The British prided
themselves on their tolerance and openhandedness.
It would be their downfall. It wasn't difficult to get
into Britain. The fact that it was an isolated island,
cut off from the mainland of Europe, did little to
impair entry.

Malik already had his people in place. Outwardly,
they were living the quiet life in London's suburbia.
In reality they were waiting for the command from
Malik. Ilyana Petrocovich's creation, once perfected
and presented to Malik, would be sent to this cell,
and under his meticulous guidance they would com-
mence their well-orchestrated campaign.

Which brought Malik back to Lec Pavlic. He
would have to keep a strong hand on Pavlic's reckless moods. Malik wanted Pavlic's input, his people
and his desire for vengeance. At the same time he
didn't want the man's unrestrained wildness to drag
them all down into a pit of chaos. That wouldn't
profit anyone. In the end, if Pavlic did prove to be
out of control Malik would cut him down without a
second thought. As with all men with a cause, the

right of the individual would take precedence over someone who was getting in the way.

Malik wouldn't let that happen.

His cause was the most important. As much as he wanted to help Pavlic and the FAP, the testing time for comradeship would be on the day it came down to one or the other.

Malik had no qualms as far as that was concerned.

In his eyes Lec Pavlic and the FAP were expendable.

If the time came when Pavlic's extremes placed Malik and his plans in jeopardy, the FAP would feel the weight of retribution coming down with deadly force.

Sound behind him caught Malik's attention. He knew who it was before he turned, a smile already on his lips.

"Ilyana, how nice to see you."

Ilyana Petrocovich returned his smile a little awkwardly. She wasn't used to the niceties of social intercourse. Her life revolved around her work. She was as dedicated to it as any drug user was to his daily fix. Maybe more so because it was how she filled her time. If she wasn't physically working on one of her projects, she would be drafting new thoughts onto paper. Malik, who was dedicated himself, had long since realized that everyone, no matter how they used their lives, needed to step back sometimes and take a breath. Not Ilyana. Take her away from her work and within a short time she became restless, disinterested in her surroundings and fretting to be back in her lab. Once Malik had learned that fact about his protégé there was no problem. He gave her what she wanted most of all, and in return she showed him just how talented she was.

She was standing before him now, clad in cream slacks and a dark shirt. Malik sighed inwardly. It was a shame she had denied her femininity for her work. She wasn't an unattractive woman. She was more striking than beautiful, and Malik admitted it wouldn't be difficult to become attracted to her. But she had made her own decisions on that subject, and he didn't intend to break the unwritten rule.

As far as Ilyana Petrocovich was personally concerned, she conceded that time spent with Malik was part of the contract she had made. To his credit he treated her as an intelligent individual, keeping their meetings on a businesslike level and never outstaying his welcome.

This particular day she had only been given thirty minutes' notice of his arrival on board *Millennium Explorer*. She would have preferred longer, but it was his vessel and he could come and go whenever he wanted. With his imminent arrival she had broken off from her work, left the secure lab and made her way to the luxurious cabin she had been assigned. Like everything else on board the ship, the living quarters were excellent. The moment he had purchased the vessel, Malik had made certain that the accommodations were upgraded to a high degree. The ship would be at sea for long periods, and he needed to keep his crew comfortable and secure. The facilities were intended to keep them content, with little reason to complain. Not that many of them ever would. Every man on board had been handpicked from his own devoted followers. They were of his faith and his vision. Each saw his struggle as a global one against the common enemy. As Malik did, they knew that their battle against the nonbelievers would be long and hard. The cost was great in human terms, but none of them even thought about that. Total, unswerving loyalty was their creed.

It was to aid the struggle that Malik had contracted the biochemist Ilyana Petrocovich. He was pleased with his coup. Others had tried but had failed to employ her. The gifted Russian, as well as being the best in her field, was also a demanding, reclusive individual. At their first meeting in Geneva, Malik had listened to her expectations in silence. He made no comment until she had finished, and had then simply smiled and agreed to all her demands. It had been the first, and last, time he saw Ilyana Petrocovich lost for words. Her demands might have seemed a little excessive, even expensive, but Malik saw money only as a means to an end. The price he would have to pay to buy her total dedication was small when compared to the gain she would give him on completion of her projects.

When the Russian had seen the onboard facilities her satisfaction became complete. Malik had gone beyond her expectations. The lab complex, developed from the original setup on the exploration vessel, boasted the most sophisticated equipment available. Malik had obtained every item of apparatus she had listed, even down to the manufacturer and specific colors where stated. She had walked around the complex for a long time, checking this and that. Opening drawers, switching on equipment, even a little overawed by it all. Malik had turned the *Millennium Explorer* into her own private world, where all her dreams could come true at the touch of a switch. She decided there and then that she would be happy to spend the rest of her life on board the vessel.

Now, weeks later, after long and careful development and lab testing, Petrocovich was almost ready to deliver.

"Why didn't you give me more time to prepare?" she asked.

Malik smiled. "Was there something you needed to hide from me?" he said playfully. He had found out she sometimes liked to play childish teasing games.

Petrocovich shook her blond head.

"You should know by now, Malik, that we have no secrets."

"To be honest I was eager to come. If I recall the last time we spoke, you were hinting at a possible early breakthrough."

She didn't respond. Instead she moved by him to lean against the rail, watching the rolling swell of the calm sea around the vessel. The warm breeze disturbed her blond hair.

Malik allowed her the moment of mystery. He somehow knew she was about to impart good news.

"Ilyana?" he quizzed gently.

She turned to face him.

"We have our virus."

"The Gene Virus? Truly?"

"Malik, you gave me this ship so I could do my research in peace. Away from prying eyes and petty interference. You created all this for me. Do you believe I would lie to you?''

"Nothing is further from my thoughts. I am only teasing." Malik reached out to touch her shoulders. "This is wonderful news. Ilyana, do you realize what this means?''

"You will become a rich man, Malik."

He was genuinely shocked.

"Ilyana! You of all people should know that wealth means…"

"Oh, Malik, now I am teasing." Her face was suddenly wreathed in a satisfied smile. "Just getting my own back."

His concern faded and he gave a little bow.

"Now we are even."

"I understand the meaning this has for you. It will enable your people to move forward with your plans. Give you greater authority."

"And destroy our enemies."

"Yes. I must make certain never to incur your anger."

"Ilyana, that will never happen. In the coming months I am going to need you more than ever. What we have today is only the first step. I am not foolish enough to believe there are no more obstacles to overcome. I want this to succeed. To achieve that aim everything must work perfectly, and achieving perfection is an ongoing struggle."

His words came tumbling out in a torrent that was almost poetical, Ilyana thought. There was something of the showman inside him. A need to express himself in a way that grabbed the listeners' attention. Malik was an orator. He used his words and his presence to put across his point with impact. When she had first met him his speech seemed almost glib, rehearsed, but then she got to know him and began to realize that it was how he spoke. How he held his listener. If he had been a romantic, and she a recipient, there would have been no great struggle on Malik's part to achieve whatever he might want from a woman. She pushed the thought to the back of her mind for another time.

"Would you like to see what I have developed?" she asked briskly.

"Yes."

She led the way back inside, along the companionway to the restricted area in the center of the vessel where the lab complex lay. Access could only be achieved via a complicated security barrier. It comprised state-of-the-art retinal-scan outer doors. These were also part of an air-lock system designed to maintain a totally safe environment. Once through the outer door, visitors were scanned for prohibited items and only when cleared could they move to the second door. This security access demanded fingerprint ID, and once through there it was into the sterilizing area, where ultrasonics took care of any organisms present. The third security door gave access to the lab itself. Here were more security devices, plus TV monitoring from a number of cameras situated around the lab. Malik had installed everything from the detailed specifications Ilyana had drawn up herself. He had been greatly impressed by the depth of her knowledge in electronics, lab standards and biohazard control. When she had visited the *Millennium Explorer* on completion of the lab construction and commissioning, Ilyana had been like a child confronted by Toyland. He could still see the expression in her eyes as she had wandered around the gleaming fittings, running the fingers of one hand across smooth, cool surfaces.

Petrocovich led the way through the lab. The inner sanctum, where she completed her most delicate and sensitive experiments, was held at a cool temperature. The air was pure, having been cleaned a number of times through finer and finer mesh filters, until there was nothing left that might cause an imbalance in the biochemical cultures she was working with.

"This is the first batch of the virus," she said, holding up a sealed glass container. "At the moment it is simply designated IM-S1. If you decide to we can create a name for it."

"What does IM-S1 represent?"

"Ilyana-Malik-Strain 1."

Malik laughed. "I like that. So. How much virus exists?"

"Not a great deal. This container plus perhaps four times as much sealed in the stasis chamber. That would be enough to affect thousands."

"Ilyana, I have to ask this. How effective would this be?"

"At killing, extremely effective. Remember, this is a high-risk bioagent. There is no doubt in my mind that IM-S1 will do what you asked."

"But what about the other aspect?"

"How will the selective gene abilities work?" She spread her hands. "A normal bioweapon will attack anyone exposed to it. No selectivity. In simple terminology, it acts like a missile. You fire it and it hits a target, destroying everything within range. Now fire what is termed a smart missile, and you can preselect the target. The missile will ignore that which it is not programmed to hit and go only for the specified target. The codes set before the missile is fired make the choice.

"The gene weapon's function would be similar. It would seek out specific groups, based on their genetic makeup. Let's imagine a football stadium. In that stadium are three distinct racial types. Chinese, African and Spanish. A thousand of each. Each of those groups has within them their own specific genetic code, the concentration of genes in different sequences that decide the way they are. Why the Chinese have a different eye structure than the Spanish. The pigmentation difference between the African and the Chinese. To create the genetic virus we have to take the code of, say, the Spanish, and program it to blend with the chosen virus. When that virus is released into the football stadium, it will only attack the group who carry the genetic code it holds."

"So the Chinese and Africans would be safe?"

Petrocovich nodded. "The theory would say yes."

"Theory and practice are notorious for falling out," Malik observed.

"Of course. Absolutes are difficult to achieve in this branch of biochemistry. Remember I did qualify that at the beginning, Malik. No instant cure."

"A cure is hardly what we are looking for."

"A poor choice of words on my part."

Malik gently tapped the glass container.

"But at least we have something. A start."

"This is a prototype. The genetic material we gathered has been incorporated with a virulent germ culture. The difficulty is maintaining the balance between gene codes and the virus. They have been tending to reject each other, but at the moment I have managed to stabilize it. A field test will show us how effective it is. From that I will be able to establish a sound formula and that should allow any genetic code to be incorporated."

"The FAP have readily volunteered to try it for us. Lec Pavlic was positively drooling when I explained the way this would work."

"Where will he try it?"

"A number of locations. Belgrade, of course. New York and London. They both have Serbian groups living there. Ex-patriots maybe, but still Serbian, and hopefully defenseless against your selective virus."

"Be reminded, Malik, that this is a first batch. We need the trial to assess how much refining I might need to do."

"Ilyana, I understand. Now I'll leave you to carry on. Let me know when everything is completed. Oh, by the way, did Khan arrive safely with the package?"

"Yes. The components were exactly what I had ordered."

"Good. If you need me, I will be in the communication center."

Malik left her then, exiting the laboratory via the complex safety procedures that had allowed him to enter. He turned to wave to Ilyana as he stepped through the final door, but she had already returned her attention to her work. The heavy door pulled tight shut behind him, sealing the woman from the real world. Malik thought that she was very lucky. She had what she wanted, and in her eyes the world was perfect.

Unfortunately, it wasn't so simple on the outside of the glass bowl.

CHAPTER ELEVEN

Kosovo

The really hard treatment didn't start until the FAP terrorists had Calvin James and T.J. Hawkins inside their mountain stronghold. The journey by truck had been long, slow and extremely uncomfortable. The Phoenix Force pair were made to lie on the floor of the vehicle, hands tied behind them, with black hoods pulled over their heads. Every so often a boot or a rifle butt would be slammed into their ribs and backs. No one spoke during the ride. They didn't need to. The hostility was a tangible thing.

James and Hawkins bore the discomfort in silence. They knew from past experience there was no profit to be gained from antagonizing their captors. Survival depended on their staying reasonably uninjured. Angering their captors would encourage further violence, maybe even life-threatening injury. If that happened, the chances of escape were lessened. So the men lay still, absorbing every blow, and kept silent.

Finally, the truck began a torturous climb that took it higher into the mountains. The temperature dropped, and rain began to fall, drumming against the canvas top of the truck as it wound its way along a track that had endless twists and turns. Twice they rumbled over wooden bridges spanning some gap in the track. The rain became harder, accompanied by a wind that rocked the vehicle, forcing the driver to reduce his speed to a crawl.

James, his mind working busily to keep him alert, wondered if they had returned to the terrorist stronghold they had spotted from the air. It was probable, unless the FAP had more than one base in the area. That seemed unlikely. Whichever way it turned out, the immediate future for himself and Hawkins looked grim. James was no fatalist. At the same time he accepted that their position was becoming decidedly more precarious with each passing minute. The FAP was transporting them to their base for interrogation, which wasn't a prospect he relished. He had been through it before, and from that past experience James knew they were in for a hard time.

The prospect of torture didn't sit lightly on Calvin James's shoulders. If it came to that, he would have no choice in the matter. It would simply be another way of extracting information from him, born out of the knowledge that the human form could take only so much physical abuse before it submitted, taking the victim into an unconscious state where further pain achieved nothing. Before that threshold was reached, the victim could be put through unspeakable agony, turning him from a rational person into a babbling, wretched being whose only reason for living was the end of that pain. Whether the victim actually offered the information his captor desired became irrelevant. The victim might divulge his secrets without even knowing he had done so. His captor, if so inclined, might continue the torture even though he did have the information, and was extending the agony because he wanted to see how far he could take it—or simply because he was the kind of inquisitor who enjoyed the pain he could put his victim through.

AFTER WHAT SEEMED an eternity, the truck lurched to a stop. The sound of the engine had an echo quality to it, suggesting they had stopped between high walls. The tailgate of the truck was dropped and hands caught hold of James's clothing. He was dragged out of the truck, dropping unchecked to the ground. James gasped as the impact stunned him, and his captors laughed. He heard laughter. Then someone shouted an order and he was hauled to his feet, hands under his arms. He was dragged across the stony ground, pulled and twisted as his captors negotiated various turns. There was a short flight of stone steps, then the bang of a heavy metal door being pushed open. James was thrown bodily into what he assumed was a room, or a cell. He tried to stay upright, but a hard wall halted his movement. The side of his face crashed against the unyielding surface, and he slid to the floor in a half-stupor. Dimly he heard the sound of someone else being dealt the same treatment.

Hawkins.

The heavy door was banged shut. James waited to hear the sound of a lock being turned, or bolts being snapped into position.

He decided that it was strange not to secure two captives even though they were bound and hooded. It spoke of lax security.

Or something else.

Like they weren't alone. Someone was still in the room with them, watching and waiting. They wanted to hear anything James and Hawkins might say to each other if they believed they were on their own.

James stilled his breathing, straining his ears for any extraneous sound, and at the same time willing Hawkins not to speak himself. He didn't need to worry. There wasn't a sound from his Phoenix Force partner. There could have been a couple of reasons for that: Hawkins had figured the situation himself or he was unconscious.

James hoped it was the former.

Minutes dragged by, long minutes due to the strain of not knowing exactly what was happening. James used the time to calm himself, to attune his body to the numerous aches and pain. They weren't severe enough to cause him too much discomfort, but he would have chosen not to have them at all.

Sudden movement nearby caused him to tense up. Hands caught hold of his clothing and he was pulled to his feet, pushed back against the wall. The hood was yanked from his head, and James blinked his eyes against the intrusion of bright light. He focused and saw at least a half dozen armed figures confronting him. Dark, angry eyes returned his gaze. There was a great deal of hostility present. Out the corner of his left eye he saw Hawkins a few feet away. There was a wet mass of blood down the side of his partner's face.

"Very smart, you black bastard," someone said in heavily accented English.

James glanced at the speaker and saw a lean, black-haired man smiling at him. The man had an odd, haunted look in his eyes. He looked unstable, close to the edge.

Lec Pavlic stepped directly in front of James.

"They must be teaching you well in America these days," he said. "How do they do that? Feed you bananas and peanuts?"

"Pat me on the head and I'll roll over for you," James replied.

The brightness flared in Pavlic's sallow face as James's words stung him. He took a deep breath, stepping back, the smile returning. And then without warning he punched James in the mouth. The blow snapped the Phoenix Force commando's head back and it smacked against the wall behind him. Blood filled his mouth from a cut inner lip. Pavlic hit him again. Once in the face, then in the stomach. James doubled over in time to catch a knee to the side of his head that flipped him onto his back. He lay gasping for breath, pain searing his body. He spit blood from his mouth before it flooded the back of his throat and choked him.

"Get him on his feet!" Pavlic ordered.

The two men holding James had to support him.

"Look at me, American," Pavlic yelled. "Look at me when I speak to you. This moment will seem like heaven compared to how you will feel later. Then you will beg me to kill you. But first I need information. How you found us. Who you are and why you are here."

James stared at him through watering eyes. He was aware that Pavlic could kill him there and then. At that moment, James didn't actually give a damn. He had already put up with enough bullshit from these terrorists. There wasn't a great deal he could do to alter that at the moment. He shook his head to clear his thinking.

"This black bastard ain't talkin'," he said, then braced himself for the next round of punishment.

Stony Man Farm, Virginia

BARBARA PRICE DRAINED her coffee mug and turned her attention to what Carmen Delahunt was saying.

"Mark Slamen—Marik Slavenivic—had one close friend during his time at Tirana University. A man by the name of Lec Pavlic, the guy we're told is leader of the FAP. He's ethnic Albanian, the same as Slamen. They kept in close touch after leaving the university and when Slamen came to the U.S."

Delahunt brought a photograph into view on her monitor.

"The guy on the right is Slamen. The other one is Pavlic."

"Do we have anything on Pavlic?"

"He came from a small village in Kosovo that was destroyed by Serbians during one of their purges. Not only that, but all the inhabitants were massacred, placed in a mass grave and buried. Adults and children, including Pavlic's remaining family. His mother, brothers and very young sister. Intel we have states that those who knew Pavlic reported he was left stunned by what had happened. Not only that but it is reported he blamed everyone for the tragedy—the Serbs, the UN and NATO for allowing the killings to go on, the Brits and the U.S. for not addressing the situation. He vowed some kind of revenge. If no one else would do anything, then he would.''

''Is this leading somewhere?''

''Pavlic vanished soon after. A short time later the FAP emerged and the killings started. And the disruption of UN and NATO information channels.''

''So we're looking at Pavlic being the driving force behind the FAP?'' Price asked.

''I haven't pinned it down fully yet, but the time-scale fits. And the motivation.''

''Okay, Carmen, get into some deep digging. Find out everything you can about the FAP and Mark Slamen. He could be supplying the terrorists with aid, money, weapons, backup. I don't care what you have to do to get the information, but do it. And fast.

''Aaron, we might need to break into some databases to make this work. Carmen is going to need everything you can give her.''

Kurtzman raised a hand in acknowledgment.

''By the way, I just analyzed the last of those images we got from the satellite. I'd say that one of those people being put in the truck was Cal.''

He handed Price a printout of the digital scan, his finger jabbing at the closest figure. He gave her a magnifier. Price bent over the image and focused on the figure Kurtzman had indicated. The enhanced picture showed a tall, lean figure in combat gear.

She moved the magnifier to sharpen the image, peering at it for some time, then nodded.

"You're right, Aaron. It's Cal."

"I've got the location, too, and I'm ready to send it to Phoenix Force."

"Do it now."

Kosovo

THE MOOD IN THE HUT was one of cautious optimism. The information from Stony Man had been encouraging, though sober. No one expected an instant solution, but at least they had something to move on now.

Once the location was established, McCarter spread out their map of the area and checked the bearings Kurtzman had given him.

"The chopper went down here, not too far from the map references we received from it. The spot where the satellite identified the pickup area was here. If Cal and T.J. had been traveling southeast, they could have been at this location when they were caught. Tracking back brings us to the place where the chopper went down and the last location we received from them."

McCarter circled the area, tapping it with his pen.

"It's a good place for a base," Encizo said. "High country. Gives anyone up there a good field of fire as well as observation. They'll be able to see visitors coming for miles."

"That doesn't help us much," Manning observed.

"Not unless we make a HALO drop at night," McCarter said.

"I knew you were going to say that," Manning grumbled.

The High-Altitude-Low-Opening method of parachuting was well-known to Phoenix Force. They had made a number of drops using HALO, so the technique wasn't new to them.

"We need help on this," Encizo said. "Like an aircraft."

McCarter was already making a connection with Stony Man via the satellite radio. As soon as he got through, he spoke with Barbara Price, then Hal Brognola.

"I'll arrange for a plane to pick you up from the Macedonian LZ. It will take you to Aviano. The Air Force will have a plane standing by and all the gear you need. I'll have the coordinates transmitted to Aviano so your pilot can set his course, working on the bearings we have. This isn't the best scenario to work with. But with the information we have, it's the best we can come up with."

"It's a bloody awful scenario," McCarter said. "But we've got two mates in hostile hands and we aren't leaving without them. If we are right and this is the FAP base, as well, then we can finish what we came for."

"One more thing. Your time out there is running short. Real short. Get in and finish the job quick as you can. There's some heavy weather coming in."

Brognola cut the connection, leaving McCarter staring at the handset, a frown on his face. He went over the big Fed's words a few times, concentrating on Brognola's final words.

There's some heavy weather coming in.

What did he mean?

Heavy weather?

McCarter pushed away from the small desk holding the communication gear. Brognola had been unable to speak plainly due to the risk of being overheard, so what he had been saying had nothing to do with the weather. He had been trying to pass information to McCarter via a simple verbal code.

Not weather. Probably something to do with an upcoming event. Whatever it was, it seemed likely to affect the presence of Phoenix Force in the area— or more likely once they crossed over the border back into Kosovo. Not a local thing. Not the way Brognola had expressed himself. He had mentioned time running out, and a need for the team to leave before heavy weather arrived. Weather was a key word, McCarter felt certain. So where was the connection? Did it mean something coming from the sky? Like a storm? Dammit, McCarter swore. What the hell did Hal mean? What was coming out of the damn sky?

The answer hit him out of the blue.

Aircraft came out of the sky. In this instance planes carrying bombs, dropping them on strategic targets. Brognola had been warning McCarter that time was running out for the Serbians, and if NATO started dropping bombs it was going to make life difficult for anyone on the ground.

McCarter rejoined his team. He told them what Brognola had said and what he felt it meant. Both Manning and Encizo reached a similar conclusion.

"The sooner we move the better," Manning said.

They gathered their equipment together.

McCarter went looking for Sergeant Tanner.

"Looks like we're moving out," McCarter said.

"Going to pull your mates out of the fire?"

"Something like that."

"How're you doing it?"

"We'll take a plane from Aviano and make a HALO jump. We'll try and come down near the FAP base and take it from there."

"Just the three of you?"

"Not much bloody choice, Sarge."

Tanner stiffened. "Yes, there is, sir. You could take me along."

Over Tanner's shoulder McCarter caught a glimpse of Manning and Encizo. They had followed him out and had to have been close enough to hear what had been said. The expressions on their faces made his answer easy.

"Didn't you ever hear the expression never volunteer for anything, Tanner?"

The SAS man grinned. "It's the first thing they tell you to forget when you walk through the gates at Hereford. Or have you forgotten, sir?"

"No, I haven't. We'd better go see your CO and ask his permission before I steal one of his boys."

"I'll show you where he is, sir."

FAP Stronghold

THE METAL DOOR was now locked. Calvin James knew because he had tried to open it. The bright lights, covered with thick wire mesh to prevent their being broken, were on permanently. That made it hard to tell what time of day or night it was. James's watch had been taken, as had Hawkins's.

James wasn't sure how long he had been unconscious, or how long the savage beatings had gone on for. Time and place and effect had all become blurred. Pain was the predominant sensation. Numbing, aching, piercing. It was enough to keep James awake now, but not enough to prevent him from pacing the stone cell in an endless circle, following the contours of the rough, cold walls and flagged floor.

A few yards behind him Hawkins shuffled along like some bizarre shadow. The Phoenix Force warriors, hurt though they were, knew the need to keep moving. It would have been easier simply to lie on the floor, in their own blood, and let nature shut them down to blot out the pain. But that wasn't an option. It smacked of giving in, of letting their captors see that the brutal treatment was wearing them down. So instead they kept up a ceaseless trek around the cell. It maintained their grip on the conscious world and stopped their battered bodies from shutting down. Though every joint, every muscle, screamed for rest, James and Hawkins kept on moving, working out the stiffness that threatened to cripple them.

They talked, too. Nothing of any consequence, but simply to allow them to hear their own voices, and to make the enemy aware that they weren't about to give away any vital information. Neither man knew whether their captors were listening in. It didn't matter one way or the other because all they were doing was keeping each other awake.

"I still say you're wrong," Hawkins said.

"Wrong?"

"Yeah. The guy who played the black sheep son in *The Big Valley* was Lee Majors. The same guy who was *The Six Million Dollar Man.*"

"You're thinking about Lee Van Cleef."

"No. He was the martial arts guy in *The Master.*"

"You sure?"

"I won't ever forget *The Master.* It was so bad you just had to watch it every week to see if they could come up with another crappy episode."

The cell door crashed open and Lec Pavlic stormed in, followed by three of his men. The three were armed. They confronted James and Hawkins.

"Enough of this nonsense," Pavlic growled. "It is time to give me the answers I need."

"No," James said. "We don't have a thing to say to you."

"Your bravery will not stop me from killing you."

"That's true," Hawkins replied. "If that's the way it has be."

"We know you are not with the regular military," Pavlic said. "So why are the Americans so interested in us?"

"The FAP declared war on us," Hawkins stated. "You expect us to sit back and take it?"

"America sat back and allowed the Albanian people to be slaughtered. You did nothing. None of you. The UN. NATO. You were cowards. And because of that we are dying in our thousands."

"So you decided to punish us all? To make us pay for what's happened?" Hawkins shook his head.

"The trouble is, friend, you did it the wrong way. You expect sympathy when you attack the ones who are trying to help you."

"Help? What help have you given?"

"Peace talks. Humanitarian aid. Monitoring. That's what," James said.

"Talk! That is all? Just talk? You sit around a table and talk to murderers and monsters? You discuss our future while we die. While we suffer."

"Hell, man, what do you want from us? Making peace has to start from something. There has to be a way to resolve this. The talks bring things into the open. What else can we do?"

"You Americans are all the same. You live in your nice safe country, with your big cars and color television sets. There is no war there. No starvation. No mass graves. What do you know about suffering? What do you know about our lives?"

"I get sick of you people using that damn excuse every time," Hawkins said. "You blame us for having a stable existence. You call us rich and lazy and corrupt. But every time trouble comes, you expect us to jump in and help. Send money. Send food. Even weapons so you can fight your wars. Send your soldiers to die for us. Then we're in trouble if we don't help. Man, we just can't win. But you know what ticks me off? We do it every time. We send the aid. We send the people. And sometimes they die. But we still do it. So tell me, mister, just what the hell do you want, because I think I lost the damn plot on this one."

Pavlic stared at Hawkins for long seconds. His face, already pale, turned almost gray. His shoulders sagged a little, and for a fleeting moment Hawkins was certain he saw defeat in the man's deep-set eyes.

"You will never understand." he said.

He turned and left the cell, followed by his men. The door was slammed shut, the exterior bolts snapped home.

James turned to his companion.

"That was a speech," he said.

"That old boy just got me mad."

"Remind me not to upset you too often."

"Cal, that guy is near the edge. You see the look in his eyes? He's got himself in such a state he doesn't know black from white. Something tells me what he's done up to now won't matter against what he plans to do in the future."

James had the same feelings himself. There was an obsession driving the man, an unreasoning wildness that had pushed him far beyond normal boundaries. It held nothing but disaster for anyone on his hate list, and from what James had been able to work out that included most of the world.

Stony Man Farm, Virginia

"BY THE TIME you make touchdown in Aviano, your ride will be ready and waiting. All the equipment you requested will be on board. I've updated the flight crew with the information we have so they can log it in the onboard computer for a course and setting. Sorry we can't give you an exact DZ, but we're going on what we've got. I hate to have to do this to you guys."

Barbara Price glanced at Brognola as she waited for McCarter's reply. She felt bad having to send them on a mission without the fine details. Sometimes it happened because of the nature of Phoenix Force's need to act swiftly and with little hard intel. Knowing that didn't make Price feel any better.

"We know you'd give us more if you had it. So don't go getting worry lines just because of us. As you Yanks say so quaintly—this time we'll just have to wing it."

"Don't forget the clock is ticking."

"When isn't the bloody thing ticking?"

"Take care, you guys, and come home safe. All of you."

"Will do. Over and out."

The line went dead, and Price put down the handset. Now that the mission was under way there was little Stony Man could do except wait, and pray that their people survived.

"Hey, I got some data here," Tokaido said, holding up a printout.

"What is it?"

"The FBI ran some checks on what Sonilab produces. There were some discrepancies in their production schedules, like someone had been making items off the record. So they ran a check on the computer system. It logs all production and stores it in a data bank. Someone had been tampering with it. The computers are tied in to the production setup, so no one can alter the runs without there being a record. Seems someone had deleted a run of items but they hadn't followed through with the backup system. They either forgot or didn't understand the way the computer works. So the FBI had one of their experts tap into the data bank and restore the deleted items. This is what they came up with."

The printout showed a miniature pressure container, in the shape of an oxygen bottle. Instead of a valve system to connect to a hose, this one had a pressure release operated by a small timing device. The whole object was no more than eight inches long by a couple of inches round. A separate diagram showed the pressure release and timer in detail, with dimensions and specifications.

"According to the log, Sonilab produced the timer device. About two dozen of them."

"Khan," Price said. "The day Able Team followed him to Sonilab. When he left he was carrying a metal case. He was picking up those timers. Next thing he's in Nassau where the *Millennium Explorer* is operating."

"Send this information to Able Team. Tell them they're going to have to make their move. If our guess is right, Petrocovich could be gearing up to produce something for Malik and the FAP to use," Brognola said.

"We'd better have a bioteam on standby," Price stated.

"Leave that with me," Brognola replied. "I'll talk to the Man about it."

"Hal, I need to show you something," Kurtzman said.

The big Fed crossed over to his station.

"Hunt just came up with the latest position for the *Levantine*."

On screen was the INMARSAT data. The cargo

ship was well into the Adriatic now, moving up toward the Albanian coastline.

"Okay. We'll have to risk an intercept. We need to have her stopped and searched."

Brognola straightened and searched his pockets. He found a pack of antacid tablets and thumbed out a couple. Chewing furiously, he crossed to one of the secure phones and made his call.

Royal Navy Submarine Hornblower, *Adriatic Sea*

COMMANDER ROBERT JENSON, captain of the nuclear-powered submarine *Hornblower,* took the message form from his second-in-command and glanced at the decoded information.

"All right, Number One, let's get this done."

He led the way from his cabin, along the central walkway to the control room, located directly beneath the conning tower.

"Periscope," he ordered.

As the periscope was activated, Jenson turned to speak to his weapons officer.

"Load a torpedo into Tube One. We'd better be ready in case these buggers give us the runaround."

"Yes, sir."

Jenson settled himself at the periscope and began a scan. It didn't take long for him to identify the target. The *Levantine* was running on minimum power, barely moving through the calm waters. Most of her running lights had been dimmed.

"Silly buggers," he said to himself. "Hiding in the dark isn't going to save you."

Jenson gave the order to bring the sub around so

that she was between the cargo ship and the shore. Once they were in position he checked that the crew was on alert before bringing the *Hornblower* to the surface. With the submarine visible he climbed up into the tower and through the opened hatch. Jenson had the powerful searchlights embedded in the conning tower turned on. The beams illuminated the cargo ship. Activating the communication system, he spoke over the external amplifiers.

"Cargo ship *Levantine*. This is the captain of the submarine off your port side. You will stand down immediately. Stop all engines and drop anchor. Failure to do so will be considered a hostile act, and we will take appropriate action."

There was no immediate response from the ship.

Jenson waited. Lights were coming on, and he could see figures moving about on the vessel's deck. Faint shouts carried across the water, then an amplified voice broke the calm.

"Why have you stopped us? This is a civilian vessel going about its business. You have no right to detain us!"

"Please drop your anchor and stop all engines. I have an armed torpedo aimed at you right now. Do not force me to use it."

He heard more raised voices on the *Levantine*. All the ship's lights were blazing now. There was a short, vicious crackle of autofire from somewhere on the cargo ship. The bullets splashed harmlessly in the water well short of the submarine.

"Don't waste my time or your bullets," Jenson said, his amplified voice booming across the water. "Face it. You have nowhere to run. Surrender your vessel to me, or face the consequences. It's your choice, gentlemen. I'll leave you to decide how you want to play this.''

Jenson's Number One appeared at his side.

"The U.S. Navy is on the way, sir. A destroyer will be with us in twenty minutes with a boarding party.''

"Thank God for that. Let's hope those idiots over there don't decide to make a run for it.''

"We have blanketed their communications, too, sir. They don't have anything too sophisticated, so it wasn't difficult to block outgoing information. However, we did pick up an incoming message to the *Levantine* about twenty minutes ago. Com room is working on it now. Shouldn't take too long to break the code.''

"Thanks, Number One. Maintain position and keep us locked on to that vessel.''

"She's not going anywhere, sir.''

Jenson followed his pointing finger and saw the splash of the vessel's anchor as it struck the water.

"Small boat just hit the water, too, sir.''

"Yes, I see it. Let the U.S. Navy know. They can send out a launch to round it up.

"I'm going below, Number One. I'll be in the com room if you need me.''

Jenson made his way down into the sub and along the central walkway to where the communications room was located.

"How's it going, Chief?'' he asked the communications officer.

"Just in time, sir,'' the young officer said, passing a printed copy of the intercepted signal to Jenson.

The *Hornblower*'s commander read the information.

"Well done, Chief. Better get this off to Northwood."

Located in Middlesex, England, Northwood was the Military Command and Control Center. Deciphered messages from vessels like the *Hornblower* were analyzed and the information used to assess military options.

Jenson left the com room and returned to the control room. He checked the position of the *Levantine* on the radar screen. He was also able to identify the smaller dot that was the launched boat making a run from the cargo ship. A wry smile showed on his face when he saw that the boat was on a course that would bring it directly in the path of the oncoming U.S. Navy destroyer.

"Better send a message to the Yanks and let them know they're about to be waylaid by a boat from the *Levantine*."

"Right away, sir."

Jenson stretched his lean frame and glanced around the control room.

"Anyone got a spare cup of coffee? All this bloody excitement has made me thirsty."

Stony Man Farm, Virginia

"THIS WAS JUST SENT from Military Command and Control Center. The British navy sub that intercepted the *Levantine* picked up an incoming message she got just before they stopped her. They decoded it and sent it on."

Brognola passed the sheet of paper to Barbara Price, who read it out to the assembled cyberteam.

"The message details target assignments for the people on board the vessel. Out of one hundred on board the ship, thirty were to be moved out through Albania to the refugee camps on the German border. They would disperse throughout mainland Europe and Great Britain. Another group, twenty in all, would be sent here to the U.S. The rest would be used within Yugoslavia. There are contact addresses for the groups going to the U.S., Europe and Great Britain. We can have these staked out and make a check on who's maintaining them before we get the local authorities to move in."

"What were these people going to do?" Wethers asked.

Katz stepped forward. "They're terrorists. They would do what terrorists do—attack designated targets, set bombs, carry out assassinations. Whatever they are ordered to do. My best guess is they would be using whatever Ilyana Petrocovich has created for them. Don't forget the designs that were found at Sonilab and the timing devices manufactured there. It looks like those devices have been delivered to Petrocovich on board the *Millennium Explorer*. Add all that up, and I think we'll come close to the right answer."

"Okay," Price said. "Let's assume Katz is right. Just because we've intercepted the cargo ship and taken the terrorists off-line, it doesn't help Cal and T.J. Petrocovich and Malik are still on the loose. I don't think we can breathe easy until everything comes together."

Brognola reached for his mug of coffee, found it was cold and went looking for the pot for a refill. Price joined him. He glanced at her and shook his head, sighing.

"You know your problem, Barb," he grumbled. "You always come up with a reason not to get complacent."

"So?"

"Every time you do you're always right."

"There are times when I wish I wasn't so damned smart. Like right now. With our people still out there and the clock ticking, being right isn't any help to them."

CHAPTER TWELVE

Nassau

"That looks like her," Rosario Blancanales said, peering through the canopy of the helicopter.

Grimaldi eased the controls, turning the garishly decorated JetRanger into a long, slow descent. Below them the sleek shape of the *Millennium Explorer* moved gracefully across the azure blue water.

"Hey, hold this damn thing steady," Schwarz said testily as he aimed the video camera at the ship. The camera was fitted with a powerful telephoto lens, enabling Schwarz to get close shots of the deck. It was possible for him to see the expressions on the upturned faces of the crew. There was no way they could see he was filming them—unless someone was checking the flyby with binoculars.

"Hey, I saw one of them hide a gun when we passed over," Schwarz said as Grimaldi flew on, leaving the ship far behind.

"You recognize anyone?" Lyons asked.

"Won't know until we take a look at the tape."

"Jack, take us back."

Grimaldi turned and changed course to avoid overflying the ship again on the return to Nassau. When they touched down at the small field he saw Jess Buchanan outside her charter business hut. The blonde waved as she spotted Grimaldi and made her way across to meet them.

"Well, go ahead and thank her nicely for telling us how to find the damn ship," Blancanales said, nudging Grimaldi.

"See you guys later," the pilot said as he left them.

Lyons led the way to the rented Ford they had left parked on the edge of the tarmac. Blancanales got behind the wheel and started the engine.

"Let's get back to the hotel and take a look at that video," Lyons said.

Aboard the Millennium Explorer

MALIK WENT to the cabin that had been used as an office by the previous owners of the ship. He found Khan there, on the telephone. The big Russian completed his call before acknowledging Malik's presence.

"I have spoken to our man in Nassau and asked him to check out that helicopter. It will not be difficult. It had its company name painted all over it."

"Khan, we can't check on every aircraft that flies overhead. We are in the Bahamas. This is a vacation area. There are charter flights every day. They go back and forth all the time."

"Maybe. But it doesn't cost a great deal to be cautious. And it might be worthwhile, seeing the recent setbacks we have experienced."

"You are a very suspicious man, Khan."

The Russian nodded. "It's why I have stayed alive so long. Trust is for little children and young girls who think they are in love. Both find out how foolish it is soon enough."

Malik couldn't help laughing. "And a cynic, too." He crossed to a wall cabinet, opened it and helped himself to a tumbler of whiskey.

"I'm paid to look out for Ilyana. That is what I am doing."

"Yes, I know. Forgive me. She could not do better than to have you protect her."

Malik slumped in a padded leather seat. He was weary. He had been moving around so much in recent weeks. Between the ship and Libya. To Kosovo and the FAP. He was attempting to please everyone while neglecting his own welfare. Personal comfort didn't concern him overly, but he did realize that tiring himself out physically wouldn't help anyone. He needed to be alert, aware of everything that was going on around him. The demands on his time and on his dedication were great. So much so that he forgot to look after himself.

The problem was that as Ilyana Petrocovich moved closer to completing her development of the Gene Virus, his excitement grew with it. The concept of a selective, programmable bioweapon had captured his imagination from the first moment he heard about it. The concept was outlandish, the stuff of fantasy. Until Ilyana had shown him articles written by eminent men in the field, who had confirmed the possibility of such a weapon. They had predicted it was still years away because so much development was still needed. Of course none of them were considering Ilyana Petrocovich and her brilliant mind, her single-minded dedication to the creation of the new virus. While they tinkered around in their laboratories, Ilyana forged ahead, using her vivid mind to work on the theory and turn it into a practicality. Now she was almost there. She had a first batch, raw, untried, with no full knowledge of how it might react when directed against the target group. But they would soon know. No matter how successful, they would have at least tried.

Malik pushed to his feet and crossed to stare out of the window. He watched the soft swell of the sea beyond the *Millennium Explorer*. The ship was fitted with a sophisticated stabilizing system that kept it on an even keel in all but the severest weather. The only indication they were at sea was the bare hint of a gentle motion.

"Khan, let me know if your man contacts you about those people in the helicopter."

The burly Russian nodded as he walked to the liquor cabinet to pour himself another drink.

Malik left the office and returned to his own cabin. He had prayers to say, part of his daily ritual, part of his everyday life. As he closed the door to his cabin, he felt a great calm come over him. All the worries of the outside world slipped away as he paused for a time of meditation before making his dedication to God.

JACK GRIMALDI HAD finished checking the helicopter. He had spent a couple of hours going over the craft to make sure it was ready for liftoff whenever

Able Team wanted it. He refueled the chopper, ran a diagnostic of the systems and rechecked the emergency gear and communications. It was only when he had completed the full list that he once again turned his thoughts to Jess Buchanan.

He liked the capable young woman. She was bright and smart, no mean businesswoman, having taken on the charter operation when her father died suddenly. There had only been the two of them, her mother having left the family while Jess was still a youngster. Suddenly on her own, Jess had been forced into a decision—sell something she loved, or run the business herself. She had chosen the latter. Six years later she was still going strong.

Grimaldi made his way across to the office, hoping to persuade Buchanan to have dinner with him. It might have to be an early one if Able Team got the notion to make their move against the *Millennium Explorer* sooner rather than later.

What the hell, Grimaldi decided. If he didn't ask now he never would.

The woman wasn't in her office. He decided to check the hangar where she housed and maintained her aircraft. A car was parked outside the hangar, and the big roller doors had been pulled almost shut. Grimaldi skirted the parked car and made for the side door of the building. As he eased it open, he heard a scuffle of sound from inside, followed by what was an unmistakable slapping sound.

He heard someone give a stifled cry, a mixture of pain and anger. Grimaldi slid through the door, hugging the inside wall as he searched for the source of the sound.

And found it.

Jess Buchanan was struggling to release herself from the grip of a hard-looking man dressed in faded denims. The guy had the woman's left arm twisted around her back and he was applying a lot of pressure. She was resisting, despite being in obvious pain. A second man stood to one side, a crooked grin on his unshaven face. He was saying something in a low tone to Buchanan. Whatever it was had no effect on the young woman. Her reply was sharp and cutting, directed at the unshaven man, and it wiped the grin from his face in an instant. He leaned forward and struck her across the side of the face, almost knocking her free from the grip of the first man.

Grimaldi moved in fast then, not wanting to extend the woman's suffering any longer than he had to. His long strides brought him up behind the pair, his hand grabbing a steel bar from the workbench as he passed it.

A scant second before Grimaldi reached the pair of hard men, Buchanan's gaze settled on him. To her credit she showed no recognition that might have alerted her attackers.

Grimaldi took out the guy holding the woman first. He swung the bar and whacked the guy across the back of the skull. The hard man let out a grunt and let go of Buchanan. She twisted away, taking herself clear of the immediate area, leaving Grimaldi with a clear field.

The Stony Man pilot turned toward the second man just as the guy made a grab for the stubby autopistol stuck in the front of his pants. Grimaldi's iron bar arced around and slammed across the back of the guy's hand, cracking bone. The man yelped with pain, his features twisted with rage as he made a second try for the gun, this time with his other hand. Grimaldi rapped the bar across the side of the guy's head, the force of the blow spinning his adversary off his feet. He stumbled, losing his balance, and went down with a thump, blood coursing down the side of his face.

A rush of sound and an accompanying yell from Buchanan alerted Grimaldi to the presence of the other hard man. This time he wasn't quite fast enough. The guy slammed into him and they fell to the floor in a tangle, each struggling to gain the upper hand. As Grimaldi hit the concrete floor, the bar bounced from his grasp. He had enough to deal with as the guy went for his throat, his thick fingers digging into Grimaldi's flesh.

The Stony Man pilot sucked in a deep breath just before his air was cut off. There was no time for niceties. Grimaldi reached up and ground his thumbs into his attacker's eyes, applying as much pressure as he could. The guy resisted for short seconds, then rolled away, letting out a shrill scream against the excruciating agony as he pawed at his injured eyes.

Grimaldi pushed up off the ground, ramming the heel of his right hand against his opponent's throat. Retching violently, the man thrashed around on the hangar floor. On his feet, Grimaldi crossed over to where the first guy lay. He took the man's gun and ejected the magazine before he put the weapon aside. Then he bent over the guy and stripped off his belt, using it to bind his hands behind his back.

Satisfied, Grimaldi returned to the first attacker and repeated the maneuver.

Buchanan was on her knees, gripping her injured arm. Bending over her, Grimaldi eased her to her feet. She turned to face him, holding back the tears as she stared into his eyes. Then she hugged him like he was a long-lost favorite friend and wept quietly.

When she was composed, he took her to the charter office and sat her in a chair. Grimaldi made her a mug of hot coffee, then waited until she felt like talking.

"I thought they were going to kill me. They were so scary, Tex."

"What was it all about?"

She raised her misty eyes to his face. "You. They came in the hangar asking about you. They asked so many damn questions. Who were you. What were you doing in Nassau. Why had you flown over the *Millennium Explorer*."

"They say why they were interested?"

"Tex, I didn't have the chance to ask. Sorry."

Grimaldi raised a hand in mock surrender. "Stupid question," he said. "I guess we must have upset someone."

"Oh, sure. Come on, Tex, do I look stupid? People don't do this kind of thing without a reason. Maybe I should be asking his questions. I mean, just who are you guys? I'm having a funny feeling a film crew is the last thing you are."

"I need to do a couple of things, Jess, such as phone my partners and make sure that guy doesn't disappear. Trust me. Please."

She considered his request. Sipping the coffee she said, "I guess I don't have a choice."

Grimaldi made his call and alerted Able Team, then returned to the hangar. The guy he'd whacked with the iron bar was still unconscious. The pilot found some electrical cable and tied the guy's feet, then he crossed to where the other man lay, still moaning about his eyes. He dragged him to the far corner of the hangar and waited for him to calm down.

"Why didn't you just come and talk to me?" Grimaldi asked.

"Why don't you go to hell!" The guy blinked his watery eyes, trying to focus on his tormentor.

Grimaldi sighed. "I can see this is going to be one of those sophisticated conversations that tend to get out of hand. Maybe I should stop wasting time and just slap you silly."

Bending over the guy, Grimaldi went through his pockets and found a thick wad of one-hundred-dollar bills.

"You work cheap."

The man muttered obscenities.

Making sure the man couldn't move, Grimaldi returned to the office. He found Buchanan in the washroom, splashing water on her face. She looked around sharply as he appeared, eyes momentarily startled.

"Hey, take it easy."

"Easy for you to say."

Grimaldi tossed the money on the office desk and sat, waiting for Able Team to arrive.

Buchanan stood over him, toweling her face. There was a red mark where she had been slapped.

"So is Tex your real name?"

Grimaldi shook his head.

"Thank God for that," she said frankly. "I like you, but I didn't go too much for the name."

They were still laughing when Blancanales stuck his head in through the door.

"I thought this was serious."

Grimaldi pushed to his feet, pausing to touch the woman's cheek.

"Will you be okay?"

"I'll be fine."

Grimaldi explained what had happened as he and Blancanales joined Lyons and Schwarz beside the Ford.

"If they have us spotted, then we need to hit them now," Lyons said. "No time like the present."

"Original line," Blancanales said. "I get the idea though."

"You pick up anything from the video?" Grimaldi asked.

"One of the guys on board was that Russian son of a bitch we tangled with," Schwarz replied. "Khan."

"I need to call the Farm," Lyons said. "The guys you bagged need taking into custody. We can't afford to have them running back to whoever hired them."

"I'll get the chopper warmed up. We can load the equipment at the same time."

Lyons took out his cell phone and tapped in the Stony Man number.

Blancanales and Schwarz got into the Ford and drove off toward the chopper.

Before he followed them Grimaldi returned to the charter office and Jess Buchanan.

"We have something to do. I'll drop back to see you when it's over," he said.

She stared at him with a puzzled expression. "You can't tell me what, though?"

"No."

"Are you cops? FBI?"

Grimaldi frowned.

"I get it. You can't tell me that, either?"

"I can tell you one thing, Jess. I will come back to see you."

The woman watched as Grimaldi and Lyons walked to the helicopter. They spent some time moving equipment from the car to the JetRanger. They were still checking out the aircraft when the sound of a police siren indicated the arrival of the local law. Lyons went out to meet them and a short time later Buchanan's attackers, now cuffed, were led out to the police cruiser, deposited in the back and driven away under guard. Lyons returned to the waiting helicopter. Grimaldi had it warmed up, and as soon as Lyons was inside he took off, buzzing Buchanan's office as he took the chopper toward the coast.

The woman watched until she could no longer see the helicopter, then she went back inside the office and closed the door.

Serbian District Police Barracks

DEEP IN HIS PRIVATE thoughts, Janic Milisivic failed to hear his superior enter the cramped, musty office.

It was only when Racev kicked the leg of the desk that Milisivic dragged himself back to reality.

"Isn't the work interesting enough for you any longer?"

The sarcasm in Racev's voice was undisguised. He and Milisivic didn't get along. As far as Milisivic was concerned, Racev was nothing more than a bully in uniform, A man who used his position, and the power it gave him, to intimidate and threaten weaker individuals. He was also known for his uncontrollable violence, and worse, for his sexual appetites. The present crisis within the country had allowed Racev to seize the opportunities that came his way. He indulged himself with the females of the ethnic minority who populated the area. Racev enjoyed his notoriety, even boasted about it. No one in the police unit made comments about his behavior. In fact a good number of his subordinates were as bad as he was. The only true opposition came from Milisivic. He stood up to Racev's bullying, and that angered the man. He would have loved to have had Milisivic removed from the unit, but because of Milisivic's connections, family that reached as far as Belgrade and the government, Racev knew not to go too far. It didn't stop him from needling Milisivic at every opportunity, especially in front of the other officers.

As Racev's sneering tones disturbed his train of thought, Milisivic raised his head to meet the man's stare.

"I'm surprised to see you here," he said. "I can

only guess that we have run out of bullets, or there are no women left to rape. Which is it, Racev?''

Racev stiffened, anger darkening his features. Physically large, broad as well as tall, his menacing appearance had been heightened by having his hair cropped close to his large skull.

"One night, my friend," he said, "you will find me behind you in a dark alley. I look forward to that occasion."

Milisivic smiled. "I knew you wouldn't be facing me, Racev. That isn't your style. Always from behind so they can't fight back." Milisivic leaned forward, asking softly, "Is that the way you take your women as well?"

This time Racev was unable to hold back his rage. He clawed his way across the desk, big hands reaching out for Milisivic. He failed to reach his intended target. Milisivic, lighter and a great deal more agile than Racev, twisted aside easily, pushing his chair up on its back legs. As Racev lunged across the desk he was briefly vulnerable, and Milisivic used that time to his own advantage. As the broad shoulders of the man stretched over the desk, Milisivic pushed to his feet. He slammed both hands down on the back of his boss's thick neck and pushed hard, driving the man's head down. The sound of Racev's face hitting the desk was loud and satisfying. Milisivic stepped back, his hand reaching for the autopistol holstered on his belt. He eased the weapon partway out of the holster and waited.

The office door opened as other officers, attracted by the noise, came to see what was happening. They stared at Racev, then at Milisivic, unsure how to react. Milisivic raised a hand to keep them at bay, letting them see that he had his hand on the butt of his pistol.

Racev pushed upright, breathing hard through a nose that was bruised and bloody. He pawed at the blood, his cold eyes fixed on Milisivic. Despite his anger, Racev was astute enough to take note that Milisivic had his hand on his pistol. He stared at the man for a time until finally he backed away.

"Enjoy your little triumph. Then remember what I said about watching your back. The time is coming faster than you think."

Milisivic said nothing. He remained where he was, his gaze never wavering from Racev. The man was totally unpredictable, given to mood changes in an instant.

Racev abruptly turned on his heel and left the office. He stamped his way out of the building, and a short time later the sound of his car was heard, tires screaming as he floored the accelerator.

Milisivic knew the matter wasn't settled. Racev wasn't the kind of man to allow a personal insult to go unchallenged. He would bide his time, allowing the incident to fester until he found himself unable to contain it any longer. And then he would make his move. The dark alley threat wasn't made in jest. Racev, like all bullies, was at heart a coward. Not that it made him any less of a threat. In fact it probably made him even more of a dangerous opponent.

Milisivic had made himself another enemy. A treacherous one, and sooner or later he would have to make a decision. It would be to leave the matter as it was, or to do something to resolve it himself, taking the opportunity out of Racev's hands.

He stepped out of the office, pushing through the crowd of onlookers. The response from his colleagues was mixed.

Those who favored Racev were openly hostile but kept their distance, unsure how Milisivic might react if they stood up to him. The officers who disliked Racev gave him a muted acknowledgment. Unlike Milisivic, they didn't have family backing and needed to act with caution. It was yet another sign of the repressive society they lived in.

Though the supposed family background protected Milisivic to a degree, he was under no illusion. His life was as much in the balance as anyone's in these uncertain times. He allowed the imagined protection to remain in the minds of others because it gave him freedom in certain areas. It was a small luxury he could use for as long as he remained undiscovered. If the day came when his subterfuge *was* discovered, he would deal with it as best he could.

The same criteria was applied to his work within the resistance group. They did what they could to interfere with the regime that was slowly and surely fragmenting the country. His position within the police force gave him access to information he was able to pass to his people, to be used if and when they were able. True, it was small compared to what they might do if they became an active, combative group. Under no illusion, Milisivic knew that any change to that status would place them directly in the firing line from the Belgrade authorities. They would be just another resistance group, on the move, at risk from everyone they met, and their achievements might even go unnoticed within the greater framework of the nation's ills. The decision by the group to remain undercover, collecting and passing information, was to remain the core of their activities. Milisivic had been a little disappointed at that. He was finding his background role almost tedious. He wasn't so sure they were gaining anything either. He had a personal yearning to do something positive, something that could at least be judged as a worthwhile act of defiance against the government. In the meantime, he kept his thoughts to himself and remained where he was.

Leaving the office, he made his way out of the building. His run-in with Racev didn't worry him much. The man's bullying attitude had been bound to cause some kind of conflict between them at some point. Milisivic had experienced his share of violence and intimidation during his service. It was to be expected, but never more than now with the country in turmoil, with the people at each other's throats, the division encouraged by the regime that had the nation in its grip. Milisivic had watched his country suffer, pain added to pain, with death hanging over everyone daily.

Milisivic was saddened by the waste of it all. His was a country that could ill afford what it was going through. Wealth wasn't something visited upon the population. The power cadre held the nation's wealth and seemed wholly intent on plunging a deprived populus into chaos and the darkness of intolerance. Already countless lives had been lost, with many more to come.

And Janic Milisivic, maintaining his cover as a police officer, was finding it harder to remain a passive observer. The chance to help the foreign undercover unit complete its mission and free their comrades from the FAP had come at an opportune moment. Whatever the outcome, if he, Milisivic, became involved, then at least he had made a contribution beyond his shadowy role within the force. The phrase "a futile gesture" rose unbidden in his mind. Milisivic shrugged it off. Somewhere along the line someone had to do something. Futile or not, direct action held an appeal for him he was unable to suppress.

He climbed behind the wheel of his 4x4 and drove away from the station, heading east. A few miles down the road was a small facility where the police unit maintained its vehicle and helicopter fleet. The helicopter fleet comprised two machines. One was a small observer helicopter, while the other was a larger German machine, armed and capable of carrying at least ten people as well as the crew. When he had been a younger man, early in his military service, Milisivic had been trained to fly helicopters. He had maintained his skill, flying the police helicopters whenever he could. The larger one, with its armor and weapons, was a cumbersome craft, but Milisivic knew its capabilities. He had already decided that would be the machine he would use. It had the range and speed, it could easily accommodate the covert team and it was armed.

He swung the 4x4 into the compound and drove

over to the field building. He made his way inside and spoke to the sergeant in charge.

"I haven't had any orders about the helicopter, Captain," the sergeant said when Milisivic told him to ready the machine for flight.

"Nor have I, Sergeant. This is a precautionary measure. If something occurred tonight that required a flight it isn't going to look good if we need a couple of hours to get the machine ready to go. Is it?"

"Put that way, I suppose you're right, sir."

"Just make sure the helicopter is fully fueled and armed. Are you on duty tonight, Sergeant?"

"Yes, Captain."

"Then I hold you responsible."

"Very well, sir."

"I'll check back later."

The sergeant watched Milisivic return to his 4x4 and drive off. He called in his ground crew and gave them their orders. He watched as they hurried to prepare the helicopter. He poured himself a mug of coffee and stood at the window watching the ground crew working at the helicopter. When he had finished his coffee and smoked a cigarette, the sergeant picked up the telephone and dialed a number.

"This is Sergeant Danic. I needed to check something with you, sir."

He explained what had taken place, then listened as the speaker on the other end of the line gave his reply.

"I understand, sir. Perfectly. The helicopter will be made ready. I look forward to seeing you later, Commandant Racev."

THE LIGHT WAS FADING when Milisivic drove back to the facility. It was cold, and rain was whipping across the road. He parked the 4x4 and climbed out. Lights had been switched on inside the building, and as Milisivic paused to turn up the collar of his long coat, he thought he saw someone pull back from one of the windows, almost as if they were trying to hide. A moment of doubt crossed his mind as he turned and picked up the stubby Czech-made Skorpion machine pistol. He made sure it was cocked and ready before easing it under his coat. He made a pretence of locking the 4x4, his eyes scanning the area, suddenly needing to be sure of his safety.

Some instinct, the will to survive, warned him to be alert.

Milisivic spotted the rear end of a vehicle parked at the end of the building. He might not have paid much attention at any other time, but when he saw the thin curls of smoke trailing from the exhaust he confirmed to himself that the situation was far from normal. The parked vehicle had its engine running, prepared to make a quick getaway.

He had driven into a trap, one baited with the prepared helicopter standing on the pad no more than thirty feet away from him. He had been betrayed, most likely by the sergeant in charge.

So, Milisivic decided, his day had come.

He knew that whatever he did in the next few minutes would determine the course of his life dramatically. If he took the wrong steps, it would end here on this desolate field. If he survived and got away, his career in the police force would be over and he would become a wanted man. Oddly, he didn't feel regret over that. The deception had become a strain. It would be a relief not to have to pretend any longer. Perhaps now he would be able to make a real contribution to the opposition group. However it went, he could at least be rid of the company of many of the men he despised for their callous disregard for the suffering of others.

He saw the door open in the building, and a dark-clad figure stepped into view.

Milisivic knew who it was before a shaft of light from a window shone on the man's face—Racev.

He paused, raising a hand almost in a casual salute, as if he were greeting an old friend.

"Janic! Of all the people to be here tonight." Racev laughed at his own joke. "But of course I knew it would be you. I have known since I received the telephone call earlier today."

Racev approached. Behind him two of his most trusted officers eased out of the vehicle, flanking their superior. Both carried AK-74s.

"Not quite the dark alley you were so concerned about, but close enough for what I need to do."

"You need to do?" Milisivic looked beyond Racev at the pair of armed men. "I think they'll be doing the shooting. Yes, definitely. You're still too much of a coward to kill me face-to-face, Racev."

Racev's face flushed with the insult. He stabbed a finger at Milisivic.

"There won't be any family protection this time, Janic. No hiding behind them now."

"Racev, there never was. That was a fantasy I let you believe because it kept you off my back. I would never have let my family be put at risk. Not for a sniveling bastard like you!''

Racev's roar of anger galvanized his two gunmen into action. They skirted him and moved toward Milisivic.

Time was up. Milisivic had wanted his moment, and here it was.

He dragged his leather coat open and brought the Skorpion into play. He delivered two short, well-placed bursts, driving both of Racev's armed men to the muddy ground. They stumbled, uncoordinated, bodies punctured by the sharp, solid bursts of 9 mm rounds.

The moment he saw his shots had achieved their purpose, Milisivic moved forward quickly. He confronted the surprised Racev and brought the man to his knees by slamming the Skorpion across the side of the man's head. As his superior slumped to his knees, Milisivic hit him a second time, harder, and he fell facedown in the mud. Milisivic slung the machine pistol, bent over Racev's still form and unleathered his pistol, hurling it into the shadows. Then he picked up one of the powerful AK-74s.

The parked patrol vehicle roared into full view, reversing from behind the building. Milisivic was ready for it. He raked the driver with a long burst, adjusted his aim and riddled the fuel tank, then continued on and shredded both tires. The vehicle came to a shuddering stop, the engine stalling.

Milisivic emptied the Kalashnikov's magazine, shattering windows in the building as a warning.

He tossed aside the empty assault rifle, unslung his own weapon, then turned to Racev and used the toe of his boot to nudge him into some kind of sluggish movement.

"Get on your damned feet, Racev, or I'll shoot you where you lie. Now!"

When Racev was upright, swaying uncertainly, blood streaming down the side of his face, Milisivic pushed him in the direction of the helicopter. He opened the hatch and forced Racev inside. Slamming the hatch shut, he directed his captive to the seat next to the pilot's, which he occupied himself.

"What are you doing?" Racev asked.

"Taking you for a ride," Milisivic said. He checked out the machine. The helicopter was fueled and ready to go. Milisivic went through the start-up procedure. As the rotors began to turn, Racev cleared his throat.

"Where?"

"I'm on an errand of mercy," Milisivic said. "I have some people to help. They need to get over the border and I'm providing the transport. That's why you let the sergeant prepare this machine just like I asked. You wanted to find out what I was doing. So here we are, Racev. Sit back and enjoy the ride. It could be your last."

Milisivic took off without any interference. No one on the ground made any attempt to stop him. Not with Racev on board.

He gained height and checked his instruments. A look at the on board maps, using the bearings David McCarter had given him, and Milisivic was able to alter his course. He turned the helicopter in the direction of the mountains where the FAP stronghold was reported to be located. All he had to do now was to spot the team of men on the ground and pick them up.

Milisivic smiled to himself at the thought. He was setting himself a difficult task. But he had made a promise to those men, and he would do his best to honor it, even if he died in the attempt.

Kosovar Airspace

McCARTER WAS TALKING to Kurtzman even as the C-141 Starlifter winged its way across the night sky, already over Kosovar territory. At 22,000 feet, it was flying unseen and unheard.

"I had an idea, so I ran a satellite scan over the map reference area we got before the chopper went down. Infrared picked up a heat source on a high point. The bird took some pictures, and we came up with what you've got on the copies."

McCarter studied the data that had been sent through to the onboard computer system.

"I figured if these people have some kind of base they're going to need power. To get power you need a portable generator. Maybe a couple of medium-size ones. They wouldn't be hard to get up there in a truck. They run on gasoline or diesel and provide everything that's needed—power, light, heat. The only drawback is they produce exhaust fumes and that is what the infrared picked up. Heat from the exhaust duct."

"Great."

"Take a look at the other set of photos. On the final sweep we picked up this guy."

The image showed a man, armed with an autorifle, plainly on guard duty.

"Do we have your base or what?" Kurtzman asked.

"I'd say we do, mate."

"The updated coordinates have been fed into the onboard computer system so your navigator can predict a better DZ. That should put you guys right over that exhaust stack."

"Okay. Thanks for that. Talk to you later. Over and out."

With the DZ coming up fast, Phoenix Force made its final equipment checks.

They wore black jumpsuits and helmets, and their throat mikes were connected to compact transceivers for man-to-man communication. Night-vision goggles hung around their necks to aid them during the assault. Each man carried his own personal weapon in a high-ride holster. Sheathed knives were standard. The lead weapon was the H&K MP-5. Gary Manning also had a Barnett crossbow and a supply of cynanide-shafted bolts. In the combat harness each man wore were extra clips of ammunition for their weapons, plus a selection of stun and fragmentation grenades, plus smoke canisters. Distributed among them were a number of compact, powerful explosive packs for demolition work.

Once the Phoenix Force commandos left the Starlifter, they would have to rely on their own expertise to extract themselves from the FAP territory unless Milisivic came through with some form of transport. Before they had lifted off from Aviano, Brognola, able to speak a little clearer on the matter he had only hinted at before, had explained to McCarter that due to the possibility of NATO attacks on Kosovo, all military personnel were being kept behind the border. The UN and NATO ground forces would stay within Macedonian territory, and there would be little help available during the early stages of the NATO strikes.

"This caught us on the hop," Brognola said by way of apology.

"We'll manage," McCarter assured him. "It won't be the first time we've improvised."

"All we seem to be doing is handing you guys a bad deal on this mission," Price said over the link.

"You can buy me a Coke as a peace offering."

"That's a yes."

One of the C-141 crew was acting as jump master for the drop. As the DZ came up, he ordered Phoenix Force and Sergeant Tanner to take up their positions. They put on their oxygen masks prior to the cabin being depressurized. The rear ramp powered open, showing the inky blackness. The next minute or so was critical as the jump master checked off the time against his navigational data, waiting for the right moment to give the order to go.

As the green light flicked to red, he yelled the command, and the four heavily equipped men moved quickly forward. Moments later they were flying into the void. The jump master closed the ramp and advised the pilot. The big aircraft turned and began its flight back to Aviano.

The team dropped like stones into the unknown. The massive plane that had brought them in vanished, as invisible to the jumpers as it had been to those on the ground thousands of feet below. The only sound was the rush of the wind buffeting them as they fell, tugging at their clothes and equipment.

The long free fall ended abruptly for the four as they released their chutes, jerking to a near stop, then descending slowly. Below they were able to make out the dark shapes of the mountain slopes. Pulling their night-vision goggles into position they were able to discern sharper detail, now bathed in a ghostly green light.

McCarter saw the spread of the escarpment and controlled his descent in its direction, watching the ground blur as he dropped toward it. Then he landed, making no sound. He gathered his chute, released the rig and bundled the fabric under an outcropping.

He watched the others land safely, all within a few yards of one another. After disposing of their chutes they gathered around McCarter.

"For Ray's benefit, we have two objectives—to get our guys out and sort out the FAP. The need is to put them out of action as much as possible. When we go in, it's hard. No prisoners. Strictly with prejudice. I want all of us back walking. Now I don't give a damn how you do it. Just do it."

McCarter glanced at Tanner, who gave him a thumbs-up.

"Just like being back at Hereford."

McCarter tapped Manning on the shoulder. "Check for sentries. Take them out first."

Manning nodded and moved away, with Encizo as his cover man.

"Take it easy, Sarge," McCarter said. "We'll have a few minutes before it gets busy."

CHAPTER THIRTEEN

Aboard the Millennium Explorer

"Has your man been in contact?" Malik asked.

Khan shook his head. "I told him it was important he keep me informed."

"It's possible he has nothing to tell you yet."

The Russian frowned, toying with the thick tumbler in his hand.

"My instinct tells me something is wrong. Maybe we should move out of the area. Relocate."

Malik considered that. "It won't be any trouble. It's the advantage of being on a ship. Perhaps we should change our position."

"It will not affect Ilyana's work, so I see no reason not to."

Malik reached for one of the onboard telephones and keyed in a number.

"Kerim, I wish to speak to you. Come to the main lounge, please."

Malik stood and crossed to the window and stared out. He was content to face the open sea, drawing on its peaceful aspect. He allowed his mind to wander, his thoughts taking him far away from his physical location to a place that existed only in his dreams—a place of beauty, of tranquillity, where the struggles of the living form were banished and there was nothing but spiritual awareness. It was a place he went to often, banishing the toils of the world around him and giving him times of joy and satisfaction he couldn't find elsewhere.

"You wished to speak to me?"

Malik was drawn swiftly back to reality. He took a breath and turned to confront Kerim, his chief of security on board the ship.

"Kerim, there is a possibility that we may have been compromised. At this moment it is only a possibility. However, we are at a critical phase of the ongoing operation, and bearing that in mind I am going to move us away from this location. I want you to put the crew on its guard. Maintain around-the-clock watches. Could you also tell Captain Ghadi that I will be along to speak with him very shortly and could he start to work out a new course. In the meantime, we should make sail."

Kerim nodded. "I will do it immediately, sir. Is there anything else?"

"Yes. Make sure that the laboratory is protected at all times. I will inform Dr. Petrocovich myself."

Kerim nodded and left the lounge.

"Georgi? Are you feeling a little more comfortable now?"

The Russian raised his glass in a mock salute. "A little."

Malik smiled. Such dour people, these Russians, he thought. Never happy unless they had something to grumble about.

Making his way from the lounge to the open deck, where the hot sun contrasted with the air-conditioned coolness of the interior, Malik walked along the deck to the hatch that allowed access to the lab section. He pushed through the door that opened onto the wide area that formed the outer pressure doors and keyed the com switch. Moments later Petrocovich's voice reached him.

"What is it?"

"May I come in, Ilyana?"

The connection clicked off. Malik heard the deep hiss of air as the pressure door began to open. He stepped into the air lock and waited until the outer door closed again. The pressure altered as air was pushed back into the section, finally settling as it reached the correct pressure. He felt the warm pulse as the ultrasonic washed over him. The inner door opened, sliding on its hydraulics, and he was able to step into the clinical environment of Ilyana Petrocovich's secret world.

She was at her desk, keying information into her computer system. As Malik crossed the lab floor, she peered at him over the top of the monitor.

"Is something wrong?"

"Since that helicopter flew by, Georgi has become nervous. As a precaution, I have decided we should move from this area and relocate. I've just spoken to Kerim about increasing security around the ship. Men will be on guard outside at all times."

"Is all this going to interfere with my work?"

"Not at all. There will be nothing to interrupt you."

"In that case I don't see why you need to bother me witn the details."

"Ilyana, I bother you only out of courtesy. Your welı-being is my concern."

For a moment her mask slipped and she was as vulnerable as any normal person. Malik was sure he saw a faint flush color her cheeks. She stopped her work, clearing her throat.

"Yes. Of course. That was rude of me, Malik. Forgive me. I get involved in all this, and I behave like a child. Thank you for your kindness."

"Good. Now I will leave you."

"Now that you are here," she said, pushing to her feet and walking around the desk, "I think you should see this."

She crossed to one of the steel lockers, secured by a digital keypad. Tapping in the numbers, she waited for the door to click open before reaching inside and drawing out one of the steel cylinders she had been working on. She held it out for Malik to see.

"The first of the prepared devices."

Malik ran his gaze over the gleaming tube. The pressure valve was in place, and he realized that he was looking at one of Ilyana's gene bombs.

He wanted to reach out to take it but held back. Despite everything he knew about Petrocovich and her strict safeguards, being in such close proximity to the deadly new device made him nervous. Malik was no coward. He had placed himself in many dangerous situations as a terrorist. Armed conflict held no fear for him. He had killed a number of times, and he had been in danger more times than he could recall. Yet all that fell away as he stood inches away from the cold, sterile metal container that held the invisible virus the Russian had created. The steel container, moisture shining wetly on the burnished metal, had the look of death about it. This object killed by stealth, by releasing microscopic germs that destroyed human life without a sound. The knowledge that this particular strain had been devised to attack only a certain gene chain, and would leave anyone without it unharmed, didn't give him any comfort. It was, he realized, the natural reaction to unseen danger. A knife or a bullet, they could be understood and feared in their own right. But this virus held a different threat, and Malik feared it.

"It's safe," Petrocovich said, sensing his unease. "Until the valve is opened there is no risk."

"I don't doubt you. Nevertheless, I prefer to do my celebrating with that back in its cabinet."

He watched her return the cylinder and lock the door.

"How soon before the rest are complete?"

"A little while. I can only complete them one at a time. The process is lengthy and needs to be handled carefully."

"I'll leave you. Congratulations, Ilyana. You said you would do it. I never doubted that. I will make certain you will not be disturbed. If you need anything just ask."

"Thank you, Malik."

Kosovo

GARY MANNING, crouching behind an outcropping, leveled his crossbow, feeling the smooth stock firm against his cheek. He drew down on his target, an FAP guard who stood over a machine-gun emplacement. He had an AK-74 slung over one shoulder of his thick, padded coat, and as he paced back and forth near the machine gun he was blowing on his bare hands.

Some yards behind, Rafael Encizo checked out the area beyond and behind. With his night-vision goggles in place, the Cuban was able to make out a clearer picture of the escarpment. The guard Manning was dealing with was the only one they had spotted so far. Encizo felt certain there would be others. All they had to do was spot them and take them out before an alarm was raised.

Slipping his finger back against the crossbow's taut trigger, Manning held his target and fired, the soft whoosh of the bolt the only sound as it was hurled from the bow. He followed its flight to where it ended, buried deep in the guard's throat. The FAP man stiffened, then dropped to the rocky ground without a sound.

Manning reloaded, placing another bolt in the slide before changing position. He covered the ground to the machine gun emplacement and checked the weapon. It was a 7.62 mm Beretta MG-42/59. Manning took out the magazine and passed it to Encizo as the Cuban rejoined him. Encizo bent over the weapon and quickly stripped out the firing mechanism.

"You seen any others yet?" Manning asked.

"No. But I'm pretty sure this guy wasn't on his own."

They moved forward, searching the area. Encizo put out a hand to pause his companion. Manning followed his finger and saw a second guard on a ledge some feet higher than their position. The man leaned against the rock behind him, the glow of a cigarette tip pinpointing his position.

Manning crouched and raised the crossbow. His shot was on target, thumping into the guard's heart. The stricken man keeled over, slithering down the rock to stop in a sitting position, the cigarette still clamped between his lips.

Encizo keyed his throat mike.

"Two down," he reported to McCarter.

McCarter tapped Tanner on the shoulder and the pair moved to join Manning and Encizo. They passed the first dead guard and moments later were kneeling in a tight group with the others.

"Didn't see any movement where we were," McCarter said. "If these two were working a close area, maybe the entrance is around here."

"Can anyone smell diesel fumes?" Tanner asked.

Encizo raised his head. "Yeah. Over there."

They moved in single file. Tanner brought up the rear, constantly checking their back trail.

"Here," Manning said.

They clustered around the section of steel tubing that jutted from a crevice in the rock. The acrid smell of diesel fumes was strong now as it pumped from the blackened end of the exhaust duct.

"Here's the main tube," Tanner said, indicating the corrugated metal that snaked across the rocky surface of the escarpment.

They followed it back to where it emerged from

a narrow opening atop a shelf of rock. Looking over the edge of the shelf, McCarter saw a large opening that led into the heart of the escarpment. To his right, some ten to fifteen feet away, was another machine-gun emplacement. He rolled back from the edge and beckoned Manning.

"Machine-gun emplacement. Two-man team. One by the gun, the other to his right, back to the gun."

Manning loaded the crossbow. He handed a second bolt to McCarter, who followed him to the ledge. Leaning over at an angle to give himself a clear shot, the big Canadian fired the first bolt at the man behind the machine gun. Even as the guard slumped forward, the bolt protruding from the back of his neck, Manning was drawing back the bowstring. He took the bolt from McCarter and loaded it. The second guard was starting to turn when Manning triggered his final shot, laying the cyanide bolt in his chest. The guard went down without a murmur.

"Let's go, lads," McCarter said.

He led the way over the ledge and down the rough slope. Encizo bent over the machine gun and disabled it as he had done to the one on the escarpment. Removing the parts from the first machine gun from his black suit, Encizo threw them, along with those from the second gun, far into the darkness.

The four warriors gathered at the entrance to the FAP base. Fluorescent lights were hung from the ceiling of what looked like a rough-hewn tunnel, which appeared to push deep into the escarpment.

"What the hell is this place?" Tanner asked.

"Natural caves extended into living quarters. Probably something left over from World War II," Manning said. "The FAP haven't had time to build this. I guess they just moved in and set up shop."

"I don't give a damn who the bloody builder was," McCarter growled. "All I want is to get our guys out and shut this place down."

They eased into the entrance and followed the tunnel. It was poorly lit, and the lights strung from hooks embedded in the tunnel roof flickered fitfully. It was cold in the tunnel, and the air had a musty odor to it.

McCarter held up his hand as the subdued murmur of voices reached them. Up ahead they could hear the clatter of booted feet on hard rock. As they rounded a curve, McCarter saw that the tunnel forked some yards in front of them.

"That's all we bloody well need," he whispered to Manning.

"All we can do is split," Manning said. "Take a tunnel each and keep in touch with the radios."

"Sarge, you come with me," McCarter ordered. "At least I can understand what you say."

Tanner grinned and fell in beside the Briton. McCarter took the left-hand tunnel, leaving Manning and Encizo with the right fork.

Within a few yards the tunnel began to descend. McCarter, in the lead, trained his MP-5 on the upcoming bend. Pressed tight against the tunnel wall, he peered around the bend and saw that the way ahead widened into a large cave with a curving roof. There was better light there, with a number of fluorescent lights draped around the walls. He saw military-style cots and blankets and a scattering of equipment boxes. Computers and allied pieces of hardware sat on tables, and cables snaked back and forth across the stone floor. A radio-communications station stood at the far side of the cave area. Voices were coming from a speaker. The radio was tuned to a talk show.

McCarter saw three figures, clad in an assortment of military and civilian clothing, sitting on upturned crates near the radio set. They were listening closely to what was being said. McCarter couldn't understand the language, but he did pick up some familiar references to NATO and the United Nations. There was even a reference to the U.S.A. The trio listening to the radio conversation kept interrupting. McCarter couldn't tell whether they were agreeing with the speaker or were against him.

McCarter felt Tanner's hand on his arm. He followed the sergeant's finger and saw two more men enter the cave from an access tunnel on the far side. Both men were arguing loudly. One of them was a lean, dark-haired man with features that were almost gaunt. From his manner he seemed to be the one in charge. He was disagreeing bitterly with his companion.

The pair came to a dead stop as the gaunt-faced man yelled something angrily and made a sharp, dismissive gesture at the other, then walked away.

"Wonder what that was all about?" McCarter asked.

"Don't know what it was about, but I do know we haven't got time to find out," Tanner replied urgently.

McCarter turned and as he did, he picked up the clatter of booted feet coming from the tunnel behind them.

"Bloody hell!" McCarter said.

Tanner, aware that their presence was about to be revealed, reached for a stun grenade. He plucked it from his harness, popped the pin and hurled it back along the tunnel.

"Fire in the hole," he shouted.

He and McCarter ducked their heads and covered their ears. The grenade detonated, filling the tunnel with its noise and light. Despite covering their ears, the two men still heard the crack. It left their ears ringing, but at least they were still able to function, unlike the three FAP terrorists who were stumbling around with deaf ears, and eyes that could see nothing but a bright white glare.

"Let's get out of here, Sarge," McCarter yelled.

He pushed away from the bend in the tunnel and broke into the main cave area. The three terrorists who had been sitting by the radio had jumped to their feet, grabbing at the weapons they had put aside temporarily.

McCarter took out the first man with a short burst from his MP-5 that toppled the guy as he was about to raise his AK-74. The subgun's sharp crackle filled the cave with noise. Pushing forward, McCarter traded shots with the other two terrorists. His calm approach to combat situations still as controlled as ever, the Briton had the natural ability of being able to think and act fast on his feet. He took the sudden change from concealment to violent conflict in his stride.

Beside him, Tanner was locked on to the other FAP men. His own MP-5 stuttered briefly, spitting out just enough fire to get the job done. He caught his first target on the move, cutting the guy down with a well-placed burst to the upper chest, then turned the muzzle of his weapon on the fourth terrorist. That man had the presence of mind to turn sideways, presenting a slimmer target, and he brought his AK-74 into play with the same movement, triggering in Tanner's direction. The SAS man felt something tug his left sleeve. Almost immediately his arm went numb, fingers dropping away from the MP-5. Tanner increased his grip on the weapon with his right hand, supporting it until he could return fire and drive the terrorist back with a short burst. As his target fell back, the sergeant braced the MP-5 against his side and arced the barrel around, catching the FAP gunner in his sights and firing the moment target acquisition was achieved. The burst drilled the guy in the throat, spinning him, and Tanner followed up with a second burst that ripped into the guy's exposed back. This time the target went down hard and stayed down.

McCarter, halfway across the cave, took out the remaining terrorist with a chest shot. The man went backward, stumbling and crashing into the radio communications station. The com set crashed to the floor, tearing cables free from their sockets. The action blew the lights within the cave area, plunging it into near darkness. McCarter pulled his night-vision goggles into place and scanned the area.

He saw Tanner leaning against the cave wall,

nursing a bloody arm. McCarter moved to his side and pulled the man's goggles into place.

"That's better," Tanner said. "At least I can see where I'm going now."

"How's the arm, Sarge?"

"I've had worse. Feeling's coming back now. It was only a bloody graze, but I lost the use for a minute."

"You still mobile?"

"Too bloody right, sir."

McCarter turned away from the SAS man, swinging his MP-5 around as he picked up the scrape of booted feet behind them.

Three terrorists who had been stopped by the flash-bang grenade had rounded the tunnel end and were coming on, firing as they appeared. McCarter pushed Tanner to the floor, following him down. Both men angled their weapons up and emptied their magazines into the advancing trio, knocking them off their feet in a hail of bullets.

"Persistent if nothing else," McCarter muttered.

Before they moved, both McCarter and Tanner ejected the spent magazines and replaced them with fresh ones. They cocked the MP-5s.

"You set, Sarge?"

"Give the word."

On their feet, they crossed the darkened cave and took up positions on either side of the tunnel leading off. McCarter took another flash-bang and tossed it down the tunnel. After the detonation, he and Tanner ducked into the corridor and moved forward, the MP-5 muzzles tracking ahead.

In the green image picked up by his goggles,

McCarter saw that the tunnel angled sharply to the left only yards ahead. There were untidy stacks of supply cartons, boxes and other pieces of equipment lining the walls of the tunnel. Some inner sense warned the Briton to be careful. Even as the thought formed in his mind, McCarter spotted a flurry of movement ahead of them, then the sudden, jerky movement of someone breaking into action. A dark shape erupted from behind a stack of cartons, the weapon in his hands aimed in the direction of the advancing commandos. McCarter had time to yell a warning to Tanner before the weapon he had spotted opened up with a vengeance. Firing blind, the FAP terrorist swept the tunnel, his autoweapon chattering loudly, shell casings ringing sharply as they hit the stone floor.

McCarter and Tanner hit the floor a split second before the vicious outburst. They maintained their prone position as the crisscross hail of slugs peppered the tunnel walls around them. The moment the firing stopped they raised themselves and returned fire, driving the gunner back along the tunnel. The man desperately tried to reload as he retreated, and just when he had to have been considering the rashness of his assault, one of his companions joined him, taking up the front position and raking the tunnel in a repeat performance.

Pulled in tight against the tunnel walls behind some crates, McCarter and Tanner rode out the gunfire in patient silence.

"This is bloody crazy!" Tanner yelled above the racket of shots.

McCarter had to agree. The uncontrolled firing

was bad enough. The fact that it was holding them back only increased his frustration. The Phoenix Force leader plucked a fragmentation grenade from his harness, pulled the pin and hurled the bomb toward the shadowy gunners. The firing continued up to the moment the grenade detonated, filling the tunnel with noise, smoke and flying debris. A single scream echoed along the tunnel, then the firing ceased. The crash of falling rock continued for a while.

Tanner crawled across to where McCarter was kneeling. When the air cleared, they continued along the tunnel, stepping over fallen rock and shattered equipment. One body lay against the tunnel wall, clothing shredded and still smoking.

At the bend the two men took time, checking the way ahead before moving on. At the far end of the section they were in the lights were still working, and they were able to remove their goggles.

McCarter took out his transceiver and tried to contact Manning and Encizo. All he got was a harsh blast of static, with little sound that was recognizable. He tried various settings but was unable to clear the interference.

"The signal isn't strong enough to penetrate," Tanner said after trying his own set. "Could be metal strata in the rock blocking the transmission. The FAP radios will be working off external aerials so they won't be blocked."

"Now he tells me," McCarter grumbled.

He jammed the transceiver back in his pocket and trudged on, following the rising floor of the tunnel. They came to a heavy wood and iron door set in the wall that blocked off the tunnel. McCarter tried to open it, but the door appeared to be locked.

"Buggers are trying to box us in," McCarter said. "Sarge, either we break through here or go all the bloody way back. What do you think?"

"SAS never got around to teaching us about retreating. I think some joker ripped that section out of the manual."

"No time for holding back then, Sarge," McCarter said.

He took out one of the explosive packs and checked it, setting the timer for thirty seconds before laying it against the base of the door and activating the timer.

As he and Tanner moved back along the tunnel, the SAS man nudged McCarter's arm.

"Bloody big charge just to take out a door, isn't it, sir?"

McCarter crouched down against the tunnel floor, pulling Tanner down with him.

"What's wrong, Sarge, you want to live forever?"

"The next few minutes would be nice, sir."

The charge detonated with force enough to make the floor under them ripple. The resultant blast filled the tunnel with smoke and flying debris. Shattered stone and dust rained on the two men even though they were well beyond the initial force of the explosion.

McCarter pushed to his feet and headed for the hazy outline of the wrecked doorway. He clattered over the pile of debris, pausing to scan what was on the other side before barreling through, his MP-5 crackling harshly as he encountered resistance.

Shaking his head Tanner followed, aware that he was in the presence of a warrior who upheld everything the SAS stood for. Straight-on courage, blended with a sharp brain and a streak of reckless determination to outwit and outfight the enemy regardless of the odds.

"Watch your perimeter, Sarge," McCarter yelled as Tanner broke through the shattered doorway and straight into a confrontation with a group of dazed, slightly confused, but still capable terrorists.

Tanner turned, his weapon up, eyes scanning the shadowy area. A couple of lights still worked, casting a fractured spread of illumination across the wide, cavernous area.

The rattle of AK-74s broke through and Tanner, already one step ahead of his would-be assailants, took a dive that brought him to ground level. He twisted, turning on his side, and raked the closest of the FAP gunners as they began to bring their weapons on-line again. His first burst punched through dusty clothing into yielding flesh, the target falling back without a sound. The stricken man collided with one of his companions, interrupting the man's actions. The hesitation gave Tanner his next shot, and he took it without pause. The MP-5 crackled sharply, the short burst tearing into the target's chest, turning him fully one-hundred-eighty degrees. With blood spilling from his mouth, the terrorist slumped to the stony ground.

McCarter, secure in the knowledge that Tanner had his side in hand, turned his attention to the group moving in his direction. Standing firm, he swept his MP-5 in a scything action that caught the three FAP men totally off guard. The speed at which McCarter responded was way beyond anything the terrorists could match. They were, to a man, still bringing their weapons into play when he opened fire. The controlled burst cut into them with the ease of a knife through water. There was no resistance. The 9 mm slugs hammered their targets off their feet.

"Let's go, Sarge," McCarter called, crossing the cavern and heading for the exit tunnel on the far side.

They left behind a number of downed FAP men and a storage area reduced to a chaotic mess by the blast from McCarter's door buster.

The tunnel angled in all directions, sometimes lit by fluorescent lights while other sections lay in shadow.

From some distance away they picked up the sound of autofire. The acoustics of the tunnel and the surrounding mass of rock made it difficult to pin down exactly where the sound was coming from, but McCarter guessed that somewhere within the rabbit warren of the FAP base, Manning and Encizo had found the enemy.

THE TUNNEL MANNING and Encizo traveled took them on a downward slope. The lighting here was poor and they activated their night-vision goggles. The rubber-soled boots they wore made no sound as they negotiated the twisting tunnels. After five minutes they emerged on a flat area with roughly hewn steps that dropped down a steep rock face.

"After you," Manning said.

Encizo grinned at his partner. "Only because you asked so nicely."

They negotiated the steps cautiously. There was no barrier on the outer side of the steps, just open air and a considerable drop. They reached bottom without incident, pausing to check their surroundings.

The light was stronger, with multiple tunnels leading off from the base of the steps.

"Don't you just love choices," Manning said.

The decision was made for them when the sound of a heavy door crashing shut reached their ears. The Phoenix Force commandos headed in that direction, seeking the source.

As they moved deeper into the tunnel, caution dictated their actions. Neither man expected their incursion into the FAP stronghold to be easy. They anticipated the worst and were fully prepared for any change in conditions. In the event, that caution paid off. As they approached a distinct bend in the tunnel, Encizo threw out a warning hand.

Manning glanced at his partner. "What?"

Encizo beckoned his teammate to the side of the tunnel. For the second time Encizo put out his hand, one finger extended to emphasize what he was showing Manning.

At the apex of the bend, where the inner wall curved sharply, the big Canadian spotted faint, almost indistinct shadows. On the face of it, they were nothing unusual, given the lighting conditions with the underground complex. But in this case the shadows belonged to men. They weren't the solid, immobile shadows cast by the rock walls of the tunnel. These shadows moved—fractionally perhaps, but the movement had been enough to alert Encizo and prevent the two men from walking into waiting guns.

Taking a fragmentation grenade from his combat harness, Encizo eased out the pin. He leaned away from the tunnel wall, gauging the angle of the bend before drawing back his arm and releasing the spring-loaded lever. He took a slow count, then tossed the grenade. It struck the far wall, bouncing off and curving around the inner bend.

In the instant before the detonation the Phoenix Force commandos heard cries of alarm as the waiting terrorists realized what had happened. Then their shouts were drowned out by the explosion. Smoke billowed from the bend, followed by a shower of debris. A coughing figure, smoke curling from his smoldering jacket, staggered into view. His face was bloody, but not as much as his back where he had caught the full force of the grenade blast. He stumbled past Manning and Encizo, staggering before he slumped to his knees, then fell facedown on the tunnel floor.

"Good call," Manning said as he moved past Encizo, his MP-5 up and ready.

Rounding the bend in the tunnel, Manning took in the chaotic scene at a glance. Three men down, their weapons on the ground with them. None of them were moving. Encizo's bouncing grenade had caught them off guard.

The tunnel beyond the kill zone lay open and clear. Manning took the lead, moving at a quicker pace now. The FAP would be on full alert, with armed terrorists scouring the tunnels looking for the invaders.

They reached an intersection.

"Your call this time," Encizo said.

Manning made his choice. "We go left."

They moved along the tunnel. The floor began to rise, and after a couple of minutes Manning and Encizo saw that the tunnel was widening.

Light blazed ahead of them. The illumination in this section was stronger than any they had encountered before. As the tunnel came to an end, the commandos were able to remove their goggles and check it out.

A large, natural grotto spread out before them. Scattered around the floor were numerous stacks of supplies—weapons, munitions, cartons of canned food, medical supplies. There were a couple of easels, holding large boards onto which were pinned charts and maps. The light came from a number of strategically placed powerful halogen lamps. On the far side of the grotto, heavy metal doors had been fitted to what looked like cells hewn out of the rock. The doors were solid, without any grilles. If people were inside those cells, they would be totally isolated.

The grotto was alive with movement. A number of armed men were moving back and forth, obviously under orders to stay alert.

"I'm guessing Cal and T.J. are in those cells," Manning stated.

"Only way we'll find out is to take a look," Encizo replied.

Manning unlimbered his crossbow and loaded a bolt.

"Let's reduce the odds," he said.

Encizo unclipped a couple of his flash-bang grenades and held them ready.

Manning fired the first bolt. It buried itself between the shoulders of one terrorist, dropping him silently, without any of his companions noticing. The big Canadian fitted another shaft into the bow, aimed and took out a second man. As he slumped to the floor, the shaft protruding from his neck, one of his partners was alerted. He yelled a warning and turned, raising his AK-74.

Encizo tossed the two flash-bang grenades, both he and Manning dropping for cover and turning away from the detonations. Although the area of the grotto dissipated the power of the grenades to a degree, there was still enough to disorientate the FAP terrorists for a time.

With their weapons up and ready, the Phoenix Force warriors broke from cover and raced into the grotto, firing on the run. The short, effective bursts from the MP-5s caught the terrorists even as they attempted to shake off the effects of the grenades. Three went down under the first salvo. Then Manning and Encizo parted company, each man covering a section of the grotto, their combined fire catching the FAP men before they could run for cover.

Encizo dived for cover behind a stack of crates, then leaned out to drill the terrorist who was moving in on his position. The man went down, bloody and burned by the shots to his chest. He lay kicking away the remaining seconds of his life as Encizo stepped by him and advanced across the grotto, his intense fire taking down anyone who came in his sights. The Cuban only paused long enough to reload the MP-5 before he reached the far side of the grotto, flattening himself against the rock wall, ready to face any resistance coming his way.

Manning had faced stiffer resistance initially, coming up against a pair of terrorists who had avoided the full effects of the flash-bang grenades. They took one look at the Canadian's black-clad figure and opened up with their firearms. One of the men carried an AK-74 while his partner was wielding a Makarov pistol. Manning took evasive, if drastic, action. He took two long strides and launched himself in a reckless dive over a stack of ammunition boxes. He crashed to the floor on the other side, rolling frantically. He slammed into more boxes, scattering them in all directions. He twisted his body, pulling the MP-5 tight against his chest, and triggered a long burst as the first of his pursuers appeared. The terrorist flipped backward, his face and throat bloody. Manning scrambled across the floor, still keeping his subgun on target. He caught a fleeting glimpse of the second FAP man, brandishing the Makarov pistol. The guy triggered a wild shot that chipped the floor close by Manning's feet. Bringing the pistol around, the man fired again, the slug burning across the back of the big Canadian's thigh as he pulled away.

Manning gasped as he felt the gouging action of the bullet. He steadied the MP-5 and locked on to the moving gunner, triggering a sustained blast that caught the guy chest high. The FAP man let out a shocked cry as he went down, his head smacking against the hard floor. He arched over on his back, pain etched across his face, the pistol spilling from his fingers.

Rolling to his feet, clicking a fresh magazine into place, Manning searched for Encizo. The Cuban raised a hand from the far side of the grotto. Manning joined him by the pair of heavy steel doors. The one closer to them stood ajar. Encizo dragged it open and peered into the cell, which was empty. They moved to the next cell. The closed door was secured by thick slide bolts. Encizo snapped the bolts back and dragged the door open. Bright light spilled from the cell.

Calvin James and T.J. Hawkins were slumped against the back wall. They were conscious but looked to be in a bad condition. They were beaten and bloody, their faces swollen into puffy masks. Encizo stood guard at the door while Manning entered the cell and checked out their teammates.

"Room service in this place is terrible," James mumbled through puffed, split lips. "I asked for a Canadian on the rocks and look what they sent."

"Talk like that will get you another six months in this place," Manning said.

"I love Canadians," Hawkins whispered, his words a husky croak.

"Let's get you bums out of here," Manning said.

He helped James and Hawkins to their feet. They clung to the wall for a moment until their bodies adjusted to the change.

"Man, do I need some R&R," James muttered.

At the door to the cell Encizo greeted his teammates.

"Cal, I got to say I've seen you looking better."

They moved off across the grotto, pausing only to pick up discarded weapons at the insistence of James and Hawkins. Each man, clutching an acquired handgun, admitted to feeling better. With Manning in the lead and Encizo bringing up the rear, the foursome made their way to the far tunnel. At the entrance Manning asked for a brief pause. He returned to the grotto and placed a couple of the explosive packs in position among the munitions, setting the timers for thirty minutes.

"Okay, let's go."

They traveled the tunnel for a few hundred yards, picking up the distant sounds of gunfire as they were able to hear the conflict between McCarter and Tanner and the FAP terrorists.

Emerging from their tunnel they were met by sudden autofire as waiting terrorists opened fire too soon. Pulling back, Manning plucked a fragmentation grenade from his harness and pulled the pin. He rolled the bomb along the adjoining tunnel, then waved his partners back. The grenade exploded with a harsh crack, filling the tunnels with smoke and the patter of debris as it fell from the tunnel roof. Intermingled with the rumble of the explosion they heard someone yelling in pain.

The tunnel was fogged with smoke and dust. As Manning poked his head and shoulders around the bend, the muzzle of his MP-5 ahead of him, a dusty figure stumbled toward him carrying an AK-74. The moment he saw Manning he opened fire. Stone chips exploded from the tunnel wall above Manning's head. The Kalashnikov jammed after a half dozen shots, giving the big Canadian the time he needed to aim and return fire. The 9 mm slugs pitched the terrorist back along the tunnel, where he stumbled over shattered rock and went down.

"Company coming," Encizo warned. He had heard the clatter of boots in the tunnel behind them.

Turning, the Cuban took a fragmentation grenade from his combat harness and pulled the pin. He lobbed the bomb back along the tunnel, heard it strike the hard ground, then rattle as it rolled. The detonation echoed the length of the tunnel, the clatter of falling rock following the fading sound of the explosion. Smoke billowed back to where Phoenix Force crouched.

A bloody, tattered figure lurched out of the smoke, clutching an AK-74. The terrorist slumped against the tunnel wall, his streaming eyes focusing on the four men before him. He muttered something none of them could understand as he fumbled with the autorifle.

"Just isn't your day, you son of a bitch," James gritted as he stepped forward and put two shots into the man's chest.

Manning eased around the bend in the tunnel. The way ahead was deserted, the floor littered with debris from the grenade explosion. Two bodies lay among the fallen rock. The scene was lit by flickering fluorescent lights, the fastenings on some torn loose so that they hung by the cables, swinging back and forth. The movement caused heavy shadows to flit back and forth across the tunnel walls.

"Hey, guys, how do we get back over the border?" Hawkins asked.

"They sending in a chopper for us?" James added.

"No. We have to make our own way out. The situation has changed. Looks like NATO is going to start making bombing runs to try and persuade the Serbians to back off."

"And we're right in the middle?" Hawkins asked. "I think I'll go back to my cell."

"They brought us in by truck," James said. "If we can find it maybe that's our way out."

"Sure," Encizo said. "If we can work out where the damn back door to this place is."

A distant, dull boom echoed through the tunnels. Someone had set off an explosive charge. Then the crackle of autofire sounded ahead of them. It ceased for a couple of minutes, then started again.

"I'll guess that's David and the sarge."

"Tanner came with you?" James asked.

"Yeah. He figured we needed the help."

"That's one good old boy," Hawkins said.

They moved along the tunnel, using the same formation of Manning in the lead and Encizo bringing up the rear. They met no opposition until the tunnel began to widen to form a natural cave. At one side, from a fissure some ten to twelve feet up, clear water gushed into a deep basin. The floor of this cave was littered with fallen rocks and great slabs of stone, splintered and shattered from eruptions within the escarpment decades ago.

Muzzle flashes winked in the dimly lighted area. Used shell casings, ejected from gun ports, rattled against the stones as they fell. There appeared to be a concentration of fire from just ahead of where Phoenix Force had emerged from the tunnel, and only minimal fire from the other position on the far side.

Manning checked out the disposition of the hostile force and counted at least eight of them. The FAP terrorists were exchanging heavy fire with McCarter and Tanner, who had taken cover behind a massive slab of stone.

They all checked that their weapons were fully loaded and ready before Manning gave the nod.

The concentrated fire from the new arrivals took the terrorists by surprise. As a number of their companions went down under the solid volley of slugs, a number of the terrorists turned their guns in that direction, triggering uncontrolled shots at shadows.

Manning leaned out from cover and laid a short burst into one man who was trying to move in closer. The shots caught him in full flight, punching him off balance. The terrorist went facedown, slithering across the rock slab he was on, and toppled into the pool of water filling the deep rock basin.

The firefight was merciless in its intent. No quarter was even considered by either side. The FAP terrorists were determined not to acquiesce to the invaders. Phoenix Force was equally determined to put a stop to the plans the FAP had for creating death and suffering on the U.S. mainland and to America's allies.

Manning used his remaining fragmentation grenade to clear the way through to McCarter and Tanner. As the last of the FAP terrorists stumbled from the blast area, they were cut down in a withering cross fire.

"Let's go," Manning said.

With Encizo's help, he got James and Hawkins to the far side of the cave and a brief reuniting with McCarter and Tanner.

"You can thank us later," McCarter said breezily. "Right now we need to get the hell out of this bloody place."

"Sooner rather than later," Manning advised. "I set a couple of charges in their munitions store." He glance at his watch. "We've got about twelve minutes left."

"The guys were brought in by truck," Encizo said. "We could use that to get out of the area."

McCarter nodded. He pointed to the tunnel branching off from the cave.

"We'll try that one."

As they moved out of the cave, Encizo placed one of his explosive packs at the entrance, setting the timer for eleven minutes. Pushing along the tunnel, they realized the floor was rising. They reached a junction, and set another explosive pack before they moved off.

James and Hawkins were starting to slow down. The punishment they had received at the hands of the terrorists was catching up with them. Seeing that, McCarter assigned Manning to James and Encizo to Hawkins, and the two Phoenix Force warriors lent their strength and support to their weaker colleagues.

It slowed their pace considerably, but there was no choice.

Reaching the very end of the tunnel, McCarter held up his hand. He stood for a moment before he could confirm that he had felt a cold draft of air on his face.

"This way," he said.

He strode along the tunnel, pausing as he saw a hesitant shadow around the natural bend. McCarter, aware of the diminishing time they had left, didn't hesitate. He plunged forward, moving out so that as he rounded the bend he was against the far wall, away from the terrorist who was waiting for him. By the time the FAP man realized he had been out-thought, McCarter's H&K emitted a short burst and the terrorist stumbled back with ragged holes in his chest and his blood on the tunnel wall behind him.

The tunnel led to an open plateau, with a fuel dump and the truck James had mentioned. It was old and battered, but McCarter wasn't looking for the latest-model Cadillac.

"Get the lads inside," he said briskly. "Sarge, keep watch."

McCarter took the remaining explosive packs and set one at the tunnel entrance and the final one in among the fuel drums.

"Check the fuel in this bloody thing. I don't want the tank running dry before we get down the mountain."

With James and Hawkins inside the back of the truck, Manning went to check the fuel supply and found it two-thirds full. There was a drum already set up, with a siphon pump in place. Manning pumped in gasoline until the tank overflowed. In the meantime Encizo located a couple of jerricans full of water and placed them in the rear so they could top up the radiator if it overheated.

"Look lively, lads," Tanner said. "Company coming."

"Everyone on board," McCarter yelled. "That means you too, Sarge."

Tanner backed away from the tunnel entrance. He was almost to the truck when armed figures appeared at the tunnel entrance. Tanner drove them back with a burst from his MP-5, the spray of slugs peppering the terrorists and ricocheting from the rock around the opening. He hit the same area with a second burst before turning and racing for the truck. He threw his weapon over the tailgate, grabbed the edge of the boards and hauled himself into the vehicle.

"Let's get out of here," he yelled at McCarter.

The Briton floored the clutch and pushed the heavy gearshift into first, then stepped on the gas. The engine roared, the rear tires gripping, spinning, then gaining purchase again. The lumbering vehicle moved off, picking up speed with surprising swiftness. McCarter had to wrestle with the steering. It was a true heavy truck, built for endurance rather than ease of handling. McCarter coaxed the machine along the rutted, precarious track, hauling on the steering wheel to keep the vehicle from scraping the rock face on their right-hand side.

Behind them the surviving terrorists who had come out of the tunnel raised their weapons and opened fire. Bullets peppered the rear of the truck, embedding themselves in the solid wood of its body.

Return fire took out two of them, forcing the others back inside.

In the noisy cab of the truck, Manning glanced quickly at his watch.

"First ones should be about now."

There was nothing for a few long seconds, then the deep rumble of the detonations reached them as Manning's packs went off and took the FAP munitions with them. The explosion spread along the tunnels, reaching deep below ground as well as spiraling up through the levels. Subsequent explosions told Phoenix Force the other packs had detonated, as well. Last to go were the ones at the tunnel mouth and the fuel dump. The drums of fuel erupted in a boiling mass of flame that reached high into the night sky, expanding out as well as up. The heat seared vegetation around the area. A thick cloud of smoke gushed out from the tunnel mouth, mingling with that from the fuel dump. The air was thick with debris dropping back to earth.

McCarter caught a glimpse of the explosions in the mirror attached to his cab door. He didn't pay much attention to the spectacle. He had seen it all before. He had enough on his hands controlling the truck. It was turning out to be harder to handle than he had first imagined. The vehicle had no sophistication about it. It was simply an engine on wheels, with a basic cab and body fitted to the chassis. The springing was crude, and the vehicle swayed alarmingly as McCarter fought to keep it on the steep track winding its way down the side of the escarpment.

The heavy explosions that had ripped through the

FAP base had subsided to a series of deep rumblings. The high wall of the escarpment cracked open and sent a cascade of rock tumbling down the slopes, crashing through the lower wooded sections, tearing out vegetation and leaving a thick dust cloud hanging over the area. The white snow clinging to the slopes was powdered gray from the settling cloud.

"That was the easy part," McCarter said to no one in particular. "Now all we have to do is get back across the bleeding border."

CHAPTER FOURTEEN

Millennium Explorer

The guard on watch at the stern of the *Millennium Explorer* saw the helicopter as it swept in from the east, coming up on the vessel at full speed. At first he was unable to make out any detail, except that it was a helicopter. As the craft closed in on the ship, he made out the shape, then the colorful design painted on its side. That was when he realized the aircraft was the same one that had buzzed them before. It had returned, but this time it wasn't making a lazy flypast. It was heading for the ship at high speed, and from where he was standing the guard felt sure it was about to collide with the stern of the ship.

What the guard didn't know was the name of the pilot.

JACK GRIMALDI'S INTENTION was to create a little unrest in the eye of any observer. To the watcher, it would look like he was going to crash. The natural reaction to that was for anyone in the vicinity to take cover. Or at least to step back. It might only be for a few seconds. A short time in anyone's book. But enough time for Grimaldi to deliver his cargo.

In this case it was Able Team, plus a few smoke canisters they would drop as they exited the chopper. It was a reckless way of boarding the *Millennium Explorer,* but in the circumstances it was the only way they could get on board quickly. The time factor was, as always, against them, and the stakes were too high to wait for any other opportunity. Their intervention was coming none too soon because the ship had already raised anchor and was on the move.

Seated in the rear of the cabin, Able Team was geared up and ready to go. The three men were armed with holstered handguns and carried 9 mm Uzi submachine guns on slings around their necks. Combat harnesses were hung with both fragmentation and stun grenades, and in pouch pockets they carried extra magazines for their weapons. Lyons and Blancanales also had extra shells for the SPAS shotguns they wore slung from their shoulders. They needed their hands free to put down the smoke canisters as Grimaldi took them to within a few feet of the deck. Once on board the ship they would use their combat skills to take out any opposition while Grimaldi remained in the vicinity, ready to call in the biohazard team when he was given the signal. As a basic precaution against any form of biological attack, the Able Team commandos also carried gas masks. Each man was equipped with a powerful transceiver so they could contact each other and Grimaldi.

"DZ coming up hard," Grimaldi called over the clatter of the rotors.

He pulled the JetRanger around, broadsiding it as the stern of the *Millennium Explorer* filled his field of vision. Utilizing the cyclic and the foot controls, Grimaldi brought the chopper to a midair stop. The machine swung with its own weight, then held steady.

"Go! Go! Go!" Grimaldi yelled over his shoulder.

The side door was already sliding back.

Lyons was first out. He threw his smoke canister and followed it, dropping the four feet to the deck. The moment his feet touched he reached for the SPAS.

Next out was Blancanales. His canister went to the right of the one Lyons had thrown.

In the few seconds between Lyons exiting the chopper and Schwarz making his appearance, the first canister had begun to spew out thick clouds of white smoke. Seconds later the one deposited by Blancanales did the same. The third canister added its contents to the rolling coils of smoke.

As soon as Schwarz had dropped from sight, Grimaldi eased back on the controls and the chopper slid away from the ship, clearing the vessel before Grimaldi took her up, circling in a wide, lazy arc that kept the *Millennium Explorer* in his sights the whole time.

On deck Able Team broke into their arranged configuration.

Lyons took center, with Blancanales on his right

and Schwarz on his left. In that order they advanced along the stern deck.

The guard who had spotted the approaching helicopter realized his error and reached out to hit the alarm button set into the bulkhead. Even as he heard the harsh sound of the alarm he knew that he would be held to blame for the fact the three men had set foot on board the ship. There would be no excuses. No second chance. Malik was a fair leader, but his ruthlessness in dealing with those who committed errors was known and feared.

The guard was a walking dead man. He accepted that and so took responsibility for his actions.

He checked the action of his Kalashnikov. Reciting a prayer, he moved to the edge of the upper deck where he was stationed and peered into the thick curtain of smoke that obscured the lower stern deck. The moving smoke played tricks with his eyes. More than once he imagined he saw a shape, then it dispersed and he knew he had been seeing only the smoke.

He failed to see the barrel of the SPAS combat shotgun as it emerged from the smoke below his vantage point. Nothing warned him. There was a sudden flash of light, followed by a numbing impact below his chin. He felt the world explode into bright color that quickly merged into darkness. The numbing impact rendered him unconscious and he died without knowing he had been decapitated by the near point-blank shot from Lyons's weapon.

The Able Team leader scaled the companionway, moving quickly along the upper deck. He spotted movement ahead. An armed figure clad in a white uniform fired in Lyons's direction. The hammer of the slugs against the metal bulkhead was followed by the singularly deafening boom of the SPAS. The concentrated charge took the target in the chest and slapped him to the deck, torn and bloody. Flat against the bulkhead, Lyons assessed his position before moving on.

He'd barely walked more than a few yards when armed figures clattered down a metal companionway, weapons cocked and ready. Lyons crouched, tracking the SPAS on the trio. He caught them before they reached the bottom of the steps, the blast from the shotgun taking out two of them in a mist of bloody red. They fell, screaming, bodies crashing to the deck. The surviving man twisted, shoving the muzzle of his autorifle between two of the steps, and touched the trigger. The spray of fire scored the metal over Lyons's head.

Lyons took seconds to lock onto his target. His SPAS shotgun boomed, and the gunner was caught chest high. He slammed into the bulkhead, held there by an invisible hand for a couple of seconds before the weight of his dying body dragged him down. He tumbled down the steps in a silent twist of arms and legs.

The Able Team leader raced up the companionway, the shotgun tracking ahead of him. When an angry face peered over the railing at the top of the steps, Lyons cut loose a single, powerful shot that drilled into the face and blew it apart. As he reached the next level, Lyons crouched low, taking his time to look over the last step. He saw a pair of armed gunners, clad in white, waiting for him. He freed a grenade, pulled the pin and lobbed the bomb toward his adversaries. They had to have spotted the explosive as it rattled across the deck plates, but they were too slow. The grenade detonated with a harsh bang.

Hitting the deck in a tight roll, Lyons leaped to his feet as he spotted a shadow of movement. He angled the shotgun around and pulled the trigger a split second before his attacker. The stocky, black-haired man went down with a brief yell, his abandoned weapon clattering across the deck.

Stepping over the guy Lyons advanced. He was heading for the bridge, his mission to stop the ship from continuing its voyage. Lyons knew he would meet resistance, and expected it.

He rounded a bulky ventilator unit and saw the panoramic window that fronted the *Millennium Explorer*'s bridge structure. The sound of gunfire had reached the ears of the crew inside the bridge. Armed men were scanning the deck area, and one of them spotted Lyons as the Able Team leader closed in on the bridge. The man raised the alarm, and crewmen rushed to the doors on either side of the bridge, emerging onto the deck.

Lyons took out the first pair to emerge, blowing the two men back through the door, glass shattering and peppering their faces. Lyons tossed aside the empty SPAS and unlimbered the Uzi. He ripped off a short burst, putting the 9 mm slugs into the chest of the first guy from the far side of the bridge. The man lost coordination and fell facedown on the deck, becoming an obstruction to the next man. As this one paused, only briefly, he became an ideal target for Lyons, who dropped him with a quick snap-burst to the head.

Lyons skidded into cover behind a raised hatch and rolled to the far side, bringing himself in line to trigger a burst into the running figures who had lost sight of him. They fell, struggling to bring their weapons to bear until Lyons fired again and stopped them permanently.

Reloading the Uzi, Lyons broke from cover, heading for the bridge. He raked the main window with a burst that splintered the glass, and as the crew members backed away, firing their weapons blindly, Lyons tossed in a smoke grenade. As the thick smoke filled the bridge, he sprinted to one of the doors and burst through. He emptied the Uzi into the smoke, hearing yells and moans, and then nothing.

With the smoke clearing, Lyons peered into the control room and saw that his targets were down. He checked the Uzi. Going back across the deck he retrieved his shotgun, quickly reloading the powerful weapon before he moved on.

ROSARIO BLANCANALES HIT the deck running, his SPAS shotgun cocked and ready as he took up his position. His view along the deck was momentarily obscured by the drifting coils of smoke. He waited until the cloud thinned, then moved on.

His caution was rewarded as a thickset man, wielding a stubby Uzi, came barreling out of the smoke. The man hadn't taken time to check the way ahead and ran directly into Blancanales's path. The Able Team commando ducked under the Uzi's muzzle, ramming the barrel of his shotgun into the guy's stomach. The gunner grunted, his finger jerking the trigger of the Uzi and sending a stream of slugs into the deck. Following through, Blancanales swung the SPAS into line and triggered a single shot that almost cut the target's torso in two. Before the corpse hit the deck Blancanales had moved on, merging with the smoke.

Reaching the first bulkhead, the Able Team commando saw an open hatch. He held back, checking the passage inside, and spotted a number of armed men crowding it as they rushed the hatchway.

Blancanales stepped into the opening, the SPAS leveled. He triggered a trio of shots down the passage, the spread of the charges taking out the advancing crewmen. They were cut down in a haze of red, a tangle of bodies and abandoned weapons.

The passage led Blancanales to cabins used for various shipboard operations. His main concern was the communications center, which he found at the far end. The door was closed. Blancanales slammed his boot into it and drove it open. A tall man turned from the radio, bringing his pistol to bear on the Able Team commando, but the SPAS was quicker. A single shot put the man down hard.

Blancanales checked out the radio. One of his objectives was to disable the communications. He had no time to waste, so he simply blew the set apart with a couple of shots from the SPAS. The powerful charge from the combat shotgun rendered the transceiver into shattered wreckage.

Shouldering the SPAS, Blancanales unlimbered his Uzi.

It was time to move on.

SCHWARZ MET no resistance until he was below-decks, heading for the engine room, his main objective. The problem with a vessel like the *Millennium Explorer* was the numerous passageways and doors leading off to other sections. They allowed for attack from any angle. The situation had little effect on Schwarz's movement. He had his task, and added complications had to be dealt with if and when they arose.

It took him only a couple of minutes to reach the lower deck, where the engines were situated. He could feel the pulse of the powerful diesel engines now. The vibration was transmitted through the metal deck plates and into the soles of his boots.

Schwarz abruptly stopped, listening to the murmur of voices ahead. He heard the unmistakable sound of a weapon being cocked. The metallic click was a sound that once heard was never forgotten. He took a quick look around. A few feet back he had passed a metal hatch. Backtracking, he placed his left hand on the lever that operated the hatch and pressed. It gave easily, moving on well-lubricated pins. Pushing against the door, Schwarz stepped over the bottom plate. He found he was in a small compartment that held the controls for the ship's pumping system. Schwarz partially closed the hatch and waited, the Uzi up and ready.

He didn't have to wait long. The sound of heavy boots clattering on the deck plates reached his ears and, peering through the crack in the hatch, he saw two men with AK-74s moving along the passage.

They had almost passed his hiding place when one of them nudged his companion and pointed to the hatch behind which Schwarz stood.

Schwarz realized his error. He should have closed the hatch fully. The fact that it was only partially closed had attracted the attention of the crewmen. Their safety regulations would have stipulated that such a hatch be secured at all times.

The Able Team commando took a split second to curse his carelessness, then acted while the crewmen were still responding to what they had seen. He hauled the hatch open with his left hand and stepped into view with his finger already closing on the Uzi's trigger. The crewmen were caught unprepared for such a response. The 9 mm Parabellum rounds from the Uzi cut into them at short range, the effect devastating. The pair went down without any resistance.

Schwarz moved on with added urgency. He had lost precious time by the very act of not following procedure.

The next hatch was conveniently marked Engine Room. Schwarz worked the lever and eased the heavy door open. This hatch would be expected to withstand enormous pressure in the event the ship took on water. Sealing such a hatch would prevent water from flooding the next compartment. Despite its size, the hatch opened easily on its hydraulic hinges. The moment he was through, Schwarz closed and secured the hatch.

The powerful sound of the vessel's huge diesel engines filled the compartment. Despite an air-conditioning unit, the air was warm and held the faintly oily odor of the fuel. The long, two-tier engine room spread out like a metal maze. All Schwarz could see were tubes and pipes, interwoven and occupying most of the space. Underfoot the companionway was composed of metal grids. Banks of control panels lined the bulkhead on Schwarz's right. In the center of the compartment were the twin diesel engines, the heart of the ship.

"Time for shut down," Schwarz murmured as he made his way along the companionway.

At the far end of the compartment he had spotted the open bay that housed the main controls for the engines. It was being maintained by two men clad in coveralls. One of them had an Uzi slung from one shoulder.

Schwarz was halfway along the companionway when the guy with the Uzi straightened and turned. He failed to spot Schwarz immediately, but the moment he did he went for his weapon.

"Don't!" Schwarz yelled.

The gunner ignored him and continued to go for his weapon.

Schwarz triggered a short burst into his chest and dropped him to the deck. He turned the Uzi on the other man, only to find he had hauled a bulky handgun from his workstation. The autopistol cracked sharply, the bullet clanging off metalwork above Schwarz's head. He dropped into a crouch and returned fire, driving a stream of 9 mm slugs into the attacker's chest. The man fell backward down a short flight of metal steps.

Schwarz reached the workstation and scanned the control panel. Most of the signs were in English, and it didn't take him long to work out the shutdown sequence. He heard the engine noise drop, the giant engines fading to a full stop. Schwarz opened the control panel access and checked out the wiring and circuit breakers. He flipped all the switches, then stood back and laid a short burst of 9 mm gunfire into the panel. The electrical circuits crackled and spit.

He surveyed his handiwork. The *Millennium Explorer* was adrift now. She wasn't going anywhere.

At the far end of the engine room, Schwarz heard the hatch being opened slowly. He hurried forward to confront the enemy.

The hatch was shoved open and a group of armed figures spilled into the engine room. They were met by Schwarz's Uzi on full-auto. He laid down a steady stream of fire, measured bursts that cut into the new arrivals. They stumbled and fell, weapons unfired as Schwarz's cool resistance took its toll.

Pulling back into cover, Schwarz fed a fresh magazine into the Uzi, cocking the weapon before he checked the far hatch. There didn't appear to be any other resistance. Nevertheless, his approach to the hatch was cautious and his eye searched the companionway beyond for any hint of movement. He saw nothing. Heard nothing.

Reaching the open hatch, the Able Team commando unclipped one of the flash-bang grenades he carried. He pulled the pin and tossed the grenade down the companionway, then retreated behind the hatch, clapping his hands over his ears. The detonation echoed loudly through the lower deck.

Schwarz waited until the blast had faded before he checked the way forward.

Two men had stumbled into view, shaking their heads and blinking against the effects of the grenade. Both were still armed. Schwarz didn't waste the moment. He cut the pair down and moved on, heading toward the upper decks. He mounted the metal companionway, emerging on a deck that seemed ominously quiet. A few yards ahead of him he saw two bodies. Discarded weapons lay close by their bloody forms.

The rattle of gunfire sounded from different sections of the *Millennium Explorer*. Schwarz hurried along the deck, searching for his partners and keeping an eye open for any opposition.

He sensed rather than saw movement on his left. A heavy dark shape erupted from a hatch and slammed into him. The impact pushed Schwarz across the deck, his movement stopped only when he struck the deck railing. The Uzi had been jarred from his fingers on impact. He snatched for the holstered Beretta, only to have a huge hand clamp over his own. Pain engulfed Schwarz's hand as crushing pressure was applied. He turned his head and recognized his attacker.

It was the big Russian Able Team had clashed with before, Georgi Khan.

The big man's sheer brute strength overwhelmed Schwarz. Khan yanked the pistol from its holster and threw it back across the deck, then his massive left hand swept around and delivered a stunning blow to the side of Schwarz's head. The force rolled the Able Team commando along the rail. He grabbed the rail to hold himself upright, not fast enough to avoid Khan's follow-up blow. He took hold of Schwarz's hair and drove his head against the rail. The impact shocked Schwarz into action and he kicked out at Khan, ramming the heel of his boot into the Russian's groin. Khan grunted but maintained his hold. He swung his opponent like a rag doll, flinging him across the open deck. Schwarz went down, sliding until the metal bulkhead stopped him.

Khan was already closing in when Schwarz snatched at the knife sheathed at his side. He pulled the heavy combat weapon and thrust it at the Russian. The blade sliced through the man's clothing and drew blood as it gouged his side. Khan pulled back, anger blazing in his eyes as he felt the pain from the cut. Wary now, he backed off a couple of steps, still watching Schwarz as the Able Team warrior pushed to his feet, thrusting the blade of his knife ahead of him.

Schwarz felt blood seeping from a gash in his head. It ran down his forehead and into his eyes. He shook his head to flick it away, trying to keep his eyes on Khan. The Russian moved in suddenly, arms widespread, his bulk seeming to expand as he got closer. Schwarz ducked in under the encircling arms, sweeping the knife to one side as he did, and had the satisfaction of feeling it slice through flesh. Khan grunted with the shock. Taking advantage of his gained momentum, Schwarz rounded on the Russian and caught Khan as he turned clumsily. Schwarz stepped in fast, the knife flashing in under Khan's hesitant reaction. This time the strike was hard and directly on target. Schwarz felt the blade sink into Khan's chest, cleaving through to pierce the heart. With the knife thrust in up to the hilt, Schwarz gave it a half-twist. Khan's eyes bulged, rolling back in their sockets. He tried to recover, but the wound was already taking its toll. Khan began to gasp for breath. Blood was bubbling out of the wound, around the blade. He fell and struck the deck flat on his back, his massive bulk shuddering in spasm until his system shut down.

Schwarz recovered his weapons, sleeving sweat and blood from his face. The attack by the Russian had caught him off guard and had almost become fatal. It was a lesson to learn. He holstered his handgun, put away his knife and checked that the Uzi was cocked and locked.

He was midway along the ship's length when the crack of an exploding grenade sounded. The flash and smoke came from around the superstructure ahead of him. He moved in against the bulkhead and peered around the corner. Smoke was still drifting over the scene of chaos on the deck.

A number of bodies lay on the deck. Two men were still on their feet, trading shots with a kneeling figure.

It was Lyons, and he took out one man.

Schwarz leaned around the corner and tracked his Uzi on the second man. He triggered a burst that knocked the guy off his feet and laid him facedown on the deck.

Lyons stood, reloading his Uzi as he joined Schwarz.

"What happened to you?"

"Long story," Schwarz said.

"Pol?"

"Haven't seen him yet."

"The lab complex should be in here," Lyons said. "The problem is I saw a team of shooters going in there, including the man called Malik."

They stood on either side of the open hatch.

"Toss in a couple of flash grenades?"

Lyons nodded. "Can't use fraggers until we know what's in there. We crack open any sealed lab unit, and we're in deep trouble."

"You guys waiting for me?"

It was Blancanales. He stood, reloading his Uzi, scanning the silent deck area. With the Uzi loaded he concentrated on the SPAS shotgun.

"Am I missing something?"

Lyons jabbed a finger in the direction of the open hatchway.

"We figure the lab is in there. But so is a welcoming committee."

Blancanales nodded. "No big bangs?"

"No. We can't risk any kind of leakage from the lab."

"Stun grenades?"

"That's what we were going for."

Blancanales unhooked two from his belt. He waited until his partners had checked and loaded their weapons. Lyons freed a stun grenade and Schwarz followed suit.

"We set?" Blancanales asked.

His partners nodded.

"Let's get it done!" Blancanales said, pulling the pins on the stun grenades.

He turned and threw both grenades in through the hatchway.

MALIK HAD HIS remaining force gathered in the area that fronted the lab complex. They were all armed, as he was, and ready to defend the complex to the bitter end.

There was an irony in the situation, Malik realized. The weapon they were protecting was supposed to wipe out their enemies, not lead to the destruction of the ones who created it. The moment he had the thought he admonished himself. They weren't defeated yet. From what he had been able to deduce, there were only three in the attack team.

Only three.

Yet they had already taken down most of his crew and security people in a ferocious firefight that had also left *Millennium Explorer* adrift, her engines shut down.

Damn them!

The Americans had proved their worth as adversaries. Malik had to give them that. When they had their backs to the wall, the Americans showed, as they had in the past, that they could fight well and overcome strong odds. Any threat to their national safety was repelled with fearsome resistance. Whatever else was said about the Americans, they did hold their freedom dear.

Malik was forced to admit that perhaps he had underestimated the courage of these people. His plans to introduce Ilyana's deadly bioweapons to American soil had galvanized the U.S. into action. Not only here but also in Kosovo, where the FAP had been part of his plan. The U.S. had deployed covert forces that had overcome the terrorists on their home ground. Lec Pavlic and his group had made their mistake when they had expanded their war to involve the Americans. Driven by Pavlic and his twisted desire for revenge, coupled with an intractable manifesto, the FAP had lost face with its own people as well as becoming a target for the Americans.

Now it was coming to a final reckoning with the Americans, here on board his own ship, the vessel he had thought would be his floating research and distribution center. Malik had satisfied Ilyana Petrocovich's demands and had given her everything she had asked for. The ship, with its secure base and ability to move where he desired, had seemed the ideal. A place he could also come to when he needed to be away from the pressures his life placed him under. Now even that was under threat.

Malik clutched the autorifle in his hands. If need be, he would destroy these Americans with his bare hands. It wouldn't be the first time he had been forced to kill in order to survive. Malik had taken life on more than one occasion, and he was still capable of doing it again.

Let these Americans come. If they desired a battle, then that was what they would get.

Malik caught the warning cry from one of his men.

"Stun grenade!"

He threw himself to one side, dropping his rifle so he could cover his ears and hide his eyes. Even so he felt the concussion wave as it filled the passage. A second, then a third blast rocked the area.

As the noise faded, Malik reached out for his weapon, closing his hand around it. Still on one knee, he turned to see his men staggering about, some with blood trailing from their ears. In their confusion they responded slowly, so that when the three Americans burst along the passage there was little to stop them.

The rattle of automatic fire broke through the numbness in Malik's ears. At least he was able to see, and as he swung around the muzzle of his rifle, tracking one of the Americans, he was stunned to see his own men going down under the savage volley of shots from the weapons of the three men.

Pushing to his feet, Malik pulled back on the trigger and saw one of the Americans stumble and fall. His victory was short-lived as the blond-haired member of the trio turned his weapon on him. The muzzle of the ugly shotgun loomed huge in Malik's eyes. Then it fired and a powerful hand lifted the terrorist and slammed him against the clear wall of the lab complex. The American fired again, this shot taking away a large chunk of Malik's left shoulder and almost severing his arm. With the rush of blood from the massive wound Malik lost consciousness. He slid down the lab wall, smearing it with his blood.

With Malik down, the surviving crew members realized their lives were on the line and they fought with mounting fury, aware that if the Americans captured them they would be subjected to vile tortures and humiliated in the eyes of God. They refused to surrender, fighting on with hopeless courage. Still affected by the concussion from the stun grenades, they were slow in responding, and this gave Able Team a further advantage.

The Stony Man team took the fight to the enemy, anxious to take them out before any of them decided to breach the lab complex. If the lab was opened and any of the deadly viruses contained inside were allowed to escape, the consequences might be too awful to even consider. There was no knowing just what biological horrors were secured behind the lab wall. Able Team, to a man, wanted it to stay that way. They could defeat human adversaries with bullets and explosives, but how did a person tackle an invisible microorganism?

They pushed the crewmen until they were at the end of the passage, crowded in a small space, yet still fighting back.

When the return fire slackened, then ceased, Able Team backed off, leaving their adversaries on the deck, weapons and hearts silent.

Able Team stood down, bloody but unbowed.

Blancanales had a bullet wound in his left side. He leaned against the bulkhead, one hand clamped over the wound, face pale, but refusing to give in.

Lyons keyed his transceiver.

"Jack, get that biohazard team in here fast. The ship's secure. We need medical help. Pol took a bullet. And we have Ilyana Petrocovich alive and sealed inside her lab complex. I don't know if she's coming out, but I'm damned sure we're not going in to get her."

"Will do," Grimaldi responded. "Stand fast and I'll have that team with you in ten minutes."

Lyons broke contact. He went to check out Blancanales.

"Jesus!"

It was Schwarz who had spoken.

"What?" Lyons asked.

He turned to see what the others were already witnessing.

Behind the sealed walls of her complex, Ilyana Petrocovich was at one of her benches. By the time Lyons had her in his sight she had already pushed a hypo needle into her arm, injecting something into her body. Withdrawing the needle, she turned to look at Able Team. There was nothing they could do. The lab was still fully locked down and Petrocovich was secure inside her sterile world.

Able Team had to stand and watch as she died. It took no longer than a few minutes and she died with little fuss, almost as if she were going to sleep. By the time the biohazard team arrived, there was nothing anyone could do for the woman.

The biohazard team took over the ship with their usual grim efficiency. Despite their protests, Able Team was subjected to a thorough and intimate examination. Though they didn't like the attitude of the biohazard team, the Stony Man warriors knew the need. Deadly microorganisms were tricky things to deal with. While many were instantly active, there were others that might lay dormant in a host and not show for days, maybe even weeks. By that time the unwitting host might have been in contact with hundreds, innocently passing along some sleeping hor-

ror that would come alive at some unexpected time
and create untold misery and suffering to thousands.
So Able Team suffered the checks and rechecks, the
injections and the lectures from the suited, masked
biohazard technicians.

When they were finally given the all clear and
allowed to leave the *Millennium Explorer,* it was
with a sigh of relief. They stood at the stern of the
ship, aware of what might have happened if they
hadn't boarded her and faced the savage resistance
of Malik and his people. For once there was little
talk between the three men. They were exhausted.
They stood and watched as Grimaldi touched down
on the open stern deck.

Once they were on board, Grimaldi called one of
the Navy ships and told them to expect Blancanales.
One of the medics from the biohazard team had
made a temporary bandage for his wound, but he
needed full treatment.

The JetRanger lifted off from the *Millennium Explorer* and headed toward the Navy ship. Below
them, the anchored *Millennium Explorer* was surrounded by a small flotilla of craft. Military chop-
pers circled the ship. The government had taken
control now. Everything on board the vessel was in
their hands. It was that fact alone that worried Carl
Lyons. The immediate threat from Ilyana Petrocovich and her deadly bioweapons was over. Now the
whole of her experiments and whatever she had created had fallen into the hands of the government
agencies.

Lyons wondered how long before all that knowledge would be locked away under official protec-

tion. Most likely until the day someone decided it was time to take it out and dust it off, and probably start the whole damn thing up again.

How long? Lyons wondered.

CHAPTER FIFTEEN

Kosovo

"How is everyone back there?" McCarter asked, struggling to keep the truck on the rutted, rain-soaked track.

The message was relayed through the canvas backing.

"Surviving."

The FAP base lay at least an hour behind them. During that time, they had negotiated the treacherous track down the mountain slope, finally reaching the comparative safety of the flatlands. That had been a contradiction in terms as far as David McCarter had been concerned.

The Kosovo landscape was anything but flat. They seemed to be constantly hitting slopes and hills, with open ravines and rain-swollen streams. If it hadn't been for McCarter's driving skills, plus the rugged construction of the ancient truck, they might have found themselves abandoned on foot long ago. As it was, they had to endure a nightmare ride through hostile terrain. The rain seemed set for the duration, and the temperature had plummeted again.

The truck wasn't equipped with such a thing as a heater, but it did throw a steady flow of fumes from the engine back into the cab.

"How do you think we're doing?" Manning asked.

McCarter couldn't risk taking his eyes from the road for an instant.

"Damned if I know," he shouted above the roar of the engine. "I'm just trying to keep us heading in the right direction."

The truck lurched at that moment, hitting some break in the ground. For a few seconds the front of the vehicle left the ground. It came down with a thump that shook everyone, but miraculously the vehicle kept going, seemingly impervious to damage.

The canvas flap at the back of the cab was drawn back and Tanner stuck his head through.

"Hate to tell you this, but there's a vehicle coming up behind, and it's moving bloody fast."

"Maybe it's the police going to pull me over for speeding," McCarter said.

"No, sir, I have a funny feeling whoever is in that thing has something a bloody sight worse than a speeding ticket for us."

"THIS IS MADNESS, Milisivic," Racev shouted above the roar of the helicopter's rotors. "Whatever it is you are planning, it won't work."

Despite the seriousness of his position, Milisivic found he was smiling at Racev's words.

"Shout all you want, Racev. It isn't going to do you any good. There are only the two of us here, and I don't give a damn about you."

"Then you are a dead man," Racev said. "What are you going to do now? You can't go back. You'll be shot on sight."

"So I've nothing to lose then. Now shut up. I'm sick of hearing your damned voice."

Racev fell silent, slumping back in his seat, staring out through the rain-streaked canopy. He tried to figure out where they were. The darkness and the rain made that impossible, though Milisivic seemed to know where he was going. Racev assessed his position. It wasn't good. He was unarmed, and there was no gain in trying to tackle Milisivic while they were in the air. Racev was no pilot. If Milisivic lost control of the helicopter, they would likely end up dead if it crashed. As Milisivic had also stated— correctly—there wasn't going to be a last-minute rescue. Racev was totally on his own with Milisivic, and for the moment he would have to go along with the man's plans.

After some time Racev said, "Don't you realize the position this puts your family in? They might very well be punished for what you're doing."

"Racev, my family will accept any outcome of this act. We are loyal to each other and to what we believe in. All I've done is to bring the day forward. Sooner or later our true feelings would have been aired. We are not cowards. You and your bullies in the government can't stop us from holding our beliefs. One day that maniac in Belgrade will topple and then this country can hold its head up again."

"You realize what you've just admitted? That you and your family are traitors."

Milisivic laughed at the man's pomposity.

"If only you could hear yourself, Racev. Do you think it really matters what I say to you? Hasn't it occurred to you yet that you're not going to tell this to anyone? That you are not getting out of this alive?"

The cold finality of the statement hit Racev like a physical blow. He pushed back in his seat, gripping the edges hard, a greasy knot of fear starting to coil on itself in the pit of his stomach.

Was it true what Milisivic had just said?

That he, Racev, was going to die?

He jerked his head around, face taut with the emotions welling up inside him.

"What are you going to do? Kill me? Murder me?"

"It's only what you have been doing for the past few months, Racev. Isn't it? Or am I wrong because you hide it under cozy words, convincing yourself that the atrocities you carry out are justified. That slaughtering women and children is the right thing to do. Executing fathers and sons is the right way to a glorious victory."

"What would you know, Milisivic? You've never been there. Never involved yourself in the work that has to be done if our nation is to survive. No. You always stand on the side, looking the other way. Does it unsettle your stomach to see real men doing what is needed to insure survival?"

Milisivic stared at his passenger.

"You know what I find frightening about what you've just said, Racev? That you actually believe it. Bad enough you do those vile things. But to hear you talk about them as if they are written on tablets of stone is even worse. You listen to that man in Belgrade and you devour every word he says and live by them."

"The president is going to save us," Racev said. "The nation is going through a terrible time. It needs a strong leader. One who can guide us into the light."

"Into what light? A future awash with the blood of all those slaughtered Albanians? To a future of fear and suspicion and mistrust? Wake up, Racev, you are a bloody fool."

"Better a fool than a coward," Racev roared, knowing that he was going to die and deciding that he might as well do something to try to save himself.

He lunged at Milisivic, hands reaching for the pistol in the other man's hand. For a moment he thought he had it in his grasp, but Milisivic had been expecting something like that to happen and he took evasive action, tipping the helicopter almost on its side, the action throwing Racev away from him to crash against the canopy. Ignoring the pain in his skull, Racev kicked out, the heel of his boot catching the side of Milisivic's face just over the cheek. Flesh tore and blood spurted from the gash.

Milisivic concentrated on righting the machine, giving Racev a free few seconds. The man took them and hauled himself upright, then pushed out of his seat and launched himself at his adversary again. He stumbled over Milisivic's feet, his wild punch missing its target by inches. Then he crashed down against the pilot, pinning him to his seat.

Racev gave a yell of triumph. He made a grab for the pistol in Milisivic's hand, brushed against it, then lost his grip again. Milisivic felt the helicopter level out. He felt his gun hand freed from Racev's grip and lashed out with the weapon, the heavy barrel smacking against the man's mouth, splitting his lips. Racev cursed, slumping back, spitting blood. Milisivic turned the muzzle of the weapon on the man, and without a second thought he pulled the trigger. Twice. The sound of the shots filled the cabin.

He saw Racev slip away from him as the bullets punched through his chest, an expression of pure astonishment on his face as the enormity of Milisivic's action washed over him. The pair of bullets, drilling into his heart, ended his life in moments, and all the ranting and hysterical mouthing that had been Racev's stock-in-trade meant nothing as life erupted from him in the form of bright red blood.

Milisivic tossed the gun on the seat Racev had vacated, shaking his head in stunned shock. His intention to kill the man had manifested itself in a totally different way than he had imagined. He had killed Racev in the heat of anger, while his own life had been in danger. And though it come about purely through Racev's actions, Milisivic felt a little cheated. He had wanted Racev to suffer. To go through the kind of mental torture his victims had. Now that moment had passed. Racev was dead, yes, but in a way his death had been quick and clean. It failed to have any justice in it as far as Milisivic was concerned.

His mind was still wrestling with the matter when he picked up a rising glow of fire in the mountains ahead. Milisivic banked the helicopter in the direction of the glow and watched as it expanded, shooting fiery tentacles into the dark sky.

"LEC! LEC, you will kill us all!" Drago shouted.

Lec Pavlic ignored his friend's pleas. He simply pushed his foot harder on the gas pedal, sending the rugged 4x4 crashing through undergrowth as he tried to catch up with the truck. The vehicle, stolen months ago from a Serbian police unit the FAP had ambushed and killed, was Russian-made. Pavlic had kept the vehicle concealed in a cave some distance away from the main stronghold. It was always fueled and the battery kept charged. Pavlic had maintained that one day the vehicle would serve a purpose, and that time seemed to have come.

Emerging from the ruins of his demolished base with Drago and a few other survivors, Pavlic had gone wild when he learned that the attack force had escaped in the truck, taking with them the prisoners. His anger had been frightening to see. For long minutes he had ranted and raved like a demented soul, the tortured sound of his rage ringing around the cold slopes.

Then he had calmed down. The change had been disquieting for the others. Turning to Drago, he had told him to find what weapons he could. The same instructions went to the others. While they searched for arms, Pavlic had retrieved the 4x4. He ordered them all inside, and the moment they were seated he drove off down the narrow track, following the stolen truck.

They had driven for almost an hour before they

spotted the truck's dim lights ahead of them. Pavlic had shouted with joy when he had seen the vehicle.

"Make sure everything is loaded. I want them all dead. Every last one of them."

"Is that a wise option?" Drago asked.

Pavlic had stood on the brake, bringing the vehicle to a slithering halt. He turned to stare at Drago.

"What?"

"Lec, these Americans are not fools. Or amateurs. They walked in and destroyed our base. Look what they did at the arms drop. And we were waiting for them that time."

"So what should we do, Drago? Turn around and sneak off into the night? Pretend this didn't happen? Go out for a drink and forget about it all? Maybe everything will be all right in the morning."

"All I am saying is we should take time to consider our actions."

"Consider our actions? Drago, we are in the middle of a war. Not a debate on the merits of whether tea is better for you than coffee. Because of these damned Americans many of our comrades are dead. Our base is in ruins. All our equipment destroyed. Do you really think this is the time to consider what we are doing?"

Pavlic jammed the stick into first and sent the 4x4 on its way again, driving with total disregard to the weather or the terrain.

"Have you forgotten," he suddenly said, "that we have operations already in motion? The ship from Libya will be here soon and the biocylinders are due shortly from Malik's little Russian doctor.

We can still do what we set out to do. We will overcome the obstacles."

"Then why risk putting all those things in jeopardy? Why this madness? Chasing these Americans across the country. If we catch up with them, what then? A gun battle against professionals? A better than even chance we will die? If that happens, Lec, where is your grand plan then?"

"I know what you are doing, Drago. Every time I take a risk, every time I push to gain an advantage, you want to stop me. Why, Drago? Have you lost your will to fight? Is the cause not as strong in your heart any longer? Tell me, Drago, because I do not understand you."

"Lec, you are talking nonsense. There has not been a moment during all these months when I haven't been at your side. Since the start we have been together. Fought and almost died many times. So do not make me look like a coward. I will face any man. Any odds. But there are times when the head has to rule. Not the heart. Sense and reason must prevail or we become what we are fighting against. And we are becoming as bad as the enemy, Lec."

"No! That is crazy. You stand us in the same shadow as the Serbs? As the Americans and NATO? All the ones we struggle against?"

"Lec, listen to yourself. You are losing sight of what we are fighting for. Right now it is not even for your dead family, let alone your country."

"They all have to die, Drago. Every one of them. There is no choice. If they defy me they have to die."

"My God, Lec. If they defy *you* they must die?"

Pavlic hunched his shoulders, drawing in on himself as he peered through the streaked windshield of the 4x4. He listened to the roar of the powerful engine, drowned out the sound of Drago's voice by focusing on the dark way ahead. His thoughts were confused. He could barely put together a cohesive string of them. The only clear, deliberate and creative thought he could muster was the one telling him to catch up with the Americans and destroy them. They had defiled his people and his base, had taken away much of his power and his influence, leaving him alone in the ashes of destruction. For that there was no forgiveness. In the present life or even the one that followed death.

"You are wrong, Drago. I know exactly what I am doing. Nothing has ever been clearer to me than that."

From the rear of the vehicle one of the FAP faithful said, "The truck is slowing down."

"You see, Drago, we still have God on our side. Now we can destroy these damned Americans and show that the FAP cannot be stopped."

MILISIVIC'S COURSE took him from the ruined mountain stronghold and on to pick up the trail of the truck McCarter was driving. As he flew through the driving rain, the Serb used all his knowledge of the area to try to guess the way the Briton would go. Milisivic was confident he was following the combat team, especially when, after almost an hour, he picked up two vehicles. One was in pursuit of the other. It had emerged from the foothills, following the exact course being taken by the first truck.

He kept the helicopter at a safe height, not wanting to be seen by the pursuing vehicle in case he escalated the problem on the ground.

The first vehicle was heading in roughly the right direction for the Macedonian border. The occupants were fortunate that with the weather being so bad it was unlikely there would be any military forces around. There was little out here of interest to the Serbians and in weather like this they would opt for staying on their bases. This was remote terrain, with little of interest to anyone. Blundering about in such foul weather was likely to do more damage by accident than deliberate intent.

Milisivic watched as the pursuing vehicle stopped once for a short time, then took up the chase again. He wondered why it had stopped. The important matter was that it had resumed the chase.

He flew on, concentrating on keeping the helicopter on course. The force of the wind and rain at his altitude was strong. It buffeted the aircraft, sometimes threatening to push him way off course, and Milisivic had to use all his skill to maintain an even flight path.

He almost missed the next act in the drama taking place below.

The lead vehicle came to a sudden halt.

"ARE YOU SURE this is a good idea?" Manning asked.

McCarter pulled on the hand brake, reaching for his MP-5 and checking that it held a full magazine.

"I'm sick of racing about this bloody country like

an idiot. One way or another we end this farce right now.''

He kicked open his door and climbed down out of the truck. Walking to the rear, he banged on the tailgate.

''Rise and shine, lads, we've got company.''

The group tumbled out of the truck, even James and Hawkins. They broke away from the vehicle and took cover in the shadows.

TURNING THE HELICOPTER, Milisivic watched the shadowy events taking place far below him. He struggled to keep the machine steady while he maintained a view of the proceedings.

He barely made out the figures breaking away from the truck.

Moments later the following vehicle slithered to a stop.

Milisivic swung the helicopter around and peered through the streaked canopy, trying to make some kind of sense out of the action below.

''GET THAT LAUNCHER ready,'' Pavlic ordered as he brought the 4x4 to a halt.

The FAP terrorist in the rear of the vehicle climbed out, the slim tube of the launcher over his shoulder. He had already primed the weapon. Down on one knee, he tracked in on the truck, then fired.

They all saw the fiery trail of the missile as it leaped from the launcher and sped in the direction of the truck. It impacted just behind the fuel tank, turning the truck into a fiery ball. The bulk of the vehicle left the ground for a few seconds under the tremendous power of the blast. Burning fuel arced through the darkness, some falling into shrubbery and setting it alight.

"Now they are on foot," Pavlic said.

He made a sweeping gesture with his arm to the four men around him. The FAP men eased away into the rain-swept darkness.

Pavlic hoisted his own AK-74, turning to face Drago.

"Do we do this together, Drago? Or have you lost your stomach for an open fight, as well?"

Drago didn't reply. He simply took his weapon and moved out. Pavlic followed.

THE BURNING TRUCK CAST a strange orange glow across the area. Phoenix Force moved beyond the illumination of the flames.

"You psychic or something?" Tanner asked.

"Not bloody likely. If I was, do you think I'd let myself get involved with stuff like this?"

"Coming in from both sides," Encizo called.

"We see them."

One of the FAP terrorists broke into a run, his AK-74 stuttering as he opened fire. He ran in a zig-zag pattern that was totally predictable. Tanner moved to a point that gave him a clear field of fire, tracked the running man and put him down with a controlled burst from his H&K.

At the same time another figure ran in from the opposite side, firing with a little more respect for his weapon. His shots were starting to come very close. Manning, moving around in the shadows well away from the rest of the team, came up almost alongside the terrorist. He raised his MP-5 and took the guy out with a single shot to the head. It was good shooting, especially in the semidark. The FAP terrorist dropped to the ground.

"THIS IS GOING TO GET us all killed," Drago said softly, not wanting to arouse Pavlic's rage further.

His friend glanced at him as they advanced in the direction of the enemy.

"Are you afraid of dying, my brother?"

"Any man with a semblance of reason is afraid of dying, Lec. There is no wonder awaiting us when we do die. Only a great unknown."

"No. You are wrong, Drago. Death will bring us to a new life of great beauty and contentment."

"I prefer my present condition," Drago said.

Pavlic was shocked at what he heard. He had always considered Drago to be one of the true faithful. He felt sorry for him. Drago was living a false life if he didn't believe what their faith taught them. It might even explain his reluctance to push ahead with the FAP's plans, his challenging of Pavlic's leadership.

It was also a strange time to confess to such misgivings, Pavlic thought. He was interrupted as a sudden rattle of gunfire burned into his ears.

He heard the excited cries and yells as his followers launched themselves at the Americans, weapons firing. The night was alive with the noise of battle. He heard the sharp crack of grenades going off, the increased sound of gunfire.

Pavlic ran forward, his Kalashnikov firing as he swept the way ahead.

He almost stepped on the body. Something made him look down, and he saw, with genuine shock, that it was Drago. He was dead, his body punctured by the blast from a fragmentation grenade. Seeing his friend torn and bloody, one leg severed at the thigh, Pavlic felt a great revulsion sweep over him.

All the anger, the inner rage and the lonely frustration welled up inside and burst like a sour taste in his throat. He dragged his gaze from the shattered corpse of his friend.

Now they would all die. This time he, Lec Pavlic, would show the way it should be done. Once and for all the enemy would see the terrible power of the FAP.

Because he was the FAP. The true leader. The only leader...

Pavlic walked toward his destiny, his weapon firing, ignoring the bullets that tore into him, and for a few disturbing moments he truly was a dead man walking.

RAFAEL ENCIZO LOWERED his weapon, staring at the riddled, bloody body of Lec Pavlic.

"For a minute I didn't believe he was going to stop."

"Bugger just didn't know when to die," Tanner remarked.

"Well, he's gone and done it now," McCarter said.

They stood in a loose group, aware that they had taken out the enemy, but not sure how safe they were themselves. The border was still a great distance away, and with the looming threat of the

NATO bombing coming ever closer, they needed to leave quickly.

"Bloody hell!" McCarter said. "Now what?"

They all heard the beat of a helicopter's rotors. Moments later a dark shape swooped out of the darkness, bathing them in the glare of a spotlight. The craft sank to the ground, settling awkwardly. The rotor wash sent rain into the faces of Tanner and Phoenix Force as they stood their ground, ready for any threat as the sliding door in the side of the chopper was opened. A figure clad in a long dark coat stepped out and crossed to meet them.

"I said I would do what I could to help," Janic Milisivic said. "I suggest you get on board and I will get you to the Macedonian border as quickly as possible."

McCarter shook his head in disbelief. If he lived to be a very old man, he would never understand people, he decided.

"Oh, bugger it," he said. "Okay, you miserable sods, get your arses on board and let's go home."

Stony Man Farm, Virginia

EPILOGUE

Stony Man Farm, Virginia

Hal Brognola waited until everyone assembled had taken their seats. He counted heads.

Phoenix Force was fully represented. They all bore the scars of their recent confrontation with the FAP. James and Hawkins had refused to stay away, despite still showing the signs of their brutal treatment at the hands of Lec Pavlic and his FAP terrorists. The bruising on their faces and bodies was still in evidence, the bruises having now turned to vivid colors. The swelling had started to recede. Moving around still caused them some discomfort, but they had insisted on being present at the debriefing.

Rosario Blancanales was still hospitalized. The bullet he had taken during the firefight on *Millennium Explorer,* luckily missing any vital organs, was taking time to heal and he was confined to bed.

In the days since the combat teams had returned to Stony Man, Kurtzman and his team had been busy assessing all the information gathered during the missions and continuing their delving into the earlier data they had accessed.

Brognola had called the meeting to update the teams on the outcome of their involvement and to give them the current status.

"Item one. The FAP. We won't know for a while but I'd say we've cut them apart. The destruction of their base has effectively wiped out their infrastructure, their computers and weapons."

"That place went up with one hell of a bang," Manning said. "I'd guess the access to those underground caverns has pretty much gone."

"There couldn't be much left in there," Encizo agreed.

"There hasn't been any active presence from the FAP since you pulled out. The whole organization seems to have gone into hiding," Barbara Price said. "The fact that Lec Pavlic is dead has shut the group down."

"There's no doubt that Pavlic had a great deal of influence over his followers," Brognola said. "His mistake was taking his agenda too far. In effect he went rogue. From Albanian freedom fighter to extreme terrorist. That was where he lost the trust of the very people he was supposed to be representing. Feedback we've had from the true Albanian rebels is that Pavlic had set them back. His actions were assumed to be representative of all the Albanians. Pavlic's personal grief over the massacre of his village, and especially his own family, had taken him down a bitter road. Striking out at us and the other NATO countries was his way of extending his grief.

It was a wrong move. His involvement with Malik just made things worse.''

''We haven't had much feedback from the group on board the *Levantine*,'' Price said. ''Basically, they are refusing to talk.''

''Send them back home,'' Hawkins suggested.

''The problem is finding out where they came from,'' Price told him. ''They're an odd mix of Muslims of different nationalities, all seasoned in terrorist activities.''

''Not our concern,'' Brognola cut in. ''Of more interest were the documents found on board. Interesting stuff. Mainly propaganda leaflets that would have been distributed as part of the attacks planned to be carried out here in the U.S., London, Paris, Berlin. All condemned the crimes we have been committing and stated that this was why the FAP had brought the war to our streets. To give us a taste of what it was like. There were travel documents, passports, money, city and street maps, marked locations, contact names and telephone numbers.''

''Sounds as if someone went to a lot of trouble to insure this campaign went well,'' James said.

''The people on board the *Levantine* were hardline activists. If they had reached their assigned destinations, we could have been facing a hell of a time with them. The way Lec Pavlic had been pushing, even they had found the line blurred. The cause of Albanian freedom had been sidelined by a rage-motivated cause. Pavlic had been seeking pure revenge in the end. He'd allowed Malik to suck him in, supply him with whatever he needed so that Pavlic saw nothing but the need to lash out. If we hadn't stopped Malik, as well, that damned virus might have been used in a second-stage attack."

Kurtzman tapped the file in front of him.

"The notes we got from Ridivic allowed us to piece together a lot of the strands. The same names kept popping up—Malik, Ilyana Petrocovich, Mark Slamen. As a bonus, when we tracked back through the Italian charter company who hired out the plane used for the arms drop, we found the money to pay for it came from one of Slamen's subsidiary companies. The Italians are innocent parties. The guy who hired the plane had his own people fly it. What they didn't know was that the FAP were going to kill them once the plane was down. A precaution against anyone talking and revealing too much."

"Busy man, our Mr. Slamen," McCarter said.

"He is at the moment," Brognola said with some satisfaction. "As we speak, Mark Slamen is under investigation by the FBI, IRS, NSA. His whole organization is being taken apart piece by piece. I'll be very surprised if he talks his way out of all that."

"What about Desarte?" Encizo asked.

"Dupre had a long-term homosexual relationship with another Frenchman. From what Interpol has been able to piece together, it looks like he was being blackmailed into providing the information the FAP wanted. Desarte was simply greedy. He took money. The authorities have located three bank accounts he opened in different names. All around the time information and access started being compromised. A couple of other names have cropped up, as well. Money was no problem as far as Malik was concerned. It didn't mean anything to him. It just provided a means of getting what he wanted. He bought off people with large sums of money without a second thought.''

''Do we take it that the certain killings that took place were nothing more than cleaning house?'' James asked.

Brognola nodded.

''That's the way it's being judged. Once the various strategies started to come together, Malik and Pavlic must have decided there were too many loose cannons around. So they silenced them. Taking them out of the picture was a way of insuring security.''

''That must have been why Georgi Khan tailed us,'' Lyons said. ''When we turned up at Weller's place after the event, it must have made him nervous.''

''We'll never know for sure,'' Brognola said. ''If he hadn't tipped his hand it might have taken a lot longer to connect him to the whole thing.''

''Hal, has any news come through about Milisivic?'' McCarter asked.

''All I can tell you on that is that his family has moved to Austria for the duration. They decided it was safer than trying to stick around Belgrade at the moment. We got the information through our embassy people. They're looking out for the family. We owe them, seeing as how Milisivic put his life on the line for you guys. The family has decided to stay out of the country and work for the removal of the current regime from safe ground.''

''Milisivic has taken off,'' Price explained. ''From what we can gather, he's taken on some kind of covert work to do with building up a dossier of atrocities committed by the Serbian government against the ethnic Albanians. That's all we can tell you because it's all we know.''

"Good luck to him," McCarter said.

"One thing I'm concerned about," Lyons stated.

"What's that?"

"The stuff the biohazard team found in Ilyana Petrocovich's lab. What's happened to it?"

"I've been waiting for that one to come up," Brognola said. "The truth? I don't know. All I can say is the military has its hands on it. Once it reached them even I wasn't told."

"Bloody great," McCarter said. "If they've got it, we'll have the damn stuff being issued to the Army, Navy and Air Force in six months."

"That's what I'm expecting," Lyons said. "Why the hell couldn't they just burn it up?"

"I won't insult any of you by quoting that National Security line," Brognola said. "What else can I say? We stopped it from being used by the FAP and Malik. That has to be worth something, guys. Give me a break on that, huh?"

Lyons scowled. He caught McCarter's eye. The Briton made a conciliatory gesture.

"I guess so," Lyons said, far from being convinced.

"We did what we set out to do," Price stated. "Come on, guys, you pulled it off. We worked well on this. Aaron and his team did some good work and the liaison was fine. It can get better. It has to. But on the whole, not bad."

"Yeah, that stuff you pulled with the satellites

was pretty sharp,'' Hawkins said. "Thanks for that, Aaron."

"It was nothing." The Bear grinned.

"The hell it wasn't," James said. "Spotting us on that mountain was brilliant. Hey, Aaron, tell me something."

"What?"

"How do I look on TV?"

"On that particular shot you looked pretty crappy," Kurtzman replied.

After the laughter had died down, Yakov Katzenelenbogen leaned forward and asked the main question on everyone's lips.

"What's the word on the bombing, Hal? How long is it going to go on?"

"Truth? I don't know. A few weeks. Maybe months. Right now the assessment is we can't be sure how the Serbians are going to respond. They might up and quit tomorrow. Or they could dig in for the long haul."

"Make the most of the R&R, guys," McCarter said. "We aren't going into retirement yet."

"It true what I heard about Tanner?" Hawkins asked.

McCarter nodded. "Last time I spoke with him he said his unit was going in deep."

"Hope he stays alive."

"The sarge is an all-right guy," James said.

McCarter agreed with that.

"The bloody part about it is it's the all-right guys that have to go in and do the dirty work."

"Yeah," James said. "Every time."

"Thank God for the good guys," Price said softly to herself as she gazed around the War Room table. "Every damned one of them."

Blood inheritance...

DON PENDLETON's

MACK BOLAN®

STORM FRONT

A homegrown terrorist group lying dormant for more than a decade rises to continue its war against the American government. Revenge against the Feds who stalked and shut down the Cohorts years ago is the first on its agenda of terror. The group's actions are matched bullet for bullet by the Executioner, who is committed to eradicating the Cohorts and its legacy of bloodshed.

Available in July 2000 at your favorite retail outlet.

James Axler

OUTLANDERS®

HELL RISING

A fierce bid for power is raging throughout new empires of
what was once the British Isles. The force of the apocalypse
has released an ancient city, and within its vaults lies the
power of total destruction. Kane must challenge the forces
who would harness the weapon of the gods to wreak final
destruction.

JAMES AXLER

DEATHLANDS®

Pandora's Redoubt

Ryan Cawdor and his fellow survivalists emerge in a redoubt in which they discover a sleek superarmored personnel carrier bristling with weapons from predark days. As the companions leave the redoubt, a sudden beeping makes them realize why the builders were constructing a supermachine in the first place.

Desperate times call for desperate measures. Don't miss out on the action in these titles!

#61910	FLASHBACK	$5.50 U.S.	☐
		$6.50 CAN.	☐
#61911	ASIAN STORM	$5.50 U.S.	☐
		$6.50 CAN.	☐
#61912	BLOOD STAR	$5.50 U.S.	☐
		$6.50 CAN.	☐
#61913	EYE OF THE RUBY	$5.50 U.S.	☐
		$6.50 CAN.	☐
#61914	VIRTUAL PERIL	$5.50 U.S.	☐
		$6.50 CAN.	☐

(limited quantities available on certain titles)

TOTAL AMOUNT	$
POSTAGE & HANDLING	$
($1.00 for one book, 50¢ for each additional)	
APPLICABLE TAXES*	$ _____
TOTAL PAYABLE	$ _____
(check or money order—please do not send cash)	

To order, complete this form and send it, along with a check or money order for the total above, payable to Gold Eagle Books, to: **In the U.S.:** 3010 Walden Avenue, P.O. Box 9077, Buffalo, NY 14269-9077; **In Canada:** P.O. Box 636, Fort Erie, Ontario, L2A 5X3.

Name: _____

Address: _____ City: _____

State/Prov.: _____ Zip/Postal Code: _____

*New York residents remit applicable sales taxes.
 Canadian residents remit applicable GST and provincial taxes.

GSMBACK1